Crashing the Party

As we hurtled past men firing wildly at the walls of the fort, I laid my forearm on the button in the center of the wheel and let the horn scream in a long, continuous blast. There were so many shooters in the street that it looked like a plague of fireflies on a hot summer night. I aimed the truck for the black spot between and underneath the lights on the wall. From the tower to our right, a red stream of tracer fire reached out for us, rending the air just above the cab of the truck.

Roosty fired his submachine gun toward the tower, and the gun went silent. Then we were in the intersection of the streets and almost at the gates. In my peripheral vision I saw Terry put both hands on the dash and lean forward. Then, straight ahead, I saw the gates leap at us from the darkness. To the left, I caught a brief glimpse of one of the bodies dangling on the wall.

"Hang on!" I yelled.

And then, with a deafening scream of rending metal and the crash of splintering timber, we smashed through the gates like a runaway locomotive. . . .

NO MAN'S LAND

ERIC L. HANEY

BERKLEY BOOKS, NEW YORK

THE BERKLEY PUBLISHING GROUP
Published by the Penguin Group
Penguin Group (USA) Inc.
375 Hudson Street, New York, New York 10014, USA
Penguin Group (Canada), 90 Eglinton Avenue East, Suite 700, Toronto, Ontario M4P 2Y3, Canada
(a division of Pearson Penguin Canada Inc.)
Penguin Books Ltd., 80 Strand, London WC2R 0RL, England
Penguin Group Ireland, 25 St. Stephen's Green, Dublin 2, Ireland (a division of Penguin Books Ltd.)
Penguin Group (Australia), 250 Camberwell Road, Camberwell, Victoria 3124, Australia
(a division of Pearson Australia Group Pty. Ltd.)
Penguin Books India Pvt. Ltd., 11 Community Centre, Panchsheel Park, New Delhi—110 017, India
Penguin Group (NZ), 67 Apollo Drive, Rosedale, North Shore 0632, New Zealand
(a division of Pearson New Zealand Ltd.)
Penguin Books (South Africa) (Pty.) Ltd., 24 Sturdee Avenue, Rosebank, Johannesburg 2196,
South Africa

Penguin Books Ltd., Registered Offices: 80 Strand, London WC2R 0RL, England

This is a work of fiction. Names, characters, places, and incidents either are the product of the author's imagination or are used fictitiously, and any resemblance to actual persons, living or dead, business establishments, events, or locales is entirely coincidental. The publisher does not have any control over and does not assume any responsibility for author or third-party websites or their content.

NO MAN'S LAND

A Berkley Book / published by arrangement with the author

PRINTING HISTORY
Berkley mass-market edition / February 2010

Copyright © 2010 by Eric L. Haney.
Cover photographs: *Map of Africa, Graphic Light, Desert Landscape* copyright © by Stockexpert/
Jupiterimages Unlimited; *Ghardaïa, Sahara, Algeria* copyright © age footstock/SuperStock; *Figure
Running in Desert* copyright © Millennium Images/Glasshouse. Cover design by Judith Lagerman.
Interior text design by Kristin del Rosario.

ISBN: 978-0-425-23300-9

BERKLEY®
Berkley Books are published by The Berkley Publishing Group,
a division of Penguin Group (USA) Inc.,
375 Hudson Street, New York, New York 10014.
BERKLEY® is a registered trademark of Penguin Group (USA) Inc.
The "B" design is a trademark of Penguin Group (USA) Inc.

PRINTED IN THE UNITED STATES OF AMERICA

10 9 8 7 6 5 4 3 2 1

Dedicated to
the memory of
Danny Ray "Doc" Gilreath,
soldier buddy, friend of youth and middle years

CHAPTER 1

I SAILED INTO SAVANNAH ON WHAT turned out to be a high tide of rare good fortune. I hadn't planned to put in here, but then again, few of my schemes ever work out according to the original plot. It's much like the old saying in the army: "No plan survives contact with the enemy."

I had been slipping down the Atlantic coast with the vague idea of making my way to Belize and doing a little charter work. Cruising, fishing, diving, it didn't make much difference to me. Anything to put a few doubloons in the old treasure chest and keep body and soul joined as one. And Belize seemed a good backwater spot where a man could lay low for a while.

But a fast-moving storm had slammed out of the North Atlantic and into the Georgia Bight. My old boat, the *Miss Rosalie*, a fifty-six-foot former Dutch fishing vessel, had taken a pretty severe beating from that particularly nasty nor'easter, and we needed to make a run for the proverbial port in a storm.

The tides on the Georgia coast are the highest to be found between the Bay of Fundy and Argentina, and the currents of the Savannah River are notoriously swift and treacherous, but this time the forces of nature conspired in our favor, and we scudded upriver on the crest of a surging spring tide. And then, after making repairs, I'd found an old shrimp dock where the space was neither too expensive nor the neighbors too discerning, and tied *Miss Rosalie* down for a period of well-needed rest and recuperation.

All in all, it was a pretty good spot. The way the yachting crowd avoided the place you'd think it was a quarantine dock for transient syphilis cases, which suited me right to the ground. And before long I came to know and become accepted by the fishermen, shrimpers, tidewater bums, and other human and animal denizens that called this little portion of out-of-the-way waterfront their home.

The shade thrown by the magnificent live oak trees at the top of the slight bluff gave a blessed protection from the powerful afternoon sun. Captain Flynt's Bucket o' Blood, a ramshackle bar down past the end of the docks, was within crawling-home distance. And the view, up and down the saltwater creek and out across the vast waving-green prairie of salt marsh stretching away eastward toward Tybee Island and the Atlantic Ocean, would have cast a spell of peace upon even Dick Cheney's calcified soul.

For hours on end, I would sit under the canopy of *Miss Rosalie*'s aft deck and fish in quiet solitude. Or think. Or stare quietly into the recesses of my memory and attempt to make right some nagging old wrongs. *Yeah, this isn't bad at all,* I often thought.

The charming old town of Savannah laid a benign

and healing hand on my psyche, and as the weeks turned to months, it seems I'd made an unconscious decision to stick around for a while. It was a welcome place of refuge I'd found here, and just when I'd needed it most. I still told myself that I was headed on down to Belize, that I was just waiting for the right conditions and would hoist sail again when the spirit moved me and the weather forecast was right.

But as the tides continued to rise and fall in their unfailing cycle, and the earth followed its ancient track around the sun, the idea of the continued trek slid further from the forefront of my mind, until eventually, it became little more than a hazy and slowly diminishing daydream.

It was an early autumn afternoon, and I was puttering away at the aft rail of *Miss Rosalie*. With a can of varnish in one hand and a brush in the other, I was going through the outward motions of work, but in reality, I was inwardly contemplating the universe with a calm sense of optimism.

Then a rogue sound caught my ear, and as I came back to the present moment, a southern breeze brought the distinct grumble of an approaching motor. There was no mistaking the uneven splutter and pop of the old Elgin outboard, and I knew who it was before I looked up.

Danny Ray Pledger was a local marsh rat. I had first cast eyes on him at the boatyard where I'd made my repairs. By birth and breeding, Danny Ray was a coastal Cracker. Thin and hollow-chested, with slumped shoulders, slack knees, and a bad stutter, he looks out on the world sort of sideways from beneath lowered brows and the brim of a greasy and omnipresent old Atlanta Braves cap. Like poor strays and castaways the world over, life has taught Danny Ray that most of the time, when someone extends a helping hand, the other hand usually hides a cruel stick behind his back.

I'd hired him to help with my boat repairs, and though at first shy as a feral cat, Danny had proven to be a surprisingly good and helpful worker. With time, a friendship had grown between us, and later he was the one who led me to this dock. As I came to know Danny Ray better, he slowly revealed himself to be a gentle and decent soul who did no harm to others and wished only the same consideration in return.

He made his way in life fishing and picking up odd jobs around the waterfront. On several occasions I had commissioned him to catch me a tub of mullet or a basket of crabs for one of my boat-deck beer socials. Danny would always help me with the cooking and the after-party cleanup. During the parties he would hover around the edges with a beer in his hand and his cap pulled low, watching the others and giving me a shy grin whenever I caught his eye.

I knew he had lost what lingering fear or doubt he had of me when he took me fishing in some of his secret speckled trout holes. I had come to enjoy the mild presence of his quiet company, but as I looked down the creek and saw him now, I knew something was very wrong.

The howling motor was running full-out, leaving a trail of oily smoke lying flat across the surface of the water. Danny was bouncing up and down on the seat and frantically waving a boat cushion in my direction. I could see his mouth moving as he called out but couldn't hear him over the rising shriek of the old outboard motor.

He was coming straight at the dock as fast as the boat would move, and it looked like he was going to plow into it head-on. I threw down the can and brush, bounded over the gunwale, and reached the end of the dock in three great jumps.

Danny arrived two seconds later. I grabbed the bow

of the boat and pushed it over so that it lay alongside the dock and threw the painter around a cleat with a fast round turn. I had not taken my eyes off Danny, who was still on the boat seat, his head downcast now as he gasped for breath.

I leaped to his end of the boat, and as I did, Danny stared at me with a pleading look on his face.

"Nuh, nuh, nuh-nuh-nuh," he stammered, his face twisted in agony with the effort to speak.

"Danny Ray, slow down. Get a breath and try again." I was kneeling on the dock and looking him in the face.

Danny shook his head fitfully from side to side and then thrust his chin forward in an attempt to cast the words from his mouth.

"It-it-it's . . ." Flinging an arm behind him to indicate downstream, he finally got it out. "Down—there."

"Can you show me where, Danny? Will you lead me?"

A wave of relief flashed across his face. He nodded vigorously and was just able to spit out the word, "Y-yes."

"Let's take my boat, and you point the way."

Danny hurled himself from his boat, dashed ahead of me, and was throwing off the dock lines to my sea skiff as I caught up to him. He jumped into the boat and was stowing lines while I primed the engine, and then a thought hit me.

"Danny, do I need to bring a gun?"

Danny Ray looked up with a profoundly saddened expression on his face. We held the look for several seconds before he was able to say, "Na-na-na—no gun—Kennesaw."

I hit the switch, the motor burst into life, and as Danny Ray pushed us away from the dock, I slammed the throttle full forward, gave the wheel a raking turn to starboard, and we roared away from the dock with such a blast of speed and a rooster tail of water that we left the GO SLOW buoy rolling violently in our wake.

From his perch on the bow of the boat, Danny Ray bird-dogged us down the creek and out into the Bull River. The tide was just starting to fall, and with a slight offshore breeze, the surface of the water lay perfectly calm and flat. Within a few minutes, we were out of sight of anything man-made and engulfed in the wilderness of the great tidal marsh.

We were flying along at full speed, just skimming the surface of the water, when Danny looked at me over his shoulder and pointed to the mouth of a creek off to the left. I started to slow down to make the turn, but Danny shook his head and pumped his fist to indicate that I should maintain speed.

I hesitated for a split second but decided to trust Danny Ray's piloting ability. He had been living on these waters, day and night, since childhood, and nobody in these parts could find their way through the maze of saltwater creeks, rivers, and sounds as well as the little man crouched in the bow of my boat.

We threaded our way through an ever-narrowing band of waterways until, as we made a sliding turn about a hairpin bend, Danny waved to me to slow down and then to cut the engine. I chopped the throttle back to idle and felt the boat settle down in the water against the falling tide. On the bank ahead, at the entry of another, smaller creek, some sort of motion caught my eye.

Danny looked back at me with a grim face, nodded his head, and pointed to the place where I had seen the flicker of movement. I idled the boat slowly forward, just making headway against the current, when through a gap in the marsh grass I got a better look at the object. It was grayish black and seemed to be slowly writhing.

Crabs, I thought as I finally realized what it was. *A*

bunch of crabs feeding on— Oh Sweet Jesus. Tell me that's not what I really see. But it was.

Danny Ray saw the look on my face and came to stand next to me at the helm. He was shaking his head slowly from side to side as he looked at the writhing mass.

It-it-it's—a girl," he managed to whisper, just as I saw a wisp of red hair.

I took a deep breath and felt the sorrow of the scene fill me down to the soles of my feet. There is no more pitiable sight or feeling to me than the first surprising view of a dead body. We looked on for just a few seconds, and then Danny touched me on the arm.

"I know," I said, reaching for the handset to the marine radio. I called the Coast Guard, told them what we had found, and requested they contact the Chatham County Police. I informed them that a man would be standing by at my dock to guide the police to the location of the body. When finished, I put the handset back on its clip and turned to my friend.

"Danny Ray, you take my boat back to the dock and guide the police back down here?"

Danny was staring out across the marsh at some unseen spot. He nodded his head in the affirmative.

"Okay then. Take the helm and put the bow up on the mud."

Danny stepped to the wheel and eased us up against the grass, just upwind of the body. I took a handheld radio out of the equipment box and put it on my belt. As I moved forward, I plucked a boat hook from its clips on the port gunwale and then stepped onto the bow platform.

"A little closer, Danny." I waved him forward. "That's it. Good."

As I felt the bow dig into the mud, I slipped out of my deck shoes and then stepped out into the marsh. I sank in the mud up to my knees, struggled to turn around, and gave the bow of the boat a shove. Danny backed the boat slowly away, then stopped and held it still in the water. He looked at me steadily, as though reluctant to leave.

"It's okay, Danny. Go on. The police will meet you at the dock. I'll be all right."

Danny nodded. "I'll—be back—fast."

He then expertly turned the boat around in the narrow channel, put it in forward, and with one last look over his shoulder, motored out of sight.

I stood and watched as he disappeared into the wall of grass. Then, slogging to my work, I settled in on a mound of oysters, and using the boat pole as best I could, tried to keep the multitude of greedy pincers off the girl's body.

I was mighty glad when later I heard the approaching boats, and very relieved when the recovery team finally arrived on site. In their ravenous hunger, the crabs were beginning to lose their fear of me, and the marsh gnats were eating me alive.

CHAPTER 2

I STOOD ON THE END OF THE DOCK, hosing the mud off my legs as I watched the ambulance pull away from the landing. It moved slowly, with no need to use its emergency lights. A police car followed in its wake, but then, turning in an opposite direction when it reached the street, it quickly sped away.

The gawkers and rubberneckers, who had assembled at the edge of the small parking lot, had finally begun to drift away. Several of them wandered down to Captain Flynt's, where the bar crowd would chew this over for days on end. I knew I'd have to make an appearance this evening and render a report of the grisly find to my tribe of fellow derelicts.

I put the hose down and accepted the towel that Danny Ray had thoughtfully retrieved from my boat. The detective had stood by patiently while I cleaned myself, but I could tell she was now ready to wrap things up and get out of here.

As I straightened up, she stepped forward, and I was surprised again at how tall she was.

Looks me straight in the eye, I thought. *Must be at least six two.* She extended a notebook and a pen.

"Would you sign here please, at the top and at the bottom?" she asked or, more correctly put, ordered.

I took the notebook, and after reading the statement, signed the document and handed it back.

"That pretty well sums it up, at least the part I know, Detective—" I hesitated as I tried to recall her name.

"Latham," she responded as she took the pad and glanced at the signature. "Patricia Latham," she said as she looked up and closed the notebook.

"Well, it's a sorry affair, Detective Patricia Latham, when dead girls are found out in the marsh."

She eyed me closely and then said in a quiet voice, "What's even sorrier, former Master Sergeant Kennesaw Tanner, is how a young woman comes to *lose* her life and then be found like that."

I was only slightly surprised that she had pulled up a bit of my background so soon. And I said nothing for a bit as I thought of her words. How *had* the life of that girl come to such a sad end? My instincts—my gut—told me that no matter what the circumstances had been, they were all wrong.

"It's bad juju, Detective. Plain bad juju."

Detective Latham looked around the dock and unconsciously wrinkled her nose as though she smelled something foul. I could understand what was at work on her.

It's going to take a lot of rum tonight to wash away that sight and smell, I thought to myself as I watched her think.

"Well," she said as she turned to me again, "I'll be able to find you—and"—she nodded toward Danny Ray, who stood like a statue just a few feet away—"Mr. Pledger, if I need to. You'll be in town, yes?"

She looked me in the eye, and I knew she meant this as a statement and not a question.

"Detective," I replied, "anytime you'd like to speak with either one of us, we can be reached through my attorney. You have his name and number there." I pointed to her notebook. "We can speak in his office. "

She listened with a slight smile and then lifted an eyebrow.

"Attorney? You feel you need an attorney? I thought you were just a concerned citizen."

"That I am, Detective, as is Mr. Pledger here. But if I"—and I nodded toward Danny Ray—"or my friend here should become persons of interest to the police—well then, things become different, don't they?"

"Do they?" she asked very pointedly.

I let her question hang in the air for a second as we held a gaze.

"The law is a blunt instrument, Detective, one that can bash about in an indiscriminate manner and cause all sorts of harm—intentional or otherwise. When I am faced with that blunt instrument, Miss Latham, I always bring a shield, as would you yourself."

She smiled, and then the smile turned to a laugh.

"Okay," she said, shaking her head. "But I have your phone number here, correct?"

"You may call it at any time, Detective. And a call doesn't have to be in the course of business only."

The smile stayed on her face, but I saw it soften just a hint. "I'll remember that," she said as she extended her hand.

We shook hands, and I was surprised at the strength of her grip.

"Sergeant Tanner," she said in conclusion.

"Next time, call me Kennesaw," I replied. "Sergeant is a 'once upon a time' title. One I haven't used in a while."

She tilted her head slightly to one side so that the breeze lifted a strand of her auburn hair.

"Kennesaw—yes, I'll do that," she said in a thought-filled voice.

She then turned and also thanked Danny Ray. And with strong and purposeful steps, she climbed the ramp to the top of the landing, got in her car, and pulled away into the gathering dusk. Danny and I stood and watched the taillights of her unmarked car until they had drifted out of sight.

"Danny Ray," I said, breaking the silence, "what say I change out of these soggy clothes and then you and I go down to Captain Flynt's and have a cold one?"

Danny nodded his head in a *yes* and we turned to walk to my boat. Just as I grabbed the handrails to step aboard, Danny Ray said, "Lu-lu—let's have more than one."

I stopped and looked again at this surprising young man.

"Yeah, Danny Ray, let's do just that."

Danny waited for me on the dock, and as I stepped aboard the *Miss Rosalie*, I looked out to the east, where the darkness of night was just falling over the marsh. For some unknown reason, the thought came to me, *It's the middle of the night out there, on the other side of that ocean.*

I quickly changed into a soft pair of ancient khakis and met Danny at the top of the ramp. And as we walked in silence toward the buzz of voices camped out on Captain Flynt's outside veranda, I composed the report I'd give to my fellow barflies:

CHAPTER 3

Pantelleria: a small Italian island off the coast of North Africa

ALAN BARNES GLANCED AT THE dimly glowing clock above the helm. It read 02:24 hours.

"Dario. Is your alarm clock broken? You're way early," he said to the man entering the bridge. "You don't come on watch for another half hour."

The man spoke no words as he stepped inside the pilothouse. Instead, he made his reply with the eight-inch blade of a KA-BAR knife, plunged, with heartfelt sincerity, into the left side of Alan Barnes's chest.

When the hilt of the fighting knife hit the chest wall, the knifeman gave the handle a violent wrench to the front and felt the edge of the blade bite deeply into Alan's sternum. It went in much more easily than he expected it would.

Must have slipped between the ribs, he thought.

The assault was so sudden that Barnes was unable to comprehend what was happening. He never felt the knife enter his body and thought instead that Dario had punched him in the side with a fist. He wanted to ask the other man what he was doing, but the words would not form.

Alan would never know that his left lung had been ripped in two and the top of his heart cut away. The frantically beating organ gushed life's liquid out the severed aorta like water from an uncapped fire hydrant, and blood completely filled the chest cavity. In an instant his blood pressure had dropped to nothing. Alan Barnes was unconscious when he hit the expensively carpeted deck. He was dead within seconds.

Dario looked at the body sprawled grotesquely at his feet, but he made no further movement. He waited, and for a full minute he listened intently for any sound in the ship, while he also brought his rapid breathing back to a normal cadence.

All was quiet. Kneeling down, he thumped the man's open eye with his middle finger. The body made no response. Satisfied with the results and elated by his success, Dario retrieved the knife from the man's chest and rolled the body underneath the instrument counter. He then stepped to the starboard hatch, opened it, and stood at the deck rail. Producing a large flashlight from a pocket of his jacket, he pointed it out to sea and fingered a series of quick double flashes: *Blink-blink. Blink-blink. Blink-blink.*

Out in the harbor, a rubber assault boat drifted silently in the darkness.

"There's the signal," whispered the man in the bow of the boat. He was the youngest and had been posted as the lookout because of his zeal and his keen eyesight. He looked back toward the steering console and was pleased with himself as he saw Commander Yagmour tap the helmsman on his shoulder and point toward the dimly seen white ship away in the distance.

Blink-blink. Blink-blink.

They all saw it now. And they all heard the commander when he said in a calm voice that carried no farther than the gunwales of the boat, "Yah lah."

The helmsman slipped the motor into gear, and the boat slid over the gentle face of the Mediterranean with the silent smoothness of a sea snake. *Now.* It was what they had been waiting for and working toward these many months. *Now.* They had been close before, but never this close, and *now* it was about to happen. *Now* they would make it happen.

On the yacht, Dario went aft along the deck until he reached the controls of the gangway. It was raised each night for security purposes, but now that was a moot point, he thought wryly to himself. He pushed the topmost button on the control box and listened as the electric motor paid out the cable that lowered the bottom of the folding stairs down to the level of the water.

The helmsman brought the black inflatable boat into the wind and alongside the gangway. Eight men dressed in dark gray poured off the boat and up the gangway. Silently, rapidly, with well-rehearsed and economical movements, the men ascended to the deck of the luxurious yacht and made straight for the bridge. Dario stood aside to maintain watch while the invaders flowed down the stairs and into the living quarters of the yacht.

Yagmour paused by a doorway and, looking left and right, saw that his men were in position, each two-man team poised at a different door. When he saw that all eyes were on him, he nodded and, turning, crashed through the door in front of him. His assistant, Mahmoud, threw on the light in the room, and before the couple in the huge bed had opened their eyes, the two men were upon them.

Yagmour smashed the forearm of his submachine gun across the left side of the man's head, splitting his ear in two and splattering the pillows and sheets with a drizzle of blood. Mahmoud lifted his knee and plunged it down across the woman's throat. Her hands flew to his knee, and her eyes bulged in terror, but she was too stunned to make further movement.

Mahmoud held his weight on the woman's larynx so that she could barely breathe, and when he saw that Yagmour had the man trussed up, he took the nylon lines that were draped around his neck and tied the woman securely, as he had practiced so many times before.

Yagmour turned his face toward the door and emitted a low whistle. He then stepped back to make room for the entrance of the other three teams.

The men guided their captives into a tight bunch at the foot of the bed. The children, three teenage girls, and a seven-year-old boy, blinked their eyes in confusion and mewled in awakening fear. Their Egyptian nanny, who had also been dragged in, shivered in wide-eyed and silent horror, as her feet and hands were bound with tape and she was tied to a chair.

All in the room were silent as four of the gray-clad men then departed and went aft to the crew quarters. The sound of doors crashing, the muted *clack-clack-clack* of the sound-suppressed German submachine guns, and the resumed quiet announced that all was under control. The four men returned, and the first one to reenter the suite merely nodded his head to Yagmour in the affirmative.

The commander now looked to the man on the bed, who had just regained consciousness and was straining against his bonds. Yagmour stuck the point of a knife under the man's chin and lifted him to a sitting position against the carved mahogany headboard.

"Observe," he said to his prisoner. "This is the reward to traitors of the faith, the corrupt and defiled, who consort and collaborate with infidels."

At the word *infidels*, swords appeared in the hands of three of the men. As suddenly as they appeared, the gleaming steel blades whistled through the air and fell simultaneously on the small necks of the three girls standing at the foot of their parents' bed.

Blood erupted onto the bed in a cascade of death, and the little bodies shot to the floor as though jerked downward by invisible cables. The head of one child bounced across the bed and rolled across the feet of her mother before tumbling to the carpet with an obscene thump.

The man and woman on the bed thrashed impotently against the ties that bound them and writhed in unimaginable horror. They gagged upon their muffled wails of anguish and chewed in torment on the rags that sealed their mouths.

Only the nanny's mouth was free to use, and she set up a keening, wailing noise that did not sound as though it were made by a human being. Mahmoud hit her dispassionately with an open hand across the side of the head, and she fell silent.

"Watch. Listen. Remember, and report all, woman," he said as she fell into compliance.

Yagmour gestured in her direction, and as she turned her stupefied gaze toward him, he casually lifted his weapon and fired. Two shots, into the head of the woman in the bed. And when he was sure the man knew that his wife had been killed and was looking back at him in madness and pain, he fired two more shots, this time into the man's face.

The maid, watching with stupefied incomprehension, lost control of her bladder and bowels, and her body went slack with terror.

For a few seconds, Yagmour surveyed the bedroom.

And then, with a slight smile of satisfaction, he produced a manila envelope from his jacket and dropped it gently on the dead man's chest.

Looking to the nanny, he pointed with his gun to the envelope on the corpse and said, "Make sure that is delivered to the father."

Turning now to his men, Commander Yagmour swept them with his eyes and then nodded slightly. Two men led off and out the doorway. The catatonic boy was carried in the arms of the third man in line, and the others filed out behind. At the rear, two commandos came up the corridor, one leading a blond woman, her hands tied in front and a robe thrown over her body.

Last to leave, Yagmour surveyed the carnage in the room. The air reeked with the coppery smell of blood and the foulness of human fear and excrement.

With a smile of contentment on his face, he looked back at the woman in the chair and said, "Now woman, you may scream all you wish."

Turning out the light and gently closing the door behind him, Yagmour moved down the passageway in the wake of his men.

In the darkened room, the woman screamed until she lost her voice. Thereafter, she babbled. She was babbling still, when they found her the next day.

CHAPTER 4

THERE HAD BEEN A THUNDERSTORM during the night, and I'd slept fitfully. I had dreamed the fire dream again, the one where I stand paralyzed with fear, unable to make myself act, and watch as a child burns to death in a house fire. Like a thief in the night, the dream comes unexpectedly and always leaves me with a sense of foreboding and unease. Perhaps the girl was still on my mind.

Perhaps, hell, of course she was. Who was she, and what had happened? I just couldn't shake it off.

The local news had goggled over the story for the obligatory fifteen minutes, and then everything had gone quiet. I'd heard nothing more from Detective Latham, but then, for some reason, I hadn't really expected to.

So I got up from my bunk just as the sky over the Atlantic was starting to show the color of a new day and took myself ashore for a good run. There's nothing like a long, hard run to get the poison out of the blood. Once everything is in rhythm—feet slapping the pavement, arms swinging naturally, heart throbbing, and air whooshing in and out of the lungs—I go into a sort of trance, my mind goes blank, and the miles slip by with an easy contentment.

I forget everything and just enjoy the sensation. But I also know that whatever I've had on my mind—whatever may have been bugging me—at the end of the run, it's made better. It is a cleansing experience, one I think of as taking a shower on the inside.

So I finished my run, cleaned up, and had a bite of breakfast while I listened to the BBC news on the short-wave. If you want propaganda, listen to any of the U.S. news outlets. It's little more than being shouted at by a bunch of carnival barkers. But if you want genuinely unbiased news, delivered in a reasonable tone and an adult manner, listen to the BBC.

I thought about my current state of affairs. All in all, things had been going pretty well recently. I'd had several charters in the last couple of weeks: dinner cruises, dolphin-watching tours, that sort of thing. The clients always loved *Miss Rosalie*, and I am gratified by how much they enjoy being aboard.

But somehow or other, there was that *something* still nagging at the back of my mind, *something* that wouldn't clearly reveal itself, but neither would it quite let go. *A premonition, perhaps,* I thought.

I had just stepped onto the deck, with a cup of coffee in hand, to give the boat a once-over and plan the day's activities, when I saw a man standing at the top of the landing, and I became alert. He looked ill at ease, like a man who knows he's in the wrong place. There was something familiar about the man. So I just stood and kept an eye on him. *He's up to something,* I thought.

He was looking down the line of boats at the dock, checking them one by one. I saw his eyes come to rest on the bow of *Miss Rosalie*. Reading the name and evidently satisfied, he started down the ramp. And then I recognized him.

Colonel Forrest Mayfield.

He hadn't noticed me yet, so I stood still and quiet until he was on the dock and near the pilothouse. Then I stepped from behind the mast and sang out.

"Mayfield," I barked in a parade-ground voice. "What powerful laxative caused you to be defecated from the bowels of the Pentagon?"

At the sound of my voice, he froze, and I saw him cringe at my words. Looking up, he saw me and lifted his fingers to his lips.

"Sergeant Tanner, for God's sake, not so loud."

"Why? What—or who—are you hiding from?" I called in a voice that rolled across the water and echoed off the trees. "And I'll remind you that I am no longer a sergeant. So you can call me what my friends call me. Try: sir."

I guess I was enjoying this more than I should have, but I felt a great sense of satisfaction as I watched him flinch at my words, as though he'd been stung with a whip.

"Please, I need to speak with you—privately," he implored in a low voice as he looked around to see who might be watching.

I stepped to the port gunwale and beckoned him to come closer. He stepped to the edge of the dock and craned his head backward to look up at me. I sincerely hoped he'd get a bad crick in his neck.

"And what would you possibly need to speak with me about? I'm no longer in your bleeding army, as you may recall," I said as I looked at his weirdly mismatched eyes—one brown, the other green.

I felt a chill shiver of pure hatred run through me at the sight of this maggot. I could strangle the bastard, right here in public, and happily serve the resulting sentence.

"It's a matter of national security," he said in a voice loaded with the gravitas of self-importance.

Well, that's an original statement if ever I've heard one, I thought, and I just looked at him. There is nothing like a prolonged silence to draw someone out and cause them to show their hand. Especially, as now, when a petty tyrant like this one wanted something so badly he was willing to demean himself for it.

Mayfield grew uncomfortable and began to shift his weight from foot to foot. His head was tilted backward to such an extent that I could see straight up his nostrils.

Man, you badly need a nose trim, I thought.

Finally, in a voice of rehearsed sincerity he said, "Your country needs you."

I let him stand there for a few more seconds before I replied.

"My country, eh? And *who*, exactly, do you speak for that represents *my* country? The people of the United States? Or some political parasite that has contributed a few hundred thousand dollars to the party in power and been awarded with a deputy-assistant-undersecretariatship of some type?"

"I come directly from the office of the Joint Chiefs of Staff, with an urgent request."

"Ah well, that caps it then. Please tell the Joint Chiefs that old Kennesaw M. Tanner, ex–master sergeant by the grace of God, says they can go pound sand for all he cares," and I turned to go inside.

I had taken two steps when he called to my back, "There's a lot of money involved in this—a lot of money."

Aha, the magic words. Why didn't you say so earlier?

I turned to look at him again, and as I did, I let my eyes roam the surrounding area until they found what I had expected to see. Quickly working out the solution to a potential difficulty, I nodded to myself and then replied.

"In that case, come aboard."

I dropped the cable across the gangway and let him step on deck. He stood looking at me, a sickly smile of faux friendship on his face and a welter of sweat on his brow. Reaching up to wipe the sweat away, he looked around the deck.

"Nice boat you have here, Kennesaw."

I was in no mood for small talk. Best to get on with it and hear what he had to say—but not here.

"Go up to the foredeck and stand by that line you see there," I instructed and pointed to the spot. "Then do as I tell you."

He nodded and scampered away like the good little lap dog he was.

I threw off the spring line that was cleated nearby and then went aft to cast off the other dock lines. That done, I went into the pilothouse, where I dropped down into the engine compartment and made the pre-start checks, and then fired up that superb Gardner diesel engine. I could crank it from the helm, but I liked to be next to her and listen closely as she rattled to life and then settled into a satisfying throb.

I then climbed back to the helm and checked that Mayfield was where I had left him. I didn't trust that man at all and had hoped he'd try something while I was out of sight, but he was still in place.

I called out to him from an open hatch, "Loosen the line. Undo the knot but leave two turns around the cleat, then hold the end of the line tight."

I watched as he fumbled with the rope but finally accomplished what I had instructed.

"Hold tight now," I called.

I hit the button for the horn, gave it a long blast, and

was pleased to see Mayfield jump in surprise at the unexpected noise. I gave the wheel a turn to port and put
the engine in forward. The transmission went into gear,
and I felt the prop bite into the water. I then gave the
throttle a slight push, and *Miss Rosalie*, snubbed down
at the head, swung her stern away from the dock and out
into the channel. I put the transmission back to neutral.

"Release your line," I ordered.

Mayfield flipped the rope so that it came off the cleat
and watched as it fell away. He started to come toward
the pilothouse, but I halted him before he made more
than a couple of steps.

"Go to the bow and stand there."

He gave me a puzzled look but did as he was told. I
slipped the gear lever into reverse, checked all around,
and then pulled away from and parallel to the dock. I
waited for a small crab boat to go by, then swung her
around in the channel and headed downstream toward
the Bull River and eventually out into Wassaw Sound.
We cruised for about a half hour, until we were swallowed by the great salt marsh.

I found a deep spot in the channel, looked to see that
I was about midway between Little Tybee and Wassaw
islands, and let drop the anchor. I then let *Miss Rosalie*
drift back with the current, until I felt the anchor dig into
the sand and take a firm hold. When the anchor chain
went tight, I cut the engine.

We were completely alone out here with not a soul
for miles around. No curious ears. No prying eyes. No
hidden surveillance agents. And unless you counted the
seagulls—no witnesses.

Mayfield looked back at me like he wanted to come
from the bow and join me, but I shook my head and
pointed for him to stay where he was. Reaching up, I
took my PPK from its hiding place above the helm and

then ran a thumbnail over the "loaded round" pin that protruded slightly just under the hammer.

Satisfied that a live one was up the spout, I stuck the pistol in the left side of my waistband, took an old pair of shorts from a drawer under the pilot's berth, and went out on deck.

Walking forward, I grabbed a bucket from its place and continued toward the bow. I stopped about five paces from where Mayfield stood, watching me now with a quizzical look. He wasn't a field operative, and I was pretty certain none of this was making the slightest sense to him. And as far as I was concerned, that was good; I didn't want it to.

Unexpectedly, I tossed the bucket to him. As he caught it clumsily in both hands, I pulled the pistol, leveled it on his nose, and clicked off the safety. He stood frozen with the bucket held in front of his chest, as though he thought it would protect him. And now, for the first time, he looked at me with real fear. I remained quiet and let him stand there as the reality of the situation sank in.

"I don't know what this is about, Kennesaw. What are you doing? I mean you no harm."

He was upwind of me, and I could smell the fear oozing from his pores.

"Take your clothes off and put them in the bucket," I ordered.

"But, but, I only wanted to . . ." he stammered.

"Forrest Mayfield, you'll do everything I tell you, or I will shoot you in the guts and throw you over for the sharks."

This man was here for an unknown reason, but one, I was sure, that was a threat to my well-being, if not my life and liberty. A chill of determination settled inside me, and I knew he could see it and feel it.

"This—I mean—I didn't expect . . ."

"I've killed better men than you, Mayfield—and you damn well know it. And if I return without you aboard—well, absent a body . . ."

I let the thought linger. He considered it for a second, nodded his understanding, and with slow and deliberate movements dropped his clothes, article by article, into the bucket until he was standing before me naked, embarrassed, and thoroughly frightened.

He stood looking at me with a pained expression on his face. His shoulders were slumped inward, and he was doing his best to hide his genitals without actually covering himself with his hands. His body language told of submission.

Looking him over very carefully, I commanded, "Turn around."

After surveying him from head to heel, I then ordered, "Bend at the waist and spread 'em."

He complied without further complaint. I was now satisfied that he was concealing no stowaways or unaccounted-for boarders or lodgers.

"Stand up and turn around," I said.

When he was facing me again, I tossed him the pair of shorts.

"Put these on," I told him, as I kept the gun leveled on the center of his chest.

With his modesty now somewhat back intact, I motioned him to move toward the aft deck.

"Let's go," I said, as I directed him with the muzzle of my pistol. "You first, and walk normally."

He did the best he could, but the tension in his back muscles told of his fear and feeling of vulnerability. When we reached the aft deck, I pointed to a chair.

"Sit," I ordered.

Mayfield lowered himself carefully into the deck

chair, all the while keeping his eyes on the gun in my hand. When we were both seated, I put the pistol back in my waistband and then gave him a sunny smile.

"So, Colonel, tell me what's so important that it brings you all the way down here?"

He took a deep breath and began to talk. I listened intently as he told me the story of the attack on the yacht and the kidnapping of the only surviving heir of the Emir Al-Jemani. And I realized then the source of the premonition that had been bugging me.

CHAPTER 5

I LISTENED WITHOUT INTERRUPTION until Mayfield finished his tale. I think he had probably expected questions, but still, I asked none. Instead, I remained quiet and just looked at him over my joined fingertips, until he could stand it no longer and broke the silence.

"So, what do you think?" he asked.

"About what?" I replied.

He scratched the side of his head and said in exasperation, "About the mission."

"What mission? All I've heard is the story of a kidnapping," I replied. "And I've heard most of it already from another source."

"The mission to recover the boy. What do you think I'm doing here, for Chris' sake?"

He was getting a little steamed now. I think he had expected a more cordial reception than the one I had given him. And it was pretty obvious he was hoping for some help.

"Emir Jemani, and the assistance he provides us, is vital to our efforts in the Persian Gulf region," he said slowly and distinctly, as though speaking to a student who was having difficulty with a lesson.

"Great. Hooray for Brother Jemani," I said with an insolent grin.

I watched Mayfield as he worked hard to contain his response. Doubtlessly, he was recalling the good old days, when he would have called me to attention and issued an order. But those days were long past, and he was struggling to find something else that would work instead. And then it must have occurred to him, something completely new to his experience: Just say it straight-out.

"We want you to go get the boy," he said.

I replied, "Why? I mean, why should I? It's none of my concern."

I think that was the one comment he was unprepared for.

"Well—because—uh, because it's important." He mopped the sweat from his face with a hand, and then wiped his hand on his shorts.

"Not to me, it isn't. And besides, send Delta. That's what they do."

He squirmed a bit before responding, "Look, Tanner—sir. The kidnappers have demanded a ransom of two hundred million euros for the return of the boy."

I interrupted, "Then tell the old Grandpa to pay it. That's the best way to handle these matters: a straight-up business deal."

"There's more to it than that, much more. The kidnappers also demand the expulsion of all U.S. forces from the emirate—that we leave our air and naval bases located there and withdraw from the region. If we do that, our counterterror operations in the lower Persian Gulf will be crippled."

He gave me a searching look before continuing, "But if we don't deliver—if we don't get the boy back, the emir himself will toss us out. He's made it quite clear that he holds the U.S. responsible for the situation and its outcome."

I shook my head and replied, "Mayfield, your problem isn't my problem, and I—"

"Look," he burst in. "You've done this sort of thing before. You rescued that English girl in the Sudan last year, and before that, the two Germans in Yemen, and others that we are aware of. You have a track record. You've been successful at this sort of thing where others have only failed."

"That was private sector, Mayfield, and I was very well paid for those jobs—extremely well," I pointed out. "But this is a government-to-government function— send in Delta Force."

"We can't," he said and looked down at his feet. "It won't work, and you know it."

I could tell from the expression on his face that he was coming clean this time—no curveballs, no subterfuge.

"The boy was taken by a group calling itself the Fist of the Mahdi. He's being held at an old foreign legion fort in an area that's claimed equally by Mali, Algeria, and Niger; NSA has pinpointed the place. But if we try to negotiate overflight approval from the governments of any of the surrounding countries, we're sure the info will go immediately to the highest bidder, and we'll be burned before we even begin."

"Then do it black—all the way," I said.

Mayfield shook his head.

"Things have changed since you were on the teams. The size of the package is too large—its footprint is too big. To send in even one team means"—and he ticked off the points on his fingers—"transport aircraft, basing rights, airborne command and control, refuel birds, medical package, military and diplomatic liaison teams . . ." His voice trailed off, and he stopped for a second before continuing.

"The chance of compromise is just too high. We would be detected before we could put a recon team on the ground," he concluded.

I watched a flock of gulls dive-bombing a shoal of baitfish nearby. "Then cut the size of the package. You don't need all that," I replied.

"It will never happen, Kennesaw. We're just not configured for that. There are just too many general officers involved. We know you've done this with a team of three or four men, but we can't, and that's the bottom line."

Yeah, I thought. *Stillbirth by oversight. A bunch of generals and staff flunkies trying to act like team leaders but from the safety of a thousand miles away, accomplishing nothing and preventing everything.*

"I'm not your man, Mayfield. And besides, you can't afford me. No government contract can pay more than an ambassador's annual salary, and even if it did, I don't want to carry your water for you."

I stood. "So what say we take you back to where I first laid eyes on you this morning, and you return to your bosses and say, 'No go.'"

Mayfield jumped to his feet and hastily replied, "Wait. This wouldn't be a government contract. You'd cut your own deal with Emir Jemani. The boy is his only male heir, the last of the royal bloodline; you know what that means to the old man. He'll pay anything to get his grandson back. You can name your price. And I'll see that you have whatever assistance and support from us that you require: Intel, logistics—you name it, it's yours."

I thought about it for a few seconds before I replied,

"And of course, this way, should the recovery effort fail, you'll be able to tell the old sheikh, 'Well, it wasn't us, Your Eminence. Uncle Sam isn't responsible.'"

Mayfield, to his credit, said, "I won't lie to you, Tanner; that is exactly so."

I pondered a bit more. Life *had* become pretty predictable of late. And like my old sergeant major used to say, "If you ain't tryin', you're dyin'."

"I'll talk to the emir," I said at last.

Mayfield's face sagged with relief. "Great. Does this mean I can put my clothes on now?"

"Yeah, go ahead."

And as Mayfield went to the bow to reassume his dignity, I watched as a formation of pelicans glided silently by. When the birds had disappeared into the distance, I walked to the pilothouse, fired the engine, and raised anchor. I would bill my time and expenses from this moment forward.

Back onshore once again, I tied the dock lines and then walked Colonel Mayfield to the top of the dock.

"I'll handle everything myself, Colonel. All I want from you is the intelligence packet you have on the group and nothing else. The only thing anyone in the government can do with this is screw it up."

I stopped, and as Mayfield turned to me, I held a finger in front of his face.

"But if I detect—no—if I even suspect any interference or surveillance of any sort, no matter the source—Pentagon, CIA, whoever—I will instantly pull the plug on this thing and hold you"—I tapped him lightly on the chest with my finger—"you personally responsible. *Comprende*?"

Mayfield nodded his head in compliance as we continued to his car. He opened the car door and started to get in, but then, hesitating a second, he looked at me with a serious eye.

"Had I actually been wearing a wire, would you have really shot me?"

I looked across the roof of his car to where a van sat parked at the convenience store across the street and then to another car with a couple of men in it under the shade of the trees down by Captain Flynt's. Mayfield followed my eyes, and when I shifted my gaze back to him, the worried look had returned to his face.

"It is illegal for the United States military to run domestic surveillance or to collect intelligence on a civilian citizen. A status, I might point out to you, that I happen to enjoy."

I let the words sink in and then gave him a friendly smile.

"Colonel, I suggest you get rid of everything you've harvested on me so far—everything. Because next time, my friend, I won't be so gentle and forbearing in my response."

He nodded his head, got in his car, and cranked the engine. He put the car in gear but held his foot on the brake.

"We'll notify the emir to expect you. Can I say when you'll arrive?"

I shook my head, "Tell him, 'Soon.'"

Mayfield sat still and stared out the windshield as something rumbled through his mind. Coming back to the moment, he returned his view to me.

"Kennesaw, it wasn't me who did you in back when—well—when all that stuff went down and you were forced out. I want you to know, I spoke up for you."

His eyes searched my face, looking for belief, or was it perhaps absolution that he hoped to find?

I cast my eyes across the parking lot to see what the van and the car were doing. They had also cranked their engines. I looked back at Mayfield.

"I won't be in contact, Colonel. Tell your masters they'll know the result when I deliver the boy."

"Right," he said.

And with that, he pulled away. As he turned onto the street, the other vehicles also moved out. And in textbook fashion, so as to appear inconspicuous, they departed in different directions.

I stood for a few seconds and thought about Mayfield and what he would report back in Washington.

Probably got a whole suite of secure offices in one of the subbasements of the Pentagon, packed to capacity with self-important drones passing info back and forth and doing their utmost to impress each other with their knowledge of clandestine activity, I thought. *If I pull this one off, several of them may well make their careers by taking the credit. Well, that's the way of it all, isn't it?*

Just then the breeze shifted, and I smelled the delicious aroma drifting up from Captain Flynt's and realized that it was barbecue day. I ambled down the dock and saw Danny Ray as he brought a stack of hickory wood to the grills. I called to him to come join me in a platter of ribs. And while we ate, I asked if he could look after *Miss Rosalie* for a little while.

CHAPTER 6

SOME PEOPLE SAY PREPARATION IS everything, and for those who never execute, maybe it is. But no matter the undertaking, and especially when it has the very real potential of getting you killed, I say it pays to lay things out in a calm and rational manner.

I sat in the captain's chair in *Miss Rosalie*'s pilot-house, cleared my mind of extraneous images, and as I gazed out across the water, I let the thoughts come of their own accord. It's my method of making haste slowly. If I get in a rush, I'm liable to miss something important, if not vital. But left alone, my bank of experience and intuition will usually present the needed answers, or something relatively close.

The first requirement for any operation is cover. Cover gives you breathing room and allows space for maneuver. And there are two kinds of cover: cover for status and cover for action.

Cover for status answers the questions: Who are you, and why do you exist? According to need and how long you may require it to hold up, it can be detailed and deep or rather shallow. Cover for status usually requires backstopping, almost always through documentation and often by verification from a third party.

Cover for action is simpler but often more critical. Cover for action answers the questions: What are you doing, and why are you doing it here? The best covers of this sort are boring, and should that fail, embarrassing to the point that you're viewed with distaste, and whoever you are dealing with just wants to get away from you.

I had started building my cover for status during lunch at Captain Flynt's. Danny Ray, in true Danny Ray fashion, had asked no questions. He merely let me know that he would take care of things until I returned. But I made a point of telling Dolores, the owner of Captain Flynt's, that I would be out of town for several weeks and that Danny Ray would be watching my boat.

Dolores pushed a shock of red hair away from her face and gave me a knowing grin.

"Finally running off with a woman, eh, Kennesaw? I knew it would happen sooner or later. I'm just hurt that you didn't ask me first," she said as she pushed out her lower lip and let a fake pout play on her striking face.

Dolores is an attractive woman of a certain age. She had kept Captain Flynt's alive after the loss of her husband, the redoubtable Bill. The place and its patrons were pretty much home and family to her, and she took a keen interest in what went on in her stretch of waterfront. And with a razor wit and powerful personality, she pretty much ruled her domain as uncontested and universally acclaimed queen.

Dolores had been trying to hook me up with one lady after another since I'd arrived here—and so far, without success. Once, in a rare state of exasperation, she had scolded me. "Damn it, boy, you don't look gay, but I'm beginning to think just maybe you are."

In response, I pulled her close and gave her a long, searching kiss and a quick pat on her delectable derriere.

She stepped back, looked me deeply in the eyes, and said breathily, "Well—maybe I *was* a little hasty in my judgment."

We were friends, and I trusted her, but your friends don't necessarily need to know everything you do.

"Got a gig down in Panama, Dolores. Client wants me to captain his boat on a cruise through the islands. Might be a week, might be a month. All depends on how enthused the client becomes about the local flora and fauna. And you know how those Panamanian girls are. They're—well—they are something else," I said with a light air.

Dolores made a fainthearted slap at me with a bar towel and laughed her throaty laugh.

"Yeah, you go on down to Panama. But don't come cryin' to me, one of those little hootchies cleans your plow."

"Never happen, Dolores. Besides, you know I'm partial to redheads."

We both laughed at the exchange, and I was sure that at least four nearby patrons had heard our banter. By the time happy hour was over this evening, it would be known far and wide that Tanner was bound for the isthmian waters of Panama.

"But if you would, Dolores, I'd appreciate it if you'd collect my mail—and anything looks like a bill, go ahead and pay it for me. I don't have an exact return date, and I don't want things to fall through the cracks."

I had taken out my checkbook and was preparing to write a check when she waved it away.

"I'll take care of things 'til you return, and you can settle with me then. Besides, it'll give me a chance to read any love letters come in."

She leaned forward with her forearms across the bar, so I'd have a maximum view of her renowned cleavage.

"Just don't forget about us while you're gone, Kennesaw," she said, a coquettish lilt in her voice.

I lifted my gaze from her bosom to her face in a slow and dramatic fashion. It was part of our act, and we both enjoyed the play.

"Ain't likely to happen, Dolores. Just ain't bloody likely."

We laughed again, and as she leaned over the bar and lifted her face, I gave her a friendly kiss on the cheek.

"See you when I return," I said as I turned to leave.

"Be well, Kennesaw. And come back in one piece."

I was a little surprised at her choice of words and stopped to look at her over my shoulder. She was looking at me with a calm and serious expression.

"I'll do that, Dolores. I will."

She nodded and gave a small wave. *Good,* she mouthed silently.

I nodded in return and then stepped out the door and into the bright autumn sunshine. As I crossed the parking lot, a car with darkened windows purposely pulled athwart my path. I turned on the balls of my feet and took a ready position. The driver's window dropped, and Patricia Latham's face came into view.

"You always so jumpy? It looked like you were ready to draw down on me." She grinned.

"I was getting ready to run. Thought you might have been one of my outlaw relatives from north Georgia, looking for a loan or a place to hide out," I quipped.

She shook her head and then, when she looked at me, her face was serious.

"I was hoping to catch you. Wanted to let you know about the girl."

"Ah, the girl," I said.

"Yeah. The girl. Her name is—was, Tonya Causey.

From up in Effingham County. We have two eyewitness reports. Said she jumped from the Talmadge Bridge four days before you found the body."

I thought about this for a second.

"Two eyewitnesses reported her by name? That's pretty incredible," I said.

"Not by name, but they did report a slightly built, redheaded girl climbing over the rail and plunging into the river. Also, autopsy showed the girl drowned."

"Nobody reported her missing? I asked.

Patricia shook her head again.

"Rest of a sad story. Family—if you can call it that—hadn't kept up with her whereabouts for the last year or so. All they knew, or thought they knew, was that she was here in Savannah. The mother was just happy when she'd get some money in the mail now and then."

"Swamp Crackers, eh?"

She nodded. "I don't like to hang names on people, but yeah, that's pretty accurate. Seems the girl got out of there the first chance she got, and well . . ."

Yeah, well, I thought as I stared across the top of the car. *When I was seventeen I ran from a situation that was probably much the same. At least I ran to the army, which was a huge improvement in my life. Who the hell knows what it was that Tonya ran to? But whatever it was, it was so bad she had made the final, the ultimate run.*

"Damn," was all I could say.

"We are in agreement there," she said. "But I wanted you to hear it from me. I thought I owed you that much."

"Thanks, Lieu—" She started to give me a hard eye. "I mean, Patricia."

She smiled. "Well, gotta go. City likes me to act like I'm busy, even if I'm not—but, hey, if you've got some time on your hands this weekend, I'm having an oyster roast at my place out on Tybee. Maybe you could stop by."

"I'd like that, I really would. But I'm headed out of

town for a spell. But I'd like to take a rain check on that invitation."

"Consider it issued, just like a ticket. Call me when you get back; I'm in the phone book, you know," she said as she put the car in gear.

"I'll do that, Patricia. I sure will."

She didn't reply, just gave me a nod and a smile, rolled up the window, and pulled away.

I returned to *Miss Rosalie*, cast a quick look around the deck, and went below to my cabin. It was time to give thought to who might be available for the operation. I would need a handful of operatives who had experience in North Africa and the Middle East. Men who could be depended on if things got rough but also had the necessary subtlety to outthink a problem if they could, rather than try to overpower it.

Terry Bailey and some of his mates would fit the bill. Terry and I had last worked together in Liberia. An English cockney by birth, Terry was a fifteen-year veteran of the French Foreign Legion and well experienced in the region and with its people. He had worked across North Africa from the Atlantic coast to the banks of the Red Sea.

Last I had heard, Terry was living on a small farm in central France, tending to his vineyards and raising a flock of little legionnaires with his Corsican wife. Maybe he was available, and if so, I hoped he was willing.

I scanned my bookshelves for a particular tome, found and plucked it from its resting spot, and went to the pilothouse. I checked to make sure of today's date, then opened the book and found the page I needed. Next I tore a sheet of paper from a legal pad, placed it on the bare wood of the chart table, and transcribed the lines I needed from the book.

That done, I turned on the single sideband radio, dialed up the correct frequency, and using the handset button as a key, sent a Morse code message out into the atmosphere. When the message was concluded, I waited five minutes then sent the message once again, and then again after another five-minute interval. I checked my watch and made note of the time. There would be a reply in exactly six hours.

I took the sheet of paper with the scribbled lines, set it afire, and held it until I had to let it flutter from my hand, where it curled to a wisp in the bottom of the brass waste can. Then I ground the ashes to nothingness, opened the door to the pilothouse, and let the breeze carry the burned paper powder back to Mother Earth. Going below, I put the book back in its place and felt sure there was nothing to trace.

What was that all about? It's a given that the National Security Agency, the NSA, harvests all e-mails and telephone calls. Not that they exactly listen to or read them all, but they can sort through them for the ones of particular concern.

I operate on the principle that if a communication can be intercepted, it will be. Mayfield's visit had confirmed what I believed, that I was under a lens of interest to the government, or at least to certain agencies and departments of government. And that was enough for me to take some precautionary steps.

E-mails and phone calls are the most rapid form of communication, but they are also the least secure. The use of a human messenger is the most secure form of commo, but it is also the slowest. But a coded message, if done properly, is both rapid and secure.

The book code I had used is for all practical purposes unbreakable. Without knowing the book being used and the dating sequence involved, it is impossible to decipher the message. And no matter who took down those random dots and dashes, without the key to the code, it was all so much useless noise.

I spent the rest of the afternoon out and about town. I first visited a few storage facilities that I kept rented for cash, where I picked out some identity documents, passports, and credit cards, all of them under various assumed names but with my smiling face where a photo was required. Then I visited a few travel agencies where I put together separate legs (under differing names, with appropriate documentation, of course) that when put together made up a circuitous route to Beirut. I was back in the pilothouse of *Miss Rosalie* in time for the radio reply I was expecting. The response was what I had hoped.

Okay, I thought, *time to make tracks*. Turning off the radio, I went to my cabin and packed a small travel bag. The light of day was just fading as I gave *Miss Rosalie* one last check before climbing the dock ramp, cranking up my old Bronco, and heading through the darkening Savannah streets to the airport on the outskirts of town.

CHAPTER 7

I THINK I'VE READ THAT THE SENSE of smell is the most primitive of our senses. I guess that's true, because to me all cities have an odor or aroma that is unique to that place alone. And once taken in, the smell will revive memories and previously experienced sensations faster than anything else I know. It had happened as soon as I walked out of the terminal at Beirut. As I took in the air of that fabulous, ancient, and tragic place, a flood of images washed through my mind, and I was momentarily transported to recollections of the past, some pleasant and some otherwise.

The traffic was the same as I remembered, with a chaotic frenzy that would frighten a Formula One driver. But the taxi man was one of those old pros who wended his way through that screeching mayhem with the ease and fluid grace of a python sliding through jungle shadows.

I had the cabby drop me at the Hotel Phoenicia. I waited outside a few seconds, and as soon as he was out of sight, I ambled to the corner and turned uphill.

It was only a short stretch of the legs to the small hotel where I was really staying, one I had used a few years ago. The owner, Rafik Hamdoun, was an acquaintance I had made through mutual friends in Syria. He was an astute man, one who knew the great value of catering to the occasional client who wished his comings and goings to remain a private affair. And cash, of almost any nationality, was the preferred method of payment in Rafik's establishment.

After checking in and dropping my bag in the tastefully appointed room, I returned downstairs, where I made a very short phone call from the desk. Then I walked outside and down the narrow street to a coffee shop that sat near a small inlet off the Mediterranean.

There is nothing like Arab coffee served at an outdoor Lebanese café. The sense of neighborliness and bonhomie is clearly evident and felt even by a foreigner. I sat at a small table and listened as two elderly Druze men discussed the latest local gossip. As I sipped my *ghahwah*, eavesdropping and watching the local life pass by on its daily business, I felt my mind and ear becoming accustomed once again to the rich and vibrant tones of the Arab dialect of the Levant.

The waiter cast me an inquisitive eye, and just as I was about to order another cup, a large late model Mercedes with darkly smoked windows stopped on the street directly in front of my table. The passenger window lowered, and as I looked inside, the driver turned his face toward me, removed his fashionable French sunglasses, and leaned in my direction.

He lifted an eyebrow in query. When I nodded *yes,* he got out and came around to open the back door. I dropped a few Lebanese pound notes on the table, pointed to them as the waiter came over, and climbed into the car.

Neither the driver nor I spoke as we made our way north along the Corniche and then turned eastward toward the mountains. We soon left the city behind, climbing steadily upward over a narrowing but quite serviceable road. Before long, the driver turned the car abruptly into a small side road that rounded a sharp bend and then took us to a massive iron gate set in the stone walls of a natural defile.

The car halted for only a second as the gate swung smoothly open. I looked up as we passed beneath the arch of the gate and caught just the fleetest glimpse of the muzzle of a machine gun mounted in the rocks above. Then, before my wondering eyes, we broke out into what looked to be a veritable Garden of Eden.

As the car followed the winding gravel drive, I marveled at the unfolding scene. Never in my life had I seen such exquisite grounds. Small waterfalls chortled over rock faces, and sparkling streams bubbled and frothed over smooth stones before running into the darkly mirrored faces of fern-shaded pools.

Courting peacocks, strutting and spreading their fans, roamed freely though the grounds. The vegetation and flowers were so rich and vibrant, it made me want to take off my shoes, roll my pants up to my knees, and stroll.

The beauty of it all and the sense of natural harmony it evoked brought rushing to my mind the words of Lebanon's most famous son, Kahlil Gibran, who told us in his masterwork, *The Prophet*:

> *And forget not that the Earth delights to feel your bare feet, and the winds long to play with your hair.*

Here, in the land of *The Prophet*, I felt the living vibrancy of Gibran's immortal and sacred words sing to me as never before.

With one last turn of the drive, we arrived at a portico. A young Somali servant leaned forward and opened the car door. When I stepped out, he smiled and indicated that I should follow him. As we proceeded, the gardens surrounding the covered walkway became even more lush and verdant.

The path led to a large roofed pavilion, where I was turned over to the majordomo of the household. He was of late middle age, somewhat on the short side of average height, with a comfortable paunch and a bald pate. His eyes were direct and bold, and an Olympic nose gave strength to his visage. His dark eyebrows and fierce mustache framed an intelligent face. Dressed in gray flannel slacks and an open collar white shirt, he was the very picture of a Lebanese gentleman's gentleman.

As the Somali turned to depart, I made a slight bow to the man and spoke in greeting, *"Salam aleikum."*

He returned the bow and replied with a raised eyebrow, *"Wa, aleikum es salam."*

He gestured me to a nook furnished with several comfortable chairs and a low table. As I took my seat, he asked in English, "Would you prefer tea or coffee, sir?"

"Tea, thank you," I replied.

The man poured the tea Bedouin style, with crushed mint and chunks of sugar, into a tall glass teacup that he set before me. As I looked around and admired the setting, I wondered how long I was to sit here drinking tea and kicking my heels before the emir deigned to grace me with his royal presence.

I'll give it fifteen minutes, I thought. *That's as long as I'll play the lackey before I go find the driver and head back to town.*

As that thought was making its way through my mind, the butler sat himself in a chair across the table from me, poured himself a cup of tea, and said, "Mr.

Tanner, at very short notice you have made a long and arduous journey to meet with me in my hour of distress. For this, I can not thank you enough."

This was the second time in my life that I've taken the principal for an assistant. And on this occasion, as with the last, I had the feeling that the small deception was purposeful and even enjoyed. I put down the cup and leaned forward in my chair.

Placing the fingertips of my right hand over my heart, I said, "Emir Jemani, Your Excellence, please know that you have my condolences on the loss of your son, daughter-in-law, and your grandchildren. And I am here to help, in whatever fashion may be best, in the recovery of your grandson."

He sat with his head lowered for a few seconds, then looked up with glistening eyes. ·

"Thank you, sir. Thank you for your words and thank you for your presence," he replied.

We spent a while getting to know one another. We talked of family, of our homes and background, and of travels. I've always found Arabs to be similar to my native Southerners in that we must first come to know the person we are dealing with, if even just a little bit, before we can settle down to business. To leap straight in without the social preliminaries is worse than rude; it borders on the offensive. After a few cups of tea and friendly conversation, we finally got down to business.

"Why you, sir?" I asked. "Why did this group—this Fist of the Mahdi—target you through your family? Though they've made political demands, this has the vicious earmarks of a feud. Was it a personal vendetta by one or more of your enemies?"

He sat deeply in his chair and pulled at his mustache before speaking again.

"I've wondered many times the same thing myself," he said in a low and pensive voice. "A man such as I has many enemies. But I can find no evidence that points in that direction. My feeling, and that of my advisors, is that this infliction is due to my support for the activities of your nation."

He was stating his conditions and letting me know who was to blame.

"That may well be the case, sir," I responded. "But I am not with the United States government nor do I represent it in any fashion whatsoever."

"But you are an American citizen, are you not?" he queried.

"By accident of birth and of long habit, yes. But I do not speak for my government," I responded.

He gave me a frank look that said: *I understand your meaning. You may proceed.*

"Have you been contacted a second time since the— the kidnapping? Have there been other demands or different timelines sent?" I asked.

"None," he replied. "There has been nothing since but utter silence."

I nodded, then sat back and thought while I sipped my tea. The man across from me also retreated into a state of quiet reflection. After a minute or so, I broke the silence.

"Sir, forgive me if in my effort to achieve clarity I seem blunt. But you do realize, do you not, that there is a great likelihood that your grandson is not alive? That this was purely a murder raid, in addition to being an extortion attempt on the grand scale. And that whatever you do, it may all come to naught."

The emir stood. He gave me a fleeting look, then turned and stared across the gardens before speaking again.

"I have considered that possibility, Mr. Tanner. But if there is the slightest chance that my grandson is alive, I want him returned to me."

"Then why not accede to the demands and pay the ransom?" I asked in an even and quiet tone of voice.

He turned to me with a face twisted in hatred and anger.

"Never!" he hissed. "These jackals—these sons of a shaitan will never cause me to grovel before them nor hear me whine or beg for mercy. I would rather spend all I have—in fact, I would break the treasury of my nation—to see their dead bodies made food for carrion eaters."

We held eyes as his words rang in the air, and I sat quietly and let the emir regain his composure before I spoke.

"Sir, there is another matter that you must consider. This is real life, not a movie. Even should I undertake the quest to recover your grandson, there is a large chance that I may not be successful, that either the rescue attempt itself will fail or that the boy may be killed during the operation. Though I will do everything I possibly can, there is just no guarantee of the outcome."

A look of resolve came over the emir, and he replied quietly, "All such matters rest in the merciful hands of Allah, Mr. Tanner. And I will abide by his will with peace and gratitude, no matter the outcome."

"Then I will do my utmost to return your grandson to you, alive and well," I replied with sincerity.

The emir sat again and took a sip of his tea.

"Now to the costs," he said as he placed his cup on the table.

I had prepared a list that outlined initial funds required, along with banking instructions and a final "success" payment. The emir reached to his shirt pocket for a pair of reading glasses and, putting them on, ran down the list with a practiced eye. Midway through, he gave me a brief glance over the top of his spectacles and then went back to reading the figures. Finished, he removed his glasses and put the list on the table, but kept his face lowered, as though lost in thought for several seconds. At length he spoke without looking up.

"These costs, sir, are excessive," he said in a flat voice.

It never fails, I thought. *The wealthier they are, the more they hate to turn it loose. And here this man sits— complaining about cost when the life of a child—his own grandson—is at stake.*

I held my words for a few seconds to make sure that when I spoke it was with composure and balance.

"Sir, I am neither a philanthropist nor a philosopher, and we are not two rug merchants in Ras Beirut, drinking tea and haggling over the price of a carpet.

"I am putting my life and the lives of my confederates at risk. I take only half my fee up front; however, I must pay my men in full and in advance for their part in the operation. I also place a quite expensive insurance policy on each of them in case of death or debilitating injury, which is always a distinct possibility.

"Additionally, the equipment required and supplies for the mission are very expensive. And there is the likelihood that the equipment may be destroyed or lost during the operation."

At this point I leaned forward and, placing a resolute emphasis in my voice, continued, "But if it is your belief that the security forces of your own nation or some other entity can do this job more effectively *and* at a cost more in line with your sensibilities, then by all means, sir, please feel free to avail yourself of that option."

I rose to depart, and making a slight bow in the direction of the emir, said, "Good day, sir. I will bill you for my travel and my time until I arrive back at my home. Perhaps you will not find *that* amount to be excessive."

I turned to go and had made three steps when he spoke.

"Mr. Tanner, please. Do not go, not yet. I ask you to forgive my rash and foolish words, and I beg of you to take no offense."

As I halted and turned, he stepped to my side and took both my hands in his. "It was unthinking of me to speak of money and act as though you were not placing your life in great hazard for the sake of me and my family. I can only attribute such an outburst to my beleaguered and battered state of mind."

I looked into his eyes and saw, for the first time, the deep grief that resided within.

"Sir, shall we proceed?" I asked.

"Yes, by all means. And with whatever it takes. My life, my country, my treasury, it is all at your disposal."

"I will be at my hotel. When I've been notified by the bank that the funds have been posted, I will get under way."

The emir held my hands until I finished speaking, then, stepping back a pace, he placed his right hand over his heart and intoned, *"Bismillah, Al Rahman, Al Rahim."*

These words are the first sura, or verse, of the Quran. They are traditionally said at the outset of an undertaking, particularly a hazardous one. I find the refrain to be very beautiful and say it as a prayer quite often. In translation it means: "In the name of God, Most Gracious, Most Merciful."

I replied, "I will return your grandson to you, if within the power given unto man—*Inshallah*."

"Inshallah," he breathed.

And with that, I turned and walked to the waiting car. The emir stood and watched as we drove out of sight.

Yes, Inshallah, I thought—*God willing, indeed.*

The funds were credited to the bank account within two hours of my return to the hotel. As soon as I received the notification, I busied myself with the next leg of the journey. Rafik provided a trusted driver, along with his own vintage Mercedes, to drive me up the coast to the port city of Byblos, where I caught the ferry to Cyprus.

The sea was calm and the air balmy as I stood at the aft rail and watched the purple and tan mountains of Lebanon fade and shift colors in the late afternoon sun.

That step concluded, and now for the next, I thought as I turned my back on that beautiful and battered land and ambled to the bow of the ship to put my nose into the wind and gaze in the direction of the divided island of Cyprus.

CHAPTER 8

A RASPY VOICE GROWLED IN MY EAR, "'Lo, mate."

I cut my eyes to the side and caught a big toothy grin, a pair of outlandish eyebrows, deeply set blue eyes, and a nose that took several incredible bends and twists before reaching its final end.

"You filthy pirate. How you are, Terry?" I was barely able to get out the greeting before being grappled in a hug, lifted off my feet, and given a resounding kiss on the lips.

I returned the hug and the kiss, and then we stepped back to arm's length to survey each other. But about that kiss: In my world, we are not afraid of showing affection to a close friend with whom you've risked your life. Nor are we afraid of touching another man.

Terry and I know the odor and color of each other's blood. On several occasions we have been prepared to die together. And later, when death had seen fit to pass us by until another time, we shared the great joy of being found among the living.

We have lived, at times, as closely as two humans can live without being lovers. So a kiss is nothing that causes shame or embarrassment—at least, not to us. But you may feel differently about the matter.

Terry is known among our tribe as Waggy, because of the animation of his eyebrows. They look like separate beings with an intellect all their own. Each eyebrow moves independently of the other and apparently in complete disregard to what Terry would have them do. As I looked at him now, they were bobbing about like two bushy red caterpillars trying to cross a burning sidewalk on a hot summer day.

"You don't know how timely your message was, Kennesaw. I've been home so long this time, the old lady and me were about to go for our knives. 'Nother few days, and well—things could'a become newsworthy," he said as he flashed me a mouthful of crooked teeth.

I grabbed Terry by the arm and led off. We maneuvered our way out of the shouting and jostling crowd, trooped out of the terminal, threw ourselves in the rental car, and sped away.

As we wheeled through the surprisingly light traffic, I briefed Terry on the kidnapping and how the situation stood at present. He listened in silence while those eyebrows of his beat a tattoo on his forehead.

"Got some intel on this Fist of the Mahdi, as they calls themselves," he said, as I dodged a teenage boy dashing across the street.

"What's that?" I asked.

"Buzz I gathered from some Mafia friends in Marseille, guys who bring hashish in through Morocco, tells me it's criminal, not political. Bloke heads it up is supposedly a former Sudanese corporal name of Abdulkader Boutari. Promoted himself to colonel, raised a gang of bandits that have been terrorizing the local neighborhood, and has now hit the big time by grabbing the kid."

"Sudanese, eh? That explains invoking the Mahdi, wouldn't you think?"

"Has some history behind it at that," he said. "And it's something always plays well with the local Baptists."

I should explain: The concept of the Mahdi, in Islamic lore, is much like the idea of the Messiah. He is "the anointed one" who has come to lead the faithful back to the paths of righteousness and glory. Periodically, one of these types comes on the scene, raises an army, and promptly leads his followers to thorough disaster and complete destruction. There had been a huge uprising in the Sudan in the 1890s that had cost the British quite a lot of effort, money, and manpower to put down.

So for a Sudanese to claim the mantle again was sort of like following along in the family line. But before you say, "Aha, those crazy Muslims again; it's just like them," think: Jim Jones or David Koresh or any of the other nutcases that pop up now and again in our own country and culture. Invoking the illuminated will of God in order to fool the ignorant and easily deluded is exclusive to no culture.

Back at the villa I'd arranged for, we settled at the kitchen table to start putting a plan together.

"Ah, you remembered," cried Terry, as I produced a couple of glasses, ice, a jug of water, and a bottle of Bushmill's.

Terry's favorite drink is, as he calls it, "That Protestant Irish whiskey." And it just happens to be one I'm pretty fond of myself. So we poured, sipped, and talked as we plotted our next moves, all the while making pencil slashes on a big Michelin map of North Africa, spread before us across the table, and referring now and again to the stack of satellite photos I had downloaded.

"Biggest question: how best to get there," Terry said, as he measured map distances with a ruler.

"Get there, and get out. Those are two of the problems. Making the hit is another. But the biggest problem, in my view, is composition of the force," I replied.

I had been thinking about this one aspect since leaving Savannah, and I wanted Terry's thoughts and insight on the matter.

"What size element are you considering?" he asked as he rocked his chair on its two back legs.

"Depends on the size of the opposing force. And right now, I don't have a firm idea what that might be," I replied. "Material I got from the States says the fort they're holed up in could house up to a couple of hundred men. But who knows?"

"Aye, bugger of a problem that. But you have to believe they're in sufficient size to have not only pulled off the raid but are also large enough to maintain control of that old fort and the adjacent town."

"My thought, too, Terry. But that could place the numbers anywhere from forty up to as many as two hundred."

"Ah, well, if that's all, it's little more than a walk in the park, I shouldn't wonder." Terry's eyebrows gave me a wave, while Terry gave me a grin over the rim of his glass. "But I think using more than a handful of Westerners is out of the question. Makes too large a presence and puts the local boys off their feed."

"That's what I've been thinking all along. I'd like to go with a core of old hands as leadership, and hire an indigenous force as the muscle," I replied.

"What you think? Three—four round eyes as subordinate leaders?" he asked.

"Sounds about right to me," I said. "Excluding aircrew."

"Yeah, we'll have to fly in, that's for certain," he said

as he leaned over the table and scanned the map.

"AN2s. Those are the birds I want to use, Terry. Rugged, get in and out easily, big payload. Got some current contacts for those?" I asked.

"Jurassic planes." He smiled. "Yeah, easy enough. How many you think we'll need?"

"Four should be just about right. Three to make the lift in and out, and a forth one for odds and ends and to act as a spare, just in case something goes wrong."

"And something always goes wrong, don't it, old mate?" Terry laughed while his eyebrows danced.

"Murphy never sleeps, my friend. At least not within the limited scope of my own experience."

Terry took a sip of his drink and then a long pull on the foul-smelling cheroot he'd been working on.

"Where do you want the planes to meet us?" he asked.

"Who can we get on short notice? Can they pop right now?"

"Some Hungarian lads, top-shelf lot they are."

"Is that Istvan and his boys?" I queried.

"The same, no less. I'll call them now; I think they can get under way before the day is finished."

"You anticipated me, didn't you, Terry?"

Terry blew a smoke ring that stopped in midair, and then he gently stuck a finger through the middle of it. It held on his finger for a few seconds before dissipating.

"Kennesaw, old chum, you're not the hardest man in the world to figure out. Besides, I just considered what I might do and knew that wouldn't be too far off the old mark."

"Small minds think alike, is that it?"

Terry shrugged his shoulders and took another pull on his cigar. "So I've heard said. Now, where do you want the boys to meet us?"

"I don't want to leave a trail from here. Too easy to pick up," I said.

I sat forward and put the point of a pencil down at a spot on the map where the Mediterranean Sea washed the coast of North Africa. "Here, day after tomorrow. At last light. You know the place?"

Terry glanced down at the map. "Right. Do they need cargo handling gear?"

"Some," I said. "Also some other equipment I want them to bring in. Probably be expensive, but tell them to not worry about the cost. "

"And your indigenes, you got some lads in mind?" he asked.

"Some folks I've worked with before. I think they wouldn't mind the venture at all. In fact, it just might be something right up their alley."

"Have a name do they, these mates of yours?" Terry asked as he relit his cigar.

"Some of their neighbors refer to them as the Corsairs of the Sahara," I replied. "Others use less flattering names. The legion knows them as the Tuaregs—which in Arabic I believe means 'the bereft of God.'"

Terry let his eyebrows have full play and emitted a low whistle before replying in a near whisper, "Blue Men of the desert. Rather colorful lot, those friends of yours. I've had some right pointed dealings with them in the past. Think you can trust them?"

"Probably not, at least not in the long term. But I believe, if we look hard enough, we can find a position where our mutual interests coincide. At least for a while, which I hope will be long enough."

Terry gave me a penetrating look.

"You don't have much time, mate, and the clock is ticking. Suppose when we get there, these friends of yours aren't too keen on it all?"

"Well, in that case, Terry, we'll have to rely on you to come up with a better idea, won't we?"

Terry leaned back in his chair and blew smoke toward the ceiling.

"Yeah, they might just do it at that. And on the cuff of the moment, I can't seem to come up with anything better."

"You think perhaps Roosty and Pope Donnelly might be available?" These being men who had served with Terry in the legion, and were "in the business."

"By some odd chance, they are," he said as he studied his cigar with a fond eye before sticking it back in the corner of his mouth.

"Then let's bring them aboard, standard rate plus fifty percent, with a performance bonus for success."

Terry nodded in reply.

"Where shall they rendezvous with us?" he asked as he turned his head and blew smoke in the other direction—away from my face for a change.

"Tunisia, Jean Marc Lavalier's place, tomorrow."

"Right," he replied as he stood. "Let me pop out and place a call. Only be a minute."

Terry went out on his errand, and I sat and studied the map. *Somewhere on here are some answers,* I thought, as I scanned that flat sheet of paper that represented so much mystery and such a wide swath of God's good earth.

Terry returned quickly and gave me a thumbs-up. "All settled," he said.

Then, pouring new drinks and putting our elbows on the table, we leaned into our work, making and remaking lists on a yellow pad while Terry scattered cigar ashes across the map. Finished at last, Terry went out to make another phone call. And I went to see a man about a ship.

CHAPTER 9

GAIL BURNS CAME AWAKE WITH complete clarity and a full recognition of where she was. She lay still for several minutes though, and listened to the small sounds of the still and darkened room, trying to gauge the time. Outside the door, she could hear the muted snores of her guard. The boy beside her, on the jute mat that served as their bed, did not stir but continued in the measured cadence and full breathing of a deep sleep. That, at least, was a blessing.

For the first few days of captivity Gail had awoken to the hope that it was all a dream—that if she just lay still and went back to sleep again that it would be all right, that it had only been a nightmare. But it wasn't a dream, and it wasn't all right. The nightmare was very real, but one of the waking hours, one of reality rather than fantasy.

Gail lifted herself quietly and lightly, so as not to disturb the sleeping boy. She stood and looked down upon the child and wondered for the ten thousandth time what was to become of them. At first the boy had been unable to speak and barely registered the fact that he even knew her.

Then, when he had begun to talk, hesitatingly at first, fitfully, tearfully, to tell her what he had witnessed, she almost wished him back into his previous condition of shock. He was sleeping peacefully now, but for most of the night hours he lay in her arms, quivering and whimpering, like a small wounded animal.

She went to the far corner of the room, where she took a long drink of water from one bucket and then made use of the other that served as the latrine. She had quickly learned to arise while it was still dark and make her toilet. This way she could avoid the leering grins and lecherous eyes of her guards.

Once, an older man had caught one of the guards in his Peeping Tom act, and with fearful oaths and a single blow had bludgeoned him to the floor. But this single act of protection, rather than stopping them, had only made the guards more surreptitious at peeking in on her.

If only she could speak to that older man—he seemed to have had a conscience, a sense of decency. Maybe he would tell her what this was all about, what was to happen to her and the boy. Maybe she could reason with him. But she had been allowed no contact with anyone. And even the old woman, who came in once a day to bring food and change the buckets, would not look at her and only made grunts of disapproval when Gail tried to communicate.

Gail washed herself with the slip of a rag she had torn from the edge of the one thin blanket she and the boy shared. And then, in the distance, somewhere far off, yet clearly heard in the cool air of the early morning, she heard the voice of the muezzin as he sang the call for the predawn prayer.

She stood, and craning her neck, looked up at the small, high window that let in her single, tiny connection to the outside world, as though she might see the source of that song. And she wondered again at the beauty of the voice that was lifted in that ancient and pious call.

Perhaps he is a good man, a kind and just man, she thought as she listened. *One who would help us, if only he knew we were here.*

And as the echoes of the final words of the call faded to nothing in the faint gray light of the false dawn, Gail Burns knelt, and leaning her small forehead against the rough stone blocks of the cell wall, she whispered her own prayers to an unseen but fervently wished-for God.

CHAPTER 10

I CHECKED THE POSITION OF THE SUN against the low ridgeline to the west. That huge orange ball was falling noticeably, rapidly now, and as it did, the sky was lit with a blaze of flaming color from one horizon to the other. The utter beauty of the sunsets and sunrises of North Africa have no competitors in the world. No place else even comes close. And I stood once again, transfixed in marvel at the sight.

At last, with one last flash of red-purple-orange, the mighty life-giving orb slipped below the far edge of the earth. And with its passage, the hour seemed quieter, the sea calmer, and the wind less insistent. I turned and looked out to sea and watched as the ship that had been hovering in the distance now turned its bow in our direction.

Terry dropped his binoculars so that they hung from the cord around his neck and descended, in several bounds, from the rooftop of the old shed and came to stand by my side.

"Coming in now," he said quietly.

I turned and looked down the length of the old air-strip. Scuffing the hard surface of the ground with the toe of my desert boot, I felt something metallic. Bending down, I picked it up and held it before my face. It was a corroded strip of metal a few inches long and less than a half of an inch wide. I passed it to Terry, who turned it over in his hand and looked at it intently.

"Stripper clip. Second World War," I remarked.

Terry gave it a last look before tossing it away.

"Lee-Enfield," he said. "British infantry. If we were of a mind to dig around, I daresay we could find lots of other interesting stuff."

He was right. This was ground that had been furiously fought over as the British clawed their way out of Egypt and up the coast of Tunisia in pursuit of Rommel's Desert Rats. This very field we stood on had been a focal point of the campaign for several days. Men had clashed and died here in the fight for this terrain. And once taken from the enemy, and left behind in an insistent and ever-moving front, it had slipped once again into forgotten obscurity. But it was an obscurity and remoteness that suited our purposes to perfection, because even the Bedouins avoided this place. I think the presence of old land mines also had a lot to do with that.

Roosty stood on the end of the old stone quay and waited for the ship to arrive. A Moroccan by birth, Roosty had made his way to France as a teenager and at the first opportunity had joined the legion. For ten years he and Pope Donnelly had been in Terry's company of paratroopers. The temper of all three had been fired in the furnace of adversity and combat and honed to a wicked edge by the legion.

As I looked back down the length of the airfield, I saw the other two men coming back in our direction. They were both trained airborne pathfinders and had put their skills to work that afternoon laying out the signals for the airstrip. The small lights weren't entirely necessary, but I didn't want to leave things to chance.

Terry was looking at the ship again.

"Should be here in fifteen minutes or so," he said, as he lit a cigar.

I fanned the smoke from my face and growled, "If you've just got to smoke, I wish at least you'd buy a decent brand."

He blew a great cloud of smoke with a wicked grin.

"You buy 'em, mate, and I'll gladly smoke 'em," he said.

"Pearls before swine, amigo. Pearls before swine," I retorted.

Terry chuckled while his eyebrows flashed like demented semaphores.

"You sure the water's deep enough for Mazhar to bring her in? Maybe he needs to anchor offshore."

I shook my head as we walked to the quay.

"He draws nine feet, max, and that's at the stern. Water off the end of the pier is sixteen. He's got plenty of depth."

As we watched, a small boat pulled away from the freighter and made its way toward the quay. It roamed back and forth in an S-shaped pattern as it made its approach.

"Checking water depth," said Terry. "Not taking any chances."

I nodded in reply. Mazhar Durukan was an expert in the business of putting into small and obscure ports during after-business hours. And he was even more expert at getting out again.

His small coastal freighter was registered as a legitimate Turkish vessel, but on most occasions the cargo he carried would never have withstood even the most cursory of customs inspections. But when it came to supplying and delivering contraband, Mazhar the Turk had few, if any, peers.

The boat came to the edge of the dock, puttering back and forth as the bosun took in his soundings. Then, with a wave to us on the end of the pier, he returned to the ship at full throttle.

Roosty and Pope came up with two cargo handling dollies and stood quietly by. Then, with perfect timing, just as the light of day was fading to dusk, we watched as Mazhar, with a smooth and careful slide, brought his ship right to the end of the pier.

Terry and I grabbed the first dock lines thrown from the side of the ship. As we made these fast to the old bollards on the quay, four sailors swarmed over the side of the vessel and caught the other lines tossed to them. Within seconds, the ship was snugged securely to the dock.

Even as that was happening, cargo was being off-loaded over the side. I looked up just as the navigation lights on the ship were turned off and saw a lone, dark figure step onto the bridge wing and lift an arm in salute.

"Tah-ner!" he called. "Long time we no hear from. My wife always ask me, 'Where Tah-ner? Why he no visit no more? He mad at you, Mazhar?'

"I say, 'I don't know, woman. Maybe because you now old and ugly!' We then fight, but then we forgive and after make love!"

He threw back his head and laughed like a fiend. "Tah-ner! It makes good see you some more again. I come down now."

Mazhar swung over the side of the bridge and slithered down the narrow ladder like a trapeze artist. He bounded through the pack of scurrying crewmen and jumped to the dock with a resounding thud.

"Tah-ner, Tah-ner. Is good. Is good," he called over and over again as we greeted each other. He then turned his head in the direction of Terry and gave a curt nod of strained acknowledgment.

"Durukan," said Terry with a slight inclination of the head. "Glad you could make it."

"Uuff," was Mazhar's gruff reply.

There was bad blood between the two, that was for sure, and for the life of me, I was never able to ascertain the reason. Neither of the men ever gave a cause for their mutual animosity. Perhaps it was a case of dislike at first sight. But whatever the cause, the years had not made it any better. But at least the bad blood had never broken out in a physical manifestation.

Ignoring Terry, Mazhar grabbed my arm and led me to the stack of boxes rapidly building at the end of the pier. He flung open the lid to a crate and lifted one of the contents of the box.

"Look," he cried, as he shook the rifle in my face. "You ask, and I find for you. Best in all world. But why you want this, I don't know why."

I took the rifle in my hand, pulled back the bolt, and gave her the once-over. The AK-47 is renowned throughout the world as the almost ubiquitous assault rifle, but it has some very real limitations. First of all, in the hands of the untrained—who always tend to fire in long automatic bursts—it burns ammo at a tremendous rate. And ammo is both heavy and bulky.

Whereas this little weapon, the one I held in my hand, the SKS, has all the robust features of the AK but is a semiautomatic. It fires one shot per pull of the trigger. It has a smaller magazine capacity than the AK. It is easier to control and allows the shooter to conserve his ammunition, something that might well become critical before this job was over.

"And the other, Mazhar?" I asked, as I placed the rifle back in the crate.

"As you ask," he replied. And with a flourish, he flung open the lids to two other boxes.

I looked inside. Everything was there: RPK machine guns, a couple of sniper rifles, the little Skorpion machine pistols, two grenade launchers, and other assorted items.

I reached into one box and picked up a couple of Czech pistols that were already in their holsters. I tossed one to Terry.

"Here you go. Try not to shoot yourself."

Terry fastened the holster to his belt, then loaded several magazines and charged the pistol. Reaching into the box, he grabbed two more pistols and a couple of boxes of ammo.

"I'll take these to the other lads, if that's all right with you, Your Grace," he said as he executed a mocking curtsy in my direction before flashing a grin and moving away.

I plucked out one of the little Skorpion machine pistols and gave it a once-over. With its pistol size and folding stock, the Skorpion makes for a compact weapon. Some folks say it's a bit low-powered, but for a close-in fight, I've found it to be more than adequate.

I loaded several magazines and then slung the little shooter around my neck. The machine pistol, my knife, a compass, and a length of parachute cord would stay on my body, night and day, until the operation was over. They were part of my "If Everything Goes to Hell Kit," and I had to make it out of Indian country on my own with nothing but what I had on my person. I turned again to Mazhar, who had been watching silently.

"And the rest, Mazhar. Did you find the other things I ordered?" I queried.

He became all business again and turned toward the ship.

"Here comes now. Just like you order. Hard to get. Cost much. But Mazhar, he find."

I looked up to see two men pushing the bikes down the ramp and onto the dock. Behind them came the other pieces of equipment. I waited for the bikes to be brought over and then wasted no time in going over them thoroughly and cranking them up. While the motors idled, I looked at the rest of the stuff. It was all there: two trailers, a generator set that hooked to the bike, fuel cans, tools, spare parts: everything I was looking for.

Roosty and Terry came over as I was checking out the rolling stock. Terry scratched his head in puzzlement at the odd-looking bikes. "What the hell are those bloody things?" he asked.

Roosty laughed and jumped astride the nearest one.

"It's a donkey," he shouted as he gave the throttle a twist and lurched away, all the while laughing and calling, *"Hee-hawww, hee-hawww."*

We watched as Roosty drove to the end of the dock, then off a steep two-foot drop to the gravel beach. From there he turned inland and went up a narrow gully until only his head was showing above the rim. In a steady and fluid movement, he climbed the bike out of the gully and then returned to where we stood.

"Best cross-country motorbike in the world," I said as Roosty climbed off and gave the seat of the bike a pat. "She can go anywhere."

"Aye, perhaps," said Terry as he gave it a closer look. "But it's a right ugly beast, ain't it."

I couldn't deny that it's ugly, but it is about the only motorbike I consider fit for operational use. Made by the Rokon company of New Hampshire, she has front and back wheel drive, fat tires, and a long range at a rather slow speed.

The wheels are hollow for use as additional fuel or water carriers or to act as floats when crossing a stream. With a trailer attached, it can do something other two-wheel rigs can't; it can support itself by hauling fuel, water, and other equipment.

With the generator kit, it can power radios, other electrical items, and also recharge batteries. When Roosty called the Rokon a donkey, he wasn't far wrong. If need be, I could cross the Sahara on one of these.

At that very instant we heard a shrill whistle from the ship. Turning, I saw a man on the bridge waving to get our attention and then pointing excitedly out to sea. Looking in the direction he indicated, I saw a light bobbing along offshore, and a few seconds later, heard the low *chug-chug-chug* of a small diesel engine.

Mazhar was staring intently at the boat that could just now be dimly seen in the rapidly gathering darkness.

"Less than kilometer out. He see us, all right," Mazhar said quietly, as though his voice would carry to the men on the alien boat.

"Maybe not," whispered Terry.

"They see, and they tell. We go now, quick," said Mazhar with urgency in his voice.

He called and waved to his men, as he headed for his ship. The crew immediately broke into what looked to be a well-rehearsed drill. The lines to the ship were rapidly tossed off as the remaining cargo was hustled to the dock.

The unloading of the cargo had been a dance of efficiency itself, but the preparation for departure was something impressive to behold. It was easy to tell they had done this sort of thing many times before.

Mazhar leaped aboard while still shouting orders to his men. Going hand-over-hand up the ladder, he arrived at the bridge, where he gave quick, short instructions to the helmsman. Then, leaning over the rail, he gave the dock and his men a quick glance.

Putting two fingers to his mouth, he cut loose with a loud whistle, and as the sound penetrated the night air, the remaining men on the dock jumped aboard, and the vessel got under way.

"Tah-ner," he called, as he waved to me. "If after, you still alive, come see family. We miss much."

"I will, Mazhar," I promised. "Did you receive the payment I sent? Was it enough?"

He waved again.

"Money in bank already. No worry, is good. I see you sometime again. We eat, we drink, we laugh, yes?"

"Yes," I called. "But you be careful."

"Hah! Careful is for you, my friend. Mazhar, he is lucky!"

He thumped himself on the chest, laughed, and waved one last time before stepping back inside the bridge and taking the wheel himself.

In a matter of seconds, the stern of the ship was to the shore, and the bow was pointing out to sea, leaving our small band of men alone in the darkness on a silently brooding and hostile shore.

CHAPTER 11

AWAY TOWARD THE NORTH, I COULD
just make out the masthead light of the boat that had
provoked the rapid departure. When I turned again,
Terry, Roosty, and the other men were hauling the boxes
from the dock and stacking them by the shed that stood
near the edge of the airfield. I hurried to join them and
lend a hand.

We worked steadily, getting the gear sorted and then
cross-loaded, so that each plane would have a similar cargo.
This way if we lost one airplane, it wouldn't have all the
rifles or all the ammo. It's a means of limiting potential loss.

Making a final inventory, I knew we had everything
ready for the arrival of the planes. Now for a contin-
gency plan. I turned to the guys.

"I have to believe that as soon as that boat reaches
port, they'll report us to the authorities," I announced.

"Likely so," said Terry. "But it may be hours 'til he
gets in."

"I don't think so," I replied. "He was pretty close in-shore, which tells me he was almost home. The closest village is only about fifteen kilometers up the coast. If that's where he's going, he'll be there within another hour or so."

"Aye, to be sure, but then he has to rouse the local constable, drink some tea while he tells his story, and even then, maybe nobody bothers. I mean, it's after dark, and who knows that we mightn't be some really bad characters out here in the dark of night, ready to kill honest but nosy citizens."

"Could be as you say, Terry, but what if some Tunisian Barney Fife is on duty, just itching to make a name for himself and move up the ladder. We can't bluff our way out of this."

And as Roosty unconsciously let his hand rest on his pistol, I continued, "And we're not going to shoot any cops. This isn't life or death."

Pope Donnelly spoke up for the first time. "'Tis so, but as for me, I don't relish kicking me heels in a Tunisian lockup, either."

"And we won't," I said.

I looked over to Pope. It was always part of the plan that he linger on the airfield after our departure, make sure the area was sterile, and then return to Tunisia. There, he would monitor the radio and act as a rear echelon during the operation, just in case we needed outside assistance.

"Pope, take the truck and return to Lavalier's place now," I said. "If anything happens before we can get out of here, at least you'll be in a position to help out. If we're nabbed, Jean Marc will be able to spring us. It will just cost a little baksheesh."

Pope looked at me, then at the other men. "Right," he said and then turned to go.

We walked with him to the truck parked behind the shed. One of the joys of working with professionals is the lack of hand-wringing and dramatic posturing. Pope instinctively knew what was best in this situation and did it without argument.

He climbed aboard and cranked the engine. As he did, I reached into my shoulder pouch, pulled out a sheaf of currency, and passed the bills though the open window.

"Here you go. Just in case you run into a rough spot that requires a little lubrication."

He stuck the money down the front of his shirt and put the truck into gear.

"See you lads when you get back," he said. "Try your best not to get killed."

And then he pulled away. Within seconds he was swallowed up by the darkness, and soon we could no longer hear the engine of the truck. But a few minutes later, we saw the headlights come on as he reached the rutted dirt roadway that paralleled the coastline. Less than a minute afterward, the desert swallowed the headlights of the truck, and we were left alone in the darkness. We turned and walked back to the shed.

I leaned against one of the crates and checked my watch. Forty minutes until we could expect the arrival of Istvan and his flying circus. I had timed this so that neither Istvan nor Mazhar would see the other. I didn't want them both exposed while we were so vulnerable, nor did I want one to know the other was involved. It's always best to keep things compartmented. But sometimes, as now, it becomes an awkward dance.

It was full dark now, and the wind blowing in off the desert had a bite to it. Before dawn it would be downright cold. I found my backpack, rooted around inside, and pulled out a jacket and my *cheche*. When Roosty and Terry saw what I was doing, they followed suit.

The *cheche* (pronounced *shesh*) is the quintessential North African head covering. It is a piece of cotton cloth, six to twelve feet long and maybe eighteen inches wide. It is wrapped in a certain fashion around the head and neck. A tail of cloth is left hanging over one shoulder so that it can be pulled across the lower portions of the face to keep dust and sand from the mouth, nose, and if need be, the eyes.

It is warm in the winter. In the heat of summer it protects from the sun. It holds the moisture of sweat against the skin and it allows it to evaporate more slowly, thus cooling the wearer. It is an indispensable item of clothing and one perfectly suited to the environment.

Every tribe and group in North Africa has a slightly different way of wearing the *cheche*, along with varying color preferences. The Tuaregs wear blue or black, according to the clan. In their language it is called a *tagelmust* and for adult men is always worn with the tail end covering the face. A symbol of the Tuareg nation, the wearer is called *Kel Tagelmust*, or "Person of the Veil." In contrast to other regions, but common among the Bedouins and other nomads, the women are not veiled.

For our clan I had selected the color green, for green is known throughout the Islamic world as the color of Prophet Mohammed (peace be upon him).

Thus suited against the evening chill, we checked all items one more time. Roosty went to stand by the barrels of gasoline, so he would be ready to refuel the planes as soon as they landed. Terry and I arranged the crates and equipment for loading so that the last items loaded aboard would be the ones we would need to offload first.

We were just finishing the positioning of gear when Terry stood sharply, cocked his head, and looked out to sea. "There they are," he said, as he pointed to a spot in the sky. "Inbound."

"You sure?" I asked. I had heard nothing, but my hearing is not nearly as acute as Terry's.

"Aye, mate. It's them, all right."

I cast my eyes back and forth in the direction Terry was pointing and at last caught view of a dark speck moving slowly against the night sky. As it came closer, I then saw several other moving specks arrrayed in a staggered row. They were coming straight for our location.

Terry and I set out at a run to pop the chemical lights that would show Istvan and the pilots the location of the leading edge and the left side of the field. As the planes came over the field at a couple of hundred feet, I took one of the small lights and spun it above my head. The planes banked and came about, swinging out to sea again, but now descending on final approach. When only seconds out, the lead plane switched on his landing lights, cut power, and was almost immediately on the ground.

Roosty swung a light to gain the pilot's attention, and as the other planes landed, he guided them to the place designated for refueling and the loading of cargo. When the last plane was on the ground, Terry and I jogged over to join them.

The AN-2 is nothing so much as a flying truck. It is the world's largest biplane. They were originally designed by the Soviets for use by their Forest and Agricultural Ministry to fly into remote and austere locations. With a thousand-horsepower radial engine, a large payload, and a remarkable design that allows it to get in and off the ground in four hundred fifty feet or less, the AN-2 is in all probability the greatest rough-country airplane ever manufactured.

They were built in the thousands, and with the fall of the Soviet Union, they found their way onto the market at a very good price. Simple, rugged, and reliable, it is everything I require in a piece of equipment.

Just as I arrived by the side of the lead plane, the cargo door popped open, and out jumped the redoubtable Istvan Laczkó. Medium height, slightly balding, and with a comfortable paunch and reflective demeanor, you would naturally assume him to be a banker, a professor, or perhaps a dentist. But he is one of the most capable aviators I've ever known.

There is a saying among fliers: "There are old pilots, and there are bold pilots, but there are no old, bold pilots." Istvan happens to personify that bit of wisdom. That is not to say that he is timid, just the contrary. He will go into places and circumstances where few others will venture. It just means that he does so in a rational and well-thought-out manner that minimizes problems and maximizes the chance of success. As he has often told me, "No one hires a pilot to crash a plane."

He and I shook hands very formally, as always. Istvan is a composed and tightly held man. Displays of emotion and affection seem alien to his nature. His speech also fits his persona. His accent is Oxfordian English and very proper, as though he were a British peer. He is so correct in all his mannerisms that when I am with Istvan I always feel downright crude in comparison.

"Istvan, glad you made it. Any trouble on the flight?" I asked as we shook hands.

"No trouble," he replied in a quiet voice. "Though we had a bit more attention from the authorities on Malta than I would have liked. But it was not problematic."

"Then what say we get these birds refueled and loaded up. I'd like to get out of here soon as possible."

"Please show me what you've arranged?" he asked.

And with that I introduced him to Roosty, who was in charge of the preparations. All hands heaved-to. As one plane would pull into position for fueling, the others were being loaded. Istvan kept a careful eye on the activities as we worked under the faint beams of hooded flashlights. As the work progressed, the mechanic on the team went from plane to plane making his checks.

Istvan and the mechanic had their heads together going over their checklist when Terry called out in a quiet voice, "Looks like we may have visitors."

I looked toward the far end of the strip and saw vehicle lights moving in the distance.

"Istvan, get everything readied for immediate take-off," I called.

"Right," he replied.

As he gathered his crew together in a huddle, I went to stand near Terry, who was staring into the distance.

"Looks like four vehicles coming down the track," he said as we watched the bobbing, bouncing lights disappearing and reappearing as they negotiated the rough roadway.

"How far out do you think?" I asked.

"Mile, maybe a little more," he replied, a slight chord of tension in his voice. "At the speed they're making, maybe five—ten minutes out."

"I think so, too," I whispered.

We both knew this in all likelihood was a police or army force. That boat had reported us after all. At that instant, the vehicles came to a halt and extinguished their lights.

"That's it," I called in a voice that carried across our little band as I ran to the planes. "They're deploying. Crank 'em up, Istvan. Clear out of here. Now. Yah lah!"

Everyone ran to their respective planes. I followed Istvan as he went plane to plane and gave succinct last-second instructions to the pilots. When we climbed aboard our bird, the others were already taxiing into takeoff position.

Istvan brought the engine to life, but rather than taking the lead, he pulled his plane to the extreme right edge of the strip while the other planes maneuvered to the left side. In seconds, the planes were in position and ready. Istvan spoke into his mike, and the group started its takeoff run.

The engines roared, and the birds began to move. As the first plane powered up, the rest were enveloped in a tremendous dust storm that immediately clouded our end of the airstrip. Istvan pulled the yoke to his chest, stood on the brakes, and shoved the throttle fully forward.

He yelled to me, "Help with the brakes and hold the yoke!"

I put my feet on the pedals, shoved with all my might, and wrapped my arms around the yoke. The thousand-horsepower radial engine howled, and the plane, trying to take wing, shuddered and jerked in defiance. Even with both of us on the brakes and the wheels locked, the huge four-blade propeller was dragging us forward, inch by inch.

Just when the sound of the engine reached the point of a mad scream and the plane felt as though it was about to shake itself to pieces, Istvan yelled, "Off brakes."

I released my foothold on the pedals at the same instant as Istvan, and it seemed the plane literally bounded into the air. Pitching nose up at a severe angle, Istvan countered by slamming the yoke forward and holding her there, thus bringing us instantly back to an even keel.

"Trim!" he yelled.

I hit the trim switch and immediately felt the controls become lighter and more manageable. Casting a quick look out the side glass of the cockpit, I saw we were skimming just above the surface, not more than ten feet in the air.

Glancing across the cockpit over Istvan's head, I saw the other planes now emerging from the dust cloud, clawing to gain altitude.

Our speed was increasing by the second now. But we were flying so low we were kicking up a rooster tail of dust and debris in our wake. And as we hurtled madly through the air, I swear I could feel the desert brush slapping the belly of the big plane.

Istvan held us on a flat trajectory that was at an acute angle away from the heading of the other planes. I looked forward, and in the darkness ahead, I saw the first red and orange muzzle flashes of gunfire. We were charging straight at the trucks!

Suddenly, the flashes became bigger, brighter, and almost continuous. The sound of gunfire reached a crescendo of intensity, and the muzzle flashes lit our cockpit like a disco strobe light gone mad. Istvan shoved the yoke forward, the big plane lunged even lower, and then, before I could even blink, we were on top of them. I whipped my head around as we skimmed just over the cabs of several military trucks.

I caught a flashing glimpse of men hurling themselves to the ground, before the scene was enveloped in our dust storm. The muzzle flashes ceased as the men dove for cover, and then we were beyond them.

We had charged the ambush and scattered it. It is a classic tactic but one that requires confidence, skill, and a real set of cojones. But these are attributes Istvan the pilot has in abundance.

Afterward, he held us on the same course and altitude for twenty seconds longer, and then, with smooth deliberation, he began to climb and bring us on a heading to link up with the rest of the planes.

From his calm demeanor you would have thought this was a normal takeoff for a commuter airline. A few minutes later the other planes came into sight, and we assumed our position in the lead.

Istvan checked his GPS and autopilot and then looked over at me.

"You have a momentous day tomorrow, and there's nothing you can do up here. Why not get some sleep," he said.

"Good idea," I replied.

As I climbed out of my seat, the mechanic, who had been standing just behind us all along, gave me a grin and slid into the vacated copilot's seat.

Climbing over crates and boxes of equipment, I went aft into the cargo bay. I found my hammock, strung it up from the ribs of the fuselage, and crawling in, was soon hummed to sleep by the monotonous growl of the engine and the gentle rocking motion of the plane. I slept for the rest of the flight like a child of God.

•

CHAPTER 12

I FELT THE PLANE BANK SLIGHTLY
and awoke to a faint gray light seeping into the interior
of the plane. Getting up, I stowed my hammock and
went forward to the cockpit. Istvan and the mechanic,
whose name was András, were sipping at cups of deli-
cious-smelling coffee.

"Any more of that?" I asked.

Istvan looked over his shoulder and gave me a smile.
"Good morning," he said as András handed me a cup
and the thermos. I poured and took a grateful sip.

"All okay?" I asked as I scanned the horizon out
front.

"No excitement. Everything normal. We should be
landing in about"—Istvan consulted his instruments—
"eight minutes."

I stood at the cockpit threshold and watched as we
began a shallow descent. A few minutes later the dry
lake bed we had selected as our destination airfield came

into view. Istvan studied the ground intently as he led the formation in a low circuit of the lake bed. And then, banking on the final approach, he brought us neatly back again to Mother Earth.

The landing, as we touched down on the hardpan surface, was surprisingly smooth. Istvan taxied us as closely as possible to the mouth of a wide ravine that opened onto the northern edge of the lake bed. At last he cut the engine, and when he did so, we were immediately engulfed in the deep silence of the great Sahara desert.

I opened the cargo door and jumped down. Terry hopped from his plane, and soon everyone was outside, stretching legs and arms and attending to the call of nature. Terry joined me under the wing of my plane as the aircrews went about their post-operational checks. Roosty came over and stood with us in a huddle.

Terry looked about at our surroundings and scratched his head. "If 'nowhere' had a place on the map, this would be it, eh?"

"Sort of the general idea," I replied as I, too, scanned the area.

"Yes, I suppose it is at that," he said. "What say we have a brew up before we start the day? Just because we're in the wilderness is no reason to abandon civilized and time-honored customs."

"Help me get my gear out first," I said.

I hopped back into the plane, put the ramp into position, and began unlashing some of the cargo straps. Roosty climbed in and helped me maneuver the bike to the door, where we handed it over to Terry. Within minutes, we had everything I was going to need for the next leg of the trip.

We hooked the small trailer to the back of the bike and carefully loaded it with supplies. Water, food, radio, batteries, a tarp for shelter, and other items were soon stowed securely aboard the bike and in the trailer. The last thing I did was load one of the rifles and slide it into a scabbard on the bike where it would rest under my left knee.

Then we got out the camp stove and put on a pot of water. While waiting for the water to boil, we broke out some MREs. As the three of us made a cold breakfast, we spread my map out on the ground and knelt around it.

With the tip of my pocketknife I pointed to a spot on the map. "This is us here," I said, as I glanced up at my comrades. "And I expect to find the clan here." I pointed to another spot. Though only a few inches on the map, it represented more than forty miles.

"That's some bad country between here and there, mate. Sure you don't want to fly a little closer?" Terry asked.

"I don't want them to know what we have, not until I've spoken with the chief and the other elders. I don't want to chance it. After all, they are a tribe of thieves, you know."

"Aye, but anything could happen to a bloke in that span of country. Why not you and Istvan, in one plane, get you to say—here." He took my knife and touched the map on a spot some twenty-five miles closer.

"You think I'm not up to the ride, Terry? Is that it?" I joshed.

"Just don't want you to get lost, mate. It's a big desert out there, that's all."

"This way they wonder just where the hell I came from. I make the approach from this distance and across this terrain, they won't be able to get any sort of idea where the planes are located. Not for a few days at least. And I better have things squared away before then, or we're in for some real trouble."

When we heard the water begin to boil in the pot, we took a few minutes to make tea. Terry was in charge of the ritual, and as he went about his business with a look of supreme contentment on his face, I marveled again at what tea means to a Brit. I don't think anything we Americans do comes as close or provides the same sense of well-being.

"Wait here until tomorrow evening," I said as I accepted a steaming cup from Terry's hand. "If you haven't heard from me by then, come looking with one plane and send the other ones back out. If I have to run for it, I'll try to make it to here."

I took my knife from his hand and pointed out the location of the rendezvous.

"And I'll thank you not to try to steal my knife," I said as I closed the blade and put it in my pocket.

"Well, if that's the way it's to be, I don't know why you're still mucking about this place," he said as we stood again.

I looked around and saw that Istvan and his men had gotten out the camouflage nets and were pulling them over the planes. Pretty soon you'd have to walk right up on them before they could be detected.

I turned to my bike and gave it a once-over as I finished the tea and had a final bite of the MRE. Then I filled an additional water bag from the nearby cans and slung it over the seat. Ready at last, I pulled on a Bedouin cloak known as a *djelaba*. Made of heavy cotton, it covered my body from the sun and would protect me also from the wind and blowing dust. Then I adjusted my cheche so that it covered my face, threw a leg over the bike, and fired her up.

The engine came to life with a cough and then settled in to a satisfying purr. I gave the boys a nod of goodbye, receiving in return a hand lifted in salute from

Roosty and an obscene gesture from Terry. With that, I pulled away and set out across the desert. I was genuinely looking forward to the trek. And for the first time since this mission kicked off, I began to feel the excitement of it all.

CHAPTER 13

*THE DESERT IS AN OCEAN IN WHICH
no oar is dipped.* I think I recalled that line from the
movie *Lawrence of Arabia.*

The Hollywood version of the desert is that it's all
sand and towering dunes, but that's just another misper-
ception. There is plenty of sand all right, but mostly, the
great desert of North Africa consists of a series of
craggy, sun-blasted mountains separated by wide and
rocky valleys. The soil, in most places, is packed hard
and swept so barren by the winds that when rain does
fall, it runs off quickly and pools in the low places. As
the ground is so impervious to the infiltration of water,
what water that does fall tends to evaporate quickly back
into the atmosphere.

But some water does find its way through hidden
cracks and crevices back into the earth, to emerge again
as springs and wells. These are the places we call oases.
My destination was just such a spot, hidden deep in the

forgotten recesses of this region. But first, I had to get there. And travel is never an easy thing in the desert.

The Tuaregs are not just one tribe, but are a vast collection of peoples that inhabit the central regions of the Sahara. In the last fifty years or so, the ones who live on the outer edges of their range and come into contact with more sedentary peoples have tended to adopt a somewhat more settled life. But those in the center of their vast territory still live the nomadic life of ages past and are a fiercely independent bunch. Where we had landed was deep within the heart of Tuareg country.

It was one of those nomadic clans I was hoping to meet at my destination. This was the driest time of the year, a few months before any rainfall, and water was scarce. The spring I was striking out for was one of those water sources that never fail. I had heard about it while heading a security detail for a pipeline construction project a few years before.

While we were passing through their area, I had hired the local clan as protection. I knew that if they were in my pay, they would leave us unmolested and keep out the guerillas that were targeting our project. It is just part of the nomad's concept of hospitality. I always figure it's better to hire the neighborhood ruffians and keep them on my side rather than add unnecessary enemies.

When I sat to negotiate with the chieftain, I made it clear that I didn't want to take on the administrative difficulty of making individual payments to the men. I asked if he would be kind enough to assume that responsibility himself. He in turn was good enough to say that he would accept the burden, large as it was, as a gesture of his personal goodwill and as a demonstration of the esteem in which he held me.

Thereafter, I made weekly payroll visits where I admired a lot of livestock, listened to many stories, and drank great quantities of sweet tea. If anything, the Tuaregs love tea more than the British, and believe me, that certainly is saying a lot.

The final week, before pulling out of their territory, I brought a gasoline tanker with me and filled all the trucks belonging to the clan. I also left them with ten additional drums of the precious stuff. And through it all, I never let on that I knew they had been stealing fuel from our camps all along. But from the present of the gasoline, the chief realized that I had been aware of the theft all along, and to him it was a great joke. Ultimately, it was a small cost that paid off well. We were never attacked by the Algerian guerillas, and in fact, I never had the slightest difficulty while in that area.

I traveled slowly and picked my way carefully as I skirted the base of the great ridge that ran from northeast to southwest. My destination was on the other side of the range, tucked up in the confines of a deep canyon. As the crow flies it was maybe twenty-five miles away, but via the route I had to take, it was an all-day trip—if everything went well.

I stayed to the low places as much as possible. The beds of ancient dry streams, or wadis, as they are called, made for good going, but I could only follow each one for a short while before it ran toward the center of the valley. Then I would have to climb out and cross the rocky and boulder-strewn intervals between. When crossing a particularly high piece of terrain, I would stop and scan the area with my binoculars. Then, after consulting my map and taking a compass bearing, I would set out again.

Thus I traveled by a series of short legs. But by traveling in this method it was very unlikely that I would stumble across anyone. I wanted to remain undetected until it suited my purpose to show myself.

The popular view of desert travel by vehicle is that it

is some sort of race in high-speed off-road rockets. But the truth is, that just ain't so. The objective is to get there with all your stuff and in one piece. And all my stuff was pretty heavy.

Water weighs about eight pounds per gallon, and I needed a minimum of two gallons a day to stay alive. I had two five-gallon cans of water in the trailer, which made for eighty pounds just there. Add to that two cans of gas and the rest of my equipment, and it came to quite a load.

The bike could make forty miles an hour on good terrain, but if I went hauling ass like that out here, there was a great chance I'd damage my rig or hurt myself, and I couldn't afford either one of those eventualities.

No, slow and steady is what crosses the desert, or any rough terrain for that matter. I was content to make five miles an hour—and that was over the easy stretches. Often I moved along no faster than I could walk. But at least I was riding and not struggling with a soul-crushing load on my back.

I followed the course of another small wadi and then, finding a low spot in its bank, I coaxed the bike and trailer up and on to the high ground beyond. It was nearing midday, and even though it was autumn, the sun was beating down with a relentless ferocity. The air was so dry now that the inside of my nostrils felt like crinkled parchment, and when I opened my mouth, I could almost feel the moisture being sucked out.

It was time for a short bivouac and rest. I rolled steadily along until I found a shallow depression with a low rock ledge on one side that was just large enough to contain my "donkey" and trailer. I pulled down into it and came to a halt. I would wait here a few hours, until the worst of the midday sun was over, and then pick up the trek once again.

It felt good to get off the bike and stretch my legs. I

lifted my binoculars and made a thorough survey in all directions. The valley stretched out below until it disappeared into the distance of the haze and the heat mirage. Behind me the mountain range rose in a series of ragged and steep layers until reaching a flat summit. The length of the mountain range ran to the horizon in both directions.

I stood and listened. Nothing moved, not even the wind. It was so quiet that when I stood still and concentrated, I could hear the blood coursing in my carotid arteries. I looked to the blue bowl of the overarching sky and felt a keen enjoyment in the realization that I was utterly alone.

Some people may find such solitude disconcerting, but I relish the sensation. To know that within the range of sight and sound—and farther even than that—I was the only human being on this piece of earth produced in me the profound joy of being alive.

I am here. I live. And nothing could be more perfect.

I went to the trailer and loosened the bungee cord tie-down straps. The tarp was on top of the load and came away easily. I unfolded the fabric across the top of the trailer and the bike and pegged it to the ground with a couple of short metal stakes. I had positioned the bike at the lower end of the depression so that I would have a space of six or eight feet between the rig and the rock shelf on the upper side. I then took the hem of the tarp and pulled it to the ledge, where I could anchor it to the top of the shelf with a few stones.

I gave the tarp a sharp pull and had just turned to the ledge when, not more than two feet in front of me, I saw a movement in the rocks. A dusty black colored wad of *something* made a slow rolling movement in a crack in the ledge, and as my eyes tried to make sense of the movement, that *something* presented itself in clear view.

The great desert cobra thrust its head and upper body

into an upright stance. The puddle of his body was at waist level on the rock shelf, and his head was even with my face. He spread his hood and looked me directly in the eyes. And as I stared wonderingly into those round pupils, I knew I was engaged with a sentient and evil being.

The snake swayed side to side, as though measuring the distance between us. I saw him flicker his tongue two—three—four times. And then, in what appeared to be slow motion, he rocked himself backward to launch his strike.

I shifted my shoulders to the right, putting weight on my right leg, and then kicked to my left with every ounce of strength in my body.

The cobra hurled himself.

I saw a dark streak and felt the touch of the serpent as he flashed by my right ear. His fall carried him over my right shoulder, half his body extending over and down my back.

I grabbed the tail that dangled from the rock shelf, and as he writhed to regain control and strike again, I swung the serpent over my head with all my might. His head and upper body hit the rocky ground with a meaty slap and the sound of crunching bones.

In a second convulsive leap, I hurled myself backward, out of striking distance, and ran from the hole and onto the top of the ledge.

The snake lay writhing on the ground before me. He wasn't dead, but his back was broken. His lower half was paralyzed and immobile, while the upper portion thrashed about in agony. The great serpent struck furiously in all directions, biting, in his rage and fury, even his own body.

Then he saw me. Collecting himself with steely purpose, he lifted his head and looked me in the eye once again. Then he came at me. One of us was going to die.

As the serpent tried to drag himself forward, I drew my pistol, took deliberate aim, and with two shots severed the head from the body. Even then, the viper continued to convulse and tried to crawl away.

I snatched up a large, flat rock, and smashing it down, crushed the head of the snake to a wet and bloody pulp. I left the rock covering the head of the snake, as I didn't want to leave those deadly fangs exposed. A dead snake, given a chance, will still kill you.

But had he gotten me? Had the fangs found my body? I'd felt the serpent brush my head when he struck, but perhaps my cheche had protected me. I didn't feel a bite anywhere, but that meant absolutely nothing. I've been shot before and not known it until the excitement of the fight had worn off. As I walked to the trailer, I took a few deep breaths and willed myself to calm down.

I got out my shaving mirror and checked the side of my face and neck. Nothing. I hurriedly pulled the djelaba over my head and made an inspection of it. Sure as hell, on the right side, halfway down the back, was a wet patch the size of my palm with two puncture marks in the middle.

My heart started racing again, and I had to make the effort to bring it back under control. But then I thought, *What the hell. If he got me, it makes no difference. I'll be dead in less than half an hour, and there's not a damn thing I can do about it.*

But I had to know. I quickly shucked out of my shirt and checked it. There was a smaller splotch of venom on the shirt, but thank God, no puncture that I could see. Still, all he needed to do was graze me, and I would be a goner.

I reached a hand around and gently felt the area of my back that corresponded to the wet spots on the shirt and djelaba. My fingers came away with a bit of sticky moisture, but I could feel no scratch in the skin.

I felt again, just to make sure. What a relief: nothing. It looked as though the loose-fitting *djelaba* had saved me from the cobra's bite. *Alhamdulillah! Yes, praise God. Indeed.*

Then, I sat down and laughed. And I laughed. And I laughed some more. There was nothing else I could do. Death—unexpected death—had passed me by at close quarters, missing its mark by the merest measurement, and I felt the greatest elation you can possibly imagine.

And as I laughed from deep down in my guts—from the very center of my being—the fear and tension that had exploded within me began to leave my body.

It is a good thing to be alive. Yes, it is a very good thing.

But I couldn't just sit here chuckling and congratulating myself. I'd stopped here for a reason, and I needed to get on with it. I took a segment of radio aerial and with that in one hand and my pistol in the other, I checked the rock ledge and the surrounding area very thoroughly. I didn't want to take the chance that another snake might be hiding anywhere nearby. I was soon satisfied that all was clear.

It was only the work of another minute, and then I had the tarp anchored firmly in place. I looked down at the body of the snake. I picked it up by the middle of its body and let the tail and severed neck drape to the ground. It must have been seven feet long, and the middle of the body was as thick as my forearm. I started to toss it far away but then had another idea and took it with me into my sun shelter.

I got out my pocketknife, laid the snake on its back, and peeled the hide away within a few short minutes. Flinging the naked carcass out into the sun for the ants and flies, I then rubbed the inside of the skin with dirt before rolling it into a tight bundle and stashing it in my rucksack. I would carry the skin home with me and honor it as *the souvenir that almost killed me*.

With that small chore accomplished, I took a long pull on the water bag and stretched out under my shelter. I dozed off for a very light nap while the sun baked the earth outside.

But several times, I snapped instantly awake whenever I thought I heard the faint yet ominous sound of reptilian scales slithering stealthily over ancient rock.

•

CHAPTER 14

THE SUN WAS WELL ALONG ON ITS downward arc as I got under way once again. Picking my way carefully over the tortured terrain, I now ranged farther out into the valley floor. And as the ground became flatter and easier to negotiate, I found my mind pondering things of a philosophical nature. It is no wonder that three of the world's great religions found birth in the desert. It is a place of reflection. It is a place where you can consider not only the smallness of individual man, as a speck within the limitless universe, but also the magnificent potential of our species.

I am no Bible thumper; however, I carry some very deep-seated spiritual beliefs, but my beliefs are for me alone. I have come to realize that over the centuries, as organized religion began to assume greater social power, it became obsessed more with gaining and enforcing power over others than with inspiring spiritual insight. It became doctrinaire, rigid, and dogmatic.

Dogma, in any form, is a writ for coercion. I believe that anyone who threatens his fellow man with the holy wrath of God, because other people fail to express the proselytizer's particular brand of religious propaganda, is nothing more than a moral terrorist.

The teachings of good men, spiritual geniuses of the ages—Abraham, Moses, Jesus, Mohammed, and others— have been so perverted over the centuries as to become little more than tools in the hands of the power mongers. But if my reading of history is any indicator, it has been ever so. I do not condemn religion, but I am extremely wary and distrustful of anyone who claims the exclusive right to speak in the name of God.

But here in the desert, as on the ocean, a man can think. And in his thinking, he can plumb mental depths greater than usual. I wonder that we exist at all, that anything actually exists, and why it should be so. Was the Great Creative Force lonely? Did it desire company and companionship? Or is this all a dream in which we play out collective and individual roles? Perhaps this is an exercise in thought or an unending cycle in an everlasting drama.

In the novel, *Moby-Dick*, as the crew of the *Pequod* were swept to their doom in the quest for the great white whale, was Captain Ahab correct when he said to Starbuck: "This whole act's immutably decreed. 'Twas rehearsed by thee and me a billion years before this ocean rolled."

Is our existence and life foreordained, or is it all a matter of chance? Does free will exist and if so, have a part in our lives? I don't know, not anymore. When I was young I had great certainty about many things. But as I've added years to the tally of my life, I've come to realize that I know almost nothing. And in a peculiar way, that very uncertainty seems to give me a sense of comfort. I have come to accept the gift of life as a treasure of incomparable worth.

I believe that I am a part of the Everything. Nothing in existence is alien to me. As every individual cell of my body is wholly a part of me, then I, too, am completely a part of that which created me. By equal measure, all of us share in that sameness, and hence, we are all of the same stuff. And we enter into grave moral danger when we think we are anything more than the rest of our fellow beings. These, and other thoughts, kept me company on my journey across the sun-blasted desert wastes.

I finally rounded the end of the mountain range and began my approach toward the wadi that was my destination. I stopped on a low rise and used my binoculars to scan the region to my front. The mountain ridge was just starting to throw its shadows across the valley floor, but in the distance, maybe four miles or so across the valley, I was just able to make out the movement of a flock of animals.

Where there are animals there are people. I was getting close. Now I must proceed more carefully. I didn't want to make an unexpected and sudden appearance that would provoke a violent protective reaction. I wanted to be seen but only at the right time.

The flock was moving slowly back in the direction of the mountain. That meant the mouth of the wadi was directly to their front. A finger ridge that ran out into the valley was between me and where they were headed. I would wait here a bit longer and then begin my approach. Tuareg boys are in charge of the herds. Boys have sharp eyes and fast feet, but they are also inquisitive.

I set out again. Swinging back in as close to the skirt of the mountain as I could, I made my way to the point of the finger. Now was the critical time. I sat awhile longer and watched the shadows lengthen on the valley floor. *Okay, time to go.*

Giving the finger of the ridge a wide berth, I wheeled out into the valley, and then, as I rounded the point, there ahead of me was the mouth of the wadi. On the other side of the valley was the flock of goats and sheep I had seen earlier. And there also, following along behind, were two Tuareg boys.

I didn't stop my movement, but continued to motor along at slow speed, just like I knew what I was doing and belonged there. The boys looked across the wadi at me and gaped in amazement. I gave them a friendly wave. One of the boys slowly and uncertainly lifted a hand in return but then dropped it as though he thought better of the whole idea.

I saw them put their heads together in quick conversation as they tried to figure out just what to do. Then one of them, probably the best runner of the two, took off up the wadi like a scalded dog. The other just stood and watched, as though I were something from Mars, while the flock continued to amble home. At length, this boy, too, found his legs and lit out in the wake of his comrade.

I trundled along up the center of the wadi until I found a slight rise in the ground from which I could see and be seen. There was a bend just ahead, and I watched as the second of the two boys gave me a backward glance over his shoulder before he quickly disappeared from view.

I brought the bike to a halt and switched off the engine. Up ahead, I watched the stragglers of the flock follow the remaining boy out of sight. And then I was alone again.

The sun was completely behind the mountain now, but its rays still blossomed across the sky and lit the summit with a dazzling glow. I got off the bike and lifted the water bag for a long, deep drink as I stood and watched for movement in the rocks above and in the wadi to my front. Company, I knew, would not be long in coming.

I didn't have long to wait. Within a few minutes, four men on horseback trotted down the wadi, their excited horses held tightly on short reins. When they spied me atop the low hill, they neither halted to gawk nor hurried their pace. Instead, as they made their approach to where I stood, they spread out in an open and tactically correct formation, one that would engulf me on all sides. The option of flight was one I no longer enjoyed.

I studied the approaching men. They were dressed in tan colored camel hair djelabas, and their *cheches* were a deep indigo blue. In their waist sashes they wore ancient hand-forged swords. Each man handled the reins of his mount with one hand and with the other balanced an old military rifle, held loosely and expertly across the pommel of the saddle.

As they came near, I placed my right hand over my heart and lifted my left out to my side.

"Peace be upon you, brothers," I called out in Arabic.

The horsemen stopped, and the one nearest me spoke.

"And peace be also upon you. But who are you, strange man, and what do you want here?"

The one who spoke was a tall man. The Tuaregs are a tall people, but this man was exceptionally so. His face, covered by the veil of his *cheche*, left only his eyes exposed, but I could see that he had a lean face and a long chin. His voice was strong, harsh, and penetrating.

I replied to the tall man, "Sir, I am a wanderer from a far place. A man alone in the desert and without the protection of his own people. I would claim the hospitality of your tents—if it were offered me."

I watched the other men out of the corner of my eye but kept my attention focused on my interrogator.

"Are you lost then, that you wander so deeply into the territory of another people?" he asked.

"Not lost."

"Are you then an outcast? A pariah? A Cain, driven from his own tribe, with the hand of every man turned against him, doomed by the crushing burden of his foul crimes and sins to wander the desolate wastes and seek solace in places where his infamy is unknown?" he inquired sternly.

"Nay, I am none of these things. But rather, I am a man who goes to and fro over the face of the earth and walks back and forth upon it. I am a man compelled by Allah to seek his will in the hidden corners of this world. I am a searcher. I am a man upon a mission," I replied, as I placed my left hand on top of my right and held them both over my heart.

The man took this in and was quiet again for perhaps half a minute. He looked from me, to my bike, and then to the other men. He finally cast a look back up the wadi before speaking once again.

"And by what name would this seeker be known? How would he be called by those who know him best?" he asked.

"I am called Tah-ner, by both man and God. I have visited your people before and have enjoyed the courtesy and protection of your nation. I have known the hospitality of your fires."

I lowered my hands to my sides. The men sat unmoving and stared at me in solemn contemplation, while their horses, tired of standing still, snorted and stamped their hooves in boredom. The silence of the men became ominous, and I was beginning to wonder if I had made a tactical mistake of epic proportions. No one made a move for a weapon, but things could change in a flash.

The man spoke at last: "Tah-ner you say. It is a name foreign to my tongue and to my comprehension. I wonder why you should present yourself here, at this, of all times."

He put his hand on his sword as he continued, "And it is my belief you are here for reasons that bode my people ill. But know you this, stranger; if that be so, your life will surely hang in the balance."

He turned to the man nearest me.

"Take his rifle," he ordered.

The man dismounted, retrieved my rifle from its scabbard on the bike, and returned to his horse. I stood still and held the eyes of my inquisitor.

"Get on your machine and come," he said.

I bowed in his direction.

"Thank you, young sir. I am much honored by your kindness and generosity," I said.

He replied with a scowl in his voice: "We will see how much you enjoy our generosity, stranger. If we determine you to be an enemy, sent to spy out our land and bring harm to our people, you may not live to like it at all."

I climbed aboard my bike; the men surrounded me front, rear, and sides; and we proceeded from the open plain into the mouth of the wadi.

CHAPTER 15

THE CLIFFS AT THE ENTRANCE TO the canyon towered above us as we threaded our way through the herds and flocks that had been brought in for the night. A series of natural basins, filled to the brim with water brought from the springs by a system of stone-lined troughs, lined the lower side of the wadi.

The animals—goats, sheep, camels, horses, and donkeys—were herded to their own watering stations, and each herd was under the care of groups of boys. An old man, sitting on a high rock, seemed to be the field marshal who, keeping watch from on high, maintained order over the critical chore of watering the animals.

We continued up the wadi past the various animal holding pens. From there we passed through a sharp bend where the walls of the canyon closed in so tightly that we could negotiate the defile only two abreast. And then we entered what appeared to my eyes to be a veritable Shangri-la.

The floor of the wadi, opening wide before us, was covered by a grove of date palms. Near one side of the cliffs the water flowed through a natural stone channel, and from there ran cascading from pool to pool in a series of low waterfalls.

Citrus trees of many varieties bowed low with the weight of their ripe burden. Grapes, pomegranates, dates, and other fruits grew in profusion. Green vegetables flourished in stone-walled beds. Here, in this hidden spot, deep within the fastness of the forbidding desert, was a place of plenty, a veritable Land of Goshen.

The garden was perhaps a quarter mile in length, and as we rode along a crushed stone pathway, I marveled at the very thought of this magnificent oasis. Then, rounding another sharp bend, we entered the camp itself.

The brown, striped tents stretched away up the wadi and into the gathering darkness. The smell of food cooking over camel dung fires filled the air with a delicious aroma. As we came into view, a crowd gathered, but at our approach parted and gave us entrance into the center of camp. At last we came to a halt in front of a very wide tent that sat at the head of a semicircle of smaller tents. As I swung off the bike and my escort dismounted from their horses, a group of four elderly men emerged from the largest of the tents.

The oldest of the four stepped forward. Everyone else remained still and quiet as the man scrutinized me from head to toe. He turned his head from side to side so that he could see me better with his one good eye. The other eye—the right—was a milky white and obviously blind.

I was becoming worried—no that's not true—I was *very* worried. I knew none of these men. It was obvious that this was a completely different tribe than the one I had expected to find here. And if this group of elders decided they didn't like what they saw of me or declared me a threat—well—the atrocities committed by the

Tuaregs were the stuff of legend among old foreign legion veterans.

Flaying alive, was an evil thought that came to my mind.

The old man finished his inspection. Clearing his throat, he hawked a gob of phlegm at my feet. When he spoke at last, his voice was a cracked and creaky whine that sounded like it came from a set of leaky bellows.

"Foreigner, you have intruded where you have no invitation. You have violated a territory that is not yours. You have entered a land where the presence of the stranger is not tolerated, for the stranger is ever the enemy."

He swept his arms to take in our surroundings.

"And you have seen the secret of our hidden citadel, something allowed no outsider. Rash man, by your intemperate and foolish actions, you have pronounced your own doom."

As he delivered the final word, "doom," the collective voice of the gathered tribe broke forth in a wild ululation, one that echoed and rebounded, gathering strength and volume, as it crashed from wall to wall in the darkened canyon. And as that fierce cry rose to the heavens above, I knew this was the final act. I was a dead man.

I bowed my head and let the sound of destiny wash over me. At last the voices quieted, and all was deathly silent. It was then I looked into the face of the old man who was still standing in front of me.

"Honored father," I said in a voice that was for him and me alone. "If I have violated the laws of your tribe and nation, I stand in anticipation of your judgment and your justice. I can say only on my behalf that I have not entered your land with the spirit of an enemy but rather with the heart of a supplicant," I said in a voice of contrition.

But then, lifting my voice in power and raising my hand on high and pointing a finger skyward as a symbol of sacred testimony, I continued, "But know ye this: I *am* a *man*, and whatever your decision, whatever the penalty, I will bear it like a man. I will not crawl, and I will not beg. That is one satisfaction you will never have. Now, wise and honored judge, act in the manner you think best."

The old man searched my face with his one rheumy old eye. Then, giving me a smirk, he turned to his companions who were gathered in a cluster in front of the tent. "What say ye, brothers? What shall be the penalty required of the interloper? What shall be the judgment levied upon his head?" he called in a wheezy gasp.

The other old men put their heads together in conference. Mumbling and gesticulating to one another for several minutes, they conferred in low voices that carried no farther than their small group. And as the minutes ticked by, I felt each and every drop of the cold sweat that trickled freely down my back.

Several times, one man in particular would turn to scowl at me, and then, turning back again, remonstrate violently with his fellow judges. Then I saw them nod their heads in agreement. Now they all turned to face me.

All murmurs and chatter came to a halt as the one-eyed chief faced the gathering and stood silently. Then, lifting his face and arms heavenward as though beseeching God himself, he called in a loud voice, "What would you have of this man? What is the price of his transgression?"

Not a soul moved. All was deadly quiet. Everyone listened intently, as though expecting word from on high.

Then, from within the tent, a jovial-sounding yet hidden voice called out, "That he sing us a song. That he sing for his life!"

What! What was that? Are they taunting me before I die?

Just then a figure threw back the flap and stepped from within the dark recesses of the tent. I looked closely, trying to make out the features of this man. The voice seemed familiar. Then the man grabbed himself around the waist, bent over double, and broke into peals of raucous laughter.

When his cackle of mirth burst forth within the encircling arena of tents, the entire gathering of people erupted with screaming howls of mirth. The laughter of the tribe built to a crescendo and echoed like the crashing of waves on a rocky shore.

I was stricken mute by this display of collective madness. And then the man who had announced my sentence stepped closer, and I knew him at last.

"Sheikh Talmun, thank you for the welcome. I am very glad to see you again. And I'm also glad to be of such entertaining value to you and your people," I said, through a rigid and rictus-like smile.

The old sheikh wiped his eyes with the back of his hand and blew his nose with his fingers.

"What a great joke. You should have seen it from inside the tent. You really thought you were about to die," he howled with a levity that bent him double again.

"A great joke indeed. Perhaps someday I can return the gesture in kind," I said, trying my best to repress the heat in my voice.

But I could feel the relief of tension and an almost giddy sensation of release that ran flooding through my body. And then I began to laugh. Everyone else was quiet for a second, but as I turned and looked at the assembly arrayed about us, the tribe joined in, and the laughter became general. It went on for a minute or more, and then, as we caught our breath, sputtered at last to an end.

"Sheikh," I said when I could finally talk again. "You look younger than when last I saw you."

"My old wife died last year, and it is not good to live without a woman in the tent. So I've taken a new wife, a young one. I think this has had a good effect on me. In fact, I have recovered many forgotten attributes. A young woman can do many good things for a man." He then gave me a wink and cackled like an old hen. "But come, you are in time for prayers, and then you can tell us from whence you come."

While several young boys were busy laying rugs in front of the tent, I greeted the other three tribal elders. Then ewers of water were brought forth so that we might wash our faces, hands, and feet. Ablutions attended to, we faced the east and made our prayers.

The Tuaregs are Muslim, but they don't go in for great public demonstrations of piety as do, say, the Saudis. Prayer is not enforced by any form of religious police and is pretty much left to the individual conscience. But this prayer at the end of the day and prior to the evening meal is one that serves to join the community in a common bond.

Following the completion of prayer, a large carpet was spread in front of the tent, and food was brought. Great piles of couscous were heaped in short volcanoes on platters, and mutton stew was ladled into the calderas. I sat with the sheikh and the other elders around one platter, and we dug in to the aromatic repast with relish.

To dine in the accepted and culturally correct manner, you sit cross-legged and lean forward on your left elbow. With the right hand you scoop up the couscous, then rake in some of the stew and knead it into a small ball. The ball of stew and couscous is then flipped into the mouth with the thumb.

Such a meal is always animated and joyful and the

source of much fun. I kept a close eye on the sheikh and was ready for him when he raised his hand near his own mouth, but then, in a lightning-swift move, leaned over and flipped a ball of stew and couscous into my mouth.

The dinner guests knew what he was up to but were surprised when I immediately returned the volley. The other guests rolled with laughter, as my host coughed and choked on the unexpected morsel while I sedately enjoyed what had been given me. When the old sheikh could finally breathe once again, he was the one who laughed loudest of all.

Dinner talk was light and animated. The sheikh regaled the gathering with stories of when I was last in this region. At last the meal was cleared away. Water was poured over our hands, and towels were offered. Tea was poured into tall cups, and the water pipes were filled with fruit-flavored tobaccos. Now was the time for serious talk.

I took a puff on the mouthpiece of the pipe, leaned against the cushion at my back, and exhaled. The smoke hovered just above our heads and then slowly dissipated in the cool night air.

"Sheikh, when did you know that it was me, and how did you know?" I asked as I leaned forward for another turn at the pipe.

Sheikh Talmun exhaled in a long sigh before he spoke.

"Our scouts saw you from the top of the mountain, just after midday. A runner was sent to camp to tell us of a strange man in the desert—a lone man. The scouts followed you from above, and then when the boys came running in with your description, I knew it was you."

"Scouts out so far this time of the year?"

"Yes. We have flung our eyes and ears in a wide net," he replied. "We have been forced to go to war. That is why the entire tribe is gathered here to reach a decision on what course we should follow. Only yesterday, we reached the decision to fight."

I could feel my heart begin to sink. If a tribal war was going on, it would spread throughout the entire region, and I'd never gain the assistance I needed.

"What is this war you speak of? Is it something of long standing? A blood feud, perhaps?" I asked.

"Nay, not of long standing but of a recent happening. There is a man who has set himself up as a king, but he is no more than a murdering thief. He has an army at his command and kills as he will. He has taken control of the town and all its inhabitants. He has declared a tax on all commerce. When we sent men into town to trade our dates and young camels for wheat flour and other necessities of life, we were surprised to hear of this tax. When our men protested this outrage, the soldiers of this would-be king tried to take our camels and produce by force.

Our men fought bravely, but they were overwhelmed. Several were jailed and others were killed before a handful fought their way clear and brought news of the travesty. And thus, we have declared war."

"And this man—this king—by what name is he called?" I asked, my mood beginning to lighten.

"He calls himself 'Fist of the Mahdi,' but we call him, 'Dung of the Dog.'"

I turned to the sheikh, took both his hands in mine, and touched my forehead to his.

"Sheikh, I see that once again, our paths run side by side. Your enemy is my enemy, and this is the reason for my arrival here. I have come to bring a reckoning upon the house of this malefactor, and I bring assistance. Let us wage this war together."

Then, over much tea, tobacco, and talk, I told the sheikh and the other elders the reason I was here and what I intended to do. We talked and planned late into the night, and I thought I had successfully sidestepped the issue of my "sentence." But just as I was saying good night, Sheikh Talmun reminded me of his edict, and he was in all seriousness that the fine should be paid.

So as a lullaby to the assembled tribesmen, I stood before the tents and in the flickering light cast by the camel dung fire, and I sang for them in Spanish my favorite song, "Cielito Lindo." It was hailed as a resounding success.

CHAPTER 16

NEXT MORNING AT FIRST LIGHT, I climbed to the top of the ridge and, after adjusting the antenna a time or two, finally raised Terry on the radio. Giving him exact coordinates for the mouth of the wadi and general landing instructions, I then scrambled down to camp where I retrieved my bike and went out into the valley floor to lay out a landing strip. I was accompanied by Amayaz, the leader of the horsemen who had met me yesterday at the mouth of the wadi.

As I placed the air signal panels on the ground to indicate to Istvan and the crews the orientation of the landing zone, I queried Amayaz about the state of affairs in the town and what he knew of conditions within the old legion fort.

In the course of our talk, it became apparent to me that Amayaz was the war leader of the tribe. He wasn't one of those hotheaded firebrands, itching to run whooping into the enemy's lair, shooting things up and in general making a lot of noise. Rather, he wanted to put to an end, once and for all, depredations his people had suffered at the hands of this self-proclaimed Mahdi. He understood that my mission was somewhat different from his but that our objectives coincided to a large degree. He was a man I knew I could work with. At least, to a point.

When the planes made a flyover of the strip, the entire tribe came boiling out of the wadi to watch. Amayaz and I had a tough time getting everyone off to one side, making them stand in place and wait so that the planes could finally land.

As the big birds came in and landed one by one, you could have heard the yelling and whoops of joy for miles across the desert. The planes landed without mishap, and many willing hands soon had them unloaded and the equipment hauled into camp.

Istvan and I conferred and came to the conclusion that the best thing to do was keep one plane here and send the others back to wait for us in the town of Tamanrasset, in Algeria. We had papers showing the aircrews to be working for a petroleum exploration company. This would allow them to ferry fuel to us here for the eventual flight back out and to be in range to support us if needed.

While Istvan and I made our plans, András and two other crewmen gave tours of the planes to the Tuaregs. Few of them had ever so much as seen a plane on the ground, much less touched or been inside of one. To a person, they were enthralled, and none more so than Sheikh Talmun. I made a mental note to see to it that he went up for a flight before we left.

Everyone was assembled: men, women, and children, near the strip where we waved and cheered the planes as they made their departure. The Tuaregs were inordinately impressed and delighted by the dust storm kicked up by the propellers. Then, with a multitude of helping hands, we manhandled the remaining plane to a cleft in the wall of the wadi, where we soon had it camouflaged with nets and hidden from overhead view. Afterward, a number of boys were set to work obliterating the wheel tracks of the planes.

Roosty took a team of workers and two of the elders with him to conduct a joint inventory of the arms and equipment. This was also intended to get the combat juices of the Tuaregs flowing as they saw the extent of the goodies we had brought with us. While that was taking place, I gathered Terry, Amayaz, and Sheikh Talmun for a closer look at the problems we faced.

The sun was getting high, so we retired to the tent for our conference. The Tuareg tent, like the tent of all Bedouins, lies low to the ground. It can be buttoned up tightly when storms strike, and all the sides can be lifted to allow the free circulation of air on days such as these. The tents are made of camel hair cloth that is not only rainproof but also has superb insulating properties. It can be put up and struck in a matter of minutes.

With rugs covering the floor, it is a snug, clean, and cozy abode. A better means of housing for use in the desert has never been devised. The tent we were sitting in (as were all others in the wadi) was brown with a pattern of cream-colored stripes. The color of the cloth and the spacing and width of the stripes identify the tribe and the clan, much like the tartans of the Scottish clans.

We four huddled near the mouth of the tent, where I threw back a rug and exposed a patch of the bare ground. Before we began our talk, I pulled a knife from beneath my djelaba and withdrew it from its sheath. It was a kard, the traditional knife used by the tribes of Persia. The blade, made of Damascus steel, is long and keen and tapers to a needle-like point. The handle, made of camel bone, was so old that it looked like ancient polished ivory.

I held the knife out in front of my chest and turned it ever so slightly in my hand, letting the light send undulating ripples and flashes of color showering off the damascened blade. The effect of the shifting and wavering light as it reflected in our eyes and across the interior of the tent was hypnotic. I then gently and reverently slid the blade back into the scabbard and presented the knife to my host.

"Sheikh Talmun, it would give me profound pleasure to know that you would accept this knife, that you would use it and carry it on your person. In the land from whence it comes, such knives are revered as tribal heirlooms. I give it with the humble realization that it is small recompense for the most important thing one man can give another: genuine hospitality and friendship, that such as you've given to me and my friends."

The sheikh's eyes glistened with joyful anticipation as he gazed at the knife. Unconsciously, he rubbed his hands on the front of his robes and then slowly reached forward. I placed the knife on his upraised palms. He held it there for several seconds and looked on it with thirsting eyes. Slowly, gently, he slid the blade from its covering and held it upright in front of his face. His eyes played up and down the length of the blade as once again the pattern of ever-shifting light cast shimmers of color undulating across his face.

"It is the most beautiful thing I have ever beheld." He breathed. Then he lifted his gaze from the knife to my face.

"Tah-ner, you have prevented me from executing a great sin. For had I known you to possess such a knife, there is nothing I would not have done to gain it for myself. I will treasure this, your most magnificent gift, for all of my life. And it will remain in my clan forever."

I replied with heartfelt sincerity, "You honor me, lord, with your acceptance of my paltry offering."

I cast a sidelong glance at Amayaz to gauge his reaction. I was slightly worried that I might have provoked envy in the younger man but was pleased to find a look of pleasure at the joy of the old man's happiness with the gift.

I will see that Amayaz has a suitable gift before this is all over, I thought, as I caught the eye of Terry and saw his wink of approval.

The sheikh then sat back and tried the fit of the knife in his waist sash. He shifted it around from side to side until he found just the right spot. He then whipped the blade from its scabbard three or four times, until at last he pronounced his satisfaction.

"It has found its place on my body and will ride ever thus," he said with reverence.

I then produced my pocket knife, which I passed to Amayaz, and indicating the bare patch of dirt where I had thrown back the rug, asked him to make a sketch of the town and the fort that was our objective.

Amayaz looked at the bare dirt in thought for several seconds and then began to rapidly and deftly outline the surrounding topography of the town, its approaches, street layout, and exterior dimensions of the old fort.

"The fort," he said as he sketched, "was built by the French invaders over one hundred years ago as a means of controlling the caravan routes. The site was a rest and watering point at the spot where two trails, one from the south, one from the east, combined for the trip north, to the city of Algiers. They built the fort around the spring-fed wells found there, thus causing all men to demonstrate obeisance or go without water."

Amayaz looked from me to Terry and back again to the dirt drawing.

"The town grew around the fort and became the center of trade for this region. We Imouhar (the name the Tuaregs call themselves; it means Free People), being a peaceful trading people by nature, established a presence in the town and for many years have brought our goods there to buy and sell. Occasionally, there has been trouble with one government or another, but that is to be expected, as governments are always ruled by distant and stupid men."

Sheikh Talmun broke in, "But we have always done everything possible to avoid conflict. As Amayaz says, we are a respectful and peace-loving people who strive to keep good relations with those we encounter in the course of life."

"The world," said Terry, speaking for the first time, "knows well of the patience and peaceful forbearance of your people, Sheikh Talmun."

I gave Terry a hard glance, then flicked my eyes to Amayaz and the sheikh and saw that Terry's words had been taken literally, with no thought of the irony of his meaning.

"Yes, young man." The sheikh nodded. "But our patient and peaceful ways are sometimes sorely tried and put upon by dishonest and unscrupulous men. Such as this one, who has set himself up as a petty king. This man, Boutari."

"Well, I think, your lordship, that if we all give it our best effort, we may just be able to teach this man the grave error of his ways," Terry said with gusto in his voice and a feral grin across his face.

"A lesson—yes, that is what we must do. Administer a lesson. One that will last for a long, long time." The sheikh nodded in agreement with Terry's pronouncement.

I steered the conversation back to the task at hand. Pointing to the sand map, I asked Amayaz, "How many men do you think Boutari has on hand, and does he have the support of the people in the town?"

Amayaz studied the drawing for a bit before speaking.

"In all truth, I have no idea as to the exact number of men. They stay in the fort. What they call a gendarme, of ten or so men, patrols the town. But they are no more than bandits, robbing and abusing honest people. As for the people of the town, they are terrified. Their property is stolen. They are arrested, fined, and beaten at a whim. Defiance is met with death. The townspeople have been made to suffer more than anyone else."

I nodded my understanding. Boutari would have few genuine supporters among the populace. But I was under no illusion that we would find anyone there willing to help us. The people had been brutalized into obedience, and a population in that condition could be counted on to curry favor with their master by reporting and turning in any suspicious person.

At that moment, two women came to the tent bearing a tray laden with tea. Tuareg women, contrary to the accepted custom in Muslim regions, do not wear the veil. And men do not take the veil until the age of twenty-five.

Farther north, women of many of the Berber tribes wear facial tattoos that are actually quite alluring. Here, the women adorn themselves by painting their fingernails and dyeing extremely elaborate patterns on their wrists and hands. I don't know if it's purposeful, but the effect tends to pull your view from the face to the hands.

One of the women was quite young, in her late teens, and from the extra attention she lavished on the sheikh, it was quite apparent that she was the new wife. I stole a glance from the girl to the sheikh and saw a slight smile on the face of each.

They are in love with each other. And why not? I

thought. She was married to one of the most powerful men of the tribe, and he had gained a young bride who would bear him the children of his old age. It was an excellent match. And as the Lebanese merchant says after a satisfactory deal has been struck, *"There's something for everyone."*

The women departed, and Amayaz poured the tea. Sheikh Talmun watched the girl as she left with a wistful look on his face.

There is nothing more poignant, I thought, *than the love of an old man for a young woman.*

We sipped our tea and sat quietly, each of us cocooned in our own thoughts. I contemplated what lay ahead and felt frustrated by how little I actually knew. There was no way I was ready to move forward. I needed more information, and hard information at that, and there was only one way to get it.

I leaned forward and put down my cup.

"I need to see the town and the fort," I said, looking from Amayaz to the sheikh to Terry. "I must see the routes in and out of the town and also take the measure of the fort. If possible, we must also find a way of determining how many men are inside."

"Aye, a recce—leader's recon," said Terry, taking another sip of tea. "When shall we go?"

"Terry, I need you and Roosty to stay here and begin assembling and training the force."

I looked then to Amayaz.

"And I was hoping that Lord Amayaz would consent to be my companion and guide."

"Of course. I would allow no one else," said Amayaz with casual elegance.

"Thank you," I replied. "If we travel by night, how long is the journey?" I asked.

"If we depart prior to sundown, we can be in town before dawn of the next day."

"Is there a place in town where we can stay, perhaps with a trusted kinsman?" I inquired.

"Nay," he replied with a shake of the head. "At present there is no man there in whom I have the least confidence."

"The town has become a nest of vipers," interjected the sheikh. "It is filled with nothing but evil and cowardly men."

Scared, more likely, I thought. But scared men can be dangerous, too.

"All the more reason to be careful. Two men, unarmed, will give no cause for alarm." said Amayaz.

I could not fault his reasoning.

"Do we go by horse or by camel?" I asked.

"We travel by that machine of yours," he said. "If we went by animal, we should have no safe place to leave them. And they may be stolen or wander off if left outside of town. We can hide the machine in a ditch and walk into town. No one will know from where we came."

"What time shall we depart?" I asked.

"You should leave when the sun is halfway to the horizon," said the sheikh. "That will give you plenty of time to make your way into town before sunrise."

Amayaz nodded his head in agreement.

"You and I should sleep the rest of the day, my friend. The night will be long, and the moon does not rise until very late."

Amayaz got to his feet.

"I will send a boy to awaken you," he said. And then with a curt nod, he left to return to his own tents.

Terry and I also stood. I turned and bowed to the sheikh. "Thank you, sir, for the tea and the wise counsel. I will see you again before we set off."

"Sleep well," he said.

But his eyes were on his young wife as she returned

for the platter of cups and the teakettle. As we walked away, I glanced over my shoulder and saw the sheikh proudly showing his bride the new knife.

Terry and I returned to the tent we shared. As we strolled through camp, people smiled and greeted us politely. We were the most novel things to appear here in quite some time, and I'm sure we were the subjects of a great deal of camp gossip.

We reached the tent and sat down in the shade of its opening. Terry produced a cigar and lit up.

"Kennesaw, anything in particular strike you as odd about this whole setup?" he asked.

I was studying a line of ants marching by. There was an outbound file and a return lane. Where they came from and where they were going was anybody's guess. I'm always amazed at the insect life in the desert. I can't imagine what they find to live on. But I, too, had been contemplating the salient oddity of this mission.

"There's no ticking clock—there's been no timetable established, Terry. There's no 'or by' date. And you always have that with a kidnapping for ransom," I said as I watched the parading ants.

"Exactly. The hit was made on the boat seven"—he counted on his fingers—"no, eight days ago. Initial demands were made but without a time requirement for meeting those demands. Strange, that," he said with a vigorous bobbing of eyebrows.

"It's more than just strange, Terry," I said, looking up from the ants. "Something is missing. I don't know what, and I haven't yet reached a conclusion as to why it should be so. Usually nothing is more clear-cut than a good old-fashioned kidnapping for ransom."

Professional kidnappings have a certain element of symmetry to them. Demands are made, and to those demands compliance dates are attached. Then negotiations are opened. Proof of life is required and is given.

The cost and currency of the ransom is negotiated and agreed upon. Means and method of the ransom exchange are negotiated and eventually determined. Then you negotiate the date, time, and place of release of the hostage after payment has been made and received. And if all goes well, you get your person back alive, in mostly one piece.

Terry took a pull on his cigar, "If it were purely political, they would have sent pieces of the boy to his grandfather; just to twist the knife, so to speak."

"More importantly, it would have made the news. A political kidnapping is no good if the public doesn't know about it. It requires the theater of the public stage," I replied. "But this one has been kept completely off the radar, and purposely so, it seems."

"So it doesn't seem to be one or the other, either criminal or political. Does it, mate?"

"No, Terry, it doesn't. And like you, that puzzles me."

Terry took a puff and blew the smoke out the front of the tent. "Do you trust the people you're dealing with in your own government, the ones who brought this to you?" he asked.

"In government, something like this is always a question of: 'What does this do *for*, or *to*, my career?'" I snorted.

"This is one of those tar babies that can really hurt you. No one wants to get tagged with failure, but if all goes well, plenty of people will be lined up to take credit. But it's credit without the associated risk they want. However, if it's just a couple of nonentities like you and me who go down in the attempt, well, who cares? No real harm done—at least not to anyone of any *real* importance."

"So no, Terry, I don't trust them. Not in the slightest. Would you?"

He gave me a look that said, *Excuse me for asking a stupid question.*

"No, mate, I guess not."

"Well, first things first," I said as I crawled back into the depths of the tent, rolled out my sleeping mat, and pulled my rucksack under my head as a pillow.

"We get the kid and get out with our skins intact, maybe we can figure the rest out as we go along—and then again, maybe not. But while I take myself a well-deserved siesta in preparation for the difficult and dangerous night ahead, why don't you and Roosty do a little preliminary screening of our potential rifle company. It'd be helpful to determine who can actually *shoot* a gun before we begin training them."

"Aye, your lordship," he said, pulling his forelock and bowing his head. "Are you comfy? Can I tuck your worship in before I take my leave?"

"No, boy. Just close the door behind you," I said, as I rolled onto my side so that my face was to the dark side of the tent.

The hissing cigar butt, as it whizzed by, just barely missed my ear. I quickly found the smoldering butt and stabbed it out in the dirt. Outside, I heard Terry chuckling as he walked away. Then it was quiet in the tent, and I drifted off to sleep.

CHAPTER 17

COLONEL ABDULKADIR BOUTARI WAS a worried man. He sat in a high-backed carved wooden chair, staring vacantly at the wall, idly swishing a fly whisk with one hand while unconsciously pulling at his mustache with the other.

This is not going according to plan, he thought. *What could be wrong? Have I missed something? Something important? Perhaps. But if so, what?*

Boutari slammed the whisk on the table and called to the man just outside the door. "Khasim!" he growled.

The man dashed inside the room and came to rigid attention. "At your orders, my colonel!"

"Tell Commander Yagmour I want him, and then bring me the American woman," ordered Boutari.

"Yes, my colonel. At once, my colonel."

The man saluted and scurried from the room.

Boutari continued staring at the wall and brooding over his ever-darkening thoughts, his mood souring by the minute. Soon, brisk steps were heard in the hallway, and then a tall figure filled the door.

"You called for me, Colonel?" the man asked.

"Boutari motioned toward a chair with the fly whisk.

"Yes, Commander. Come in—sit, sit. I wanted you here for this."

At that moment other steps were heard in the hallway. The guard appeared in the door and stood at attention once again.

"Sir, the woman is here, as you ordered," announced the guard.

"Bring her in," drawled Boutari.

Gail Burns, a guard at each elbow, was led into the room and seated in the chair indicated by Boutari.

"You may go," Boutari said to the guards, "And close the door."

The guards made an about-face and left the room, the last one quietly closing the door behind him.

Gail looked at the two men who sat staring at her as though she were a specimen under a microscope.

Who are these men, these soldiers? she thought. *What nation, what army do they belong to?*

Boutari and Yagmour continued to stare at her for several seconds. She did not know it, but Boutari's look concealed his mild shock at her condition. She was dirty, with unkempt hair and a sallow, pinched look to her face. She shaded her face with one hand and squinted, her eyes unaccustomed to the light in the room.

Boutari looked angrily at Commander Yagmour.

"The woman has been maltreated. Who is responsible for this?" he barked in Arabic.

"My colonel," responded Yagmour, "her condition is irrelevant. It is the boy who is important."

Boutari slammed his palm on the desk with the sound of a pistol shot, causing Gail to jump in her seat.

"But without her, the boy will founder! He is but a child and must have the care of the woman. He knows her and trusts her. She stands in place of the mother."

Yagmour did not flinch at the rebuke but replied in a steady voice, "Yes, my colonel. I will look into the matter."

"You will do more than that, Commander. You will move the woman and the child into the room adjacent to my quarters. They will be bathed and fed and properly cared for. And you will provide them with a woman to look after their needs."

Boutari leaned forward in his chair and drilled the other man with his eyes.

"The boy is worth a great deal—to us all. Keep that in mind."

Yagmour nodded his head in acknowledgment.

Gail had followed every word the men had spoken. Her Arabic was excellent, but she gave no indication that she understood what was being said. Better to play the helpless woman and see what transpired.

Boutari turned his attention to Gail and spoke to her in clear but rather stilted English. "You and the boy will be moved to better quarters, and you will be treated with respect."

He paused to let her respond, but Gail did no more than look at him.

Perhaps the woman is simpleminded, he thought, when Gail failed at first to reply. "Did you understand what I said to you?" he asked.

After several seconds of silence, she spoke, the words pouring out in a torrent. "Why have we been taken captive? Why are we being held? Where are we, and who are you? What is to become of us?"

Boutari looked at her closely. A faint smile spread across his face, and a sinister tone came into his voice.

"If you cooperate, you will be taken care of and soon

returned to your people. If you are difficult, you will be punished."

Gail felt the fear creep back upon her as she thought of the distant screams she had heard from her cell. She gulped and nodded to Boutari that she understood.

"Good," he replied. "For your sake and that of the boy, it is best—but," he said as he twitched the fly whisk again, "what do you know of the grandfather, this Emir Jemani? Why is he so obstinate? Does he not care for his grandson? Does he not desire the swift and safe return of his sole descendant, his only living heir?"

His only living heir? That's why Abdullah whimpers so miserably in his sleep. His entire family was killed on the boat. I didn't know. I thought it was just us, just the boy and me who were kidnapped and the watch crew killed. I didn't know they had all been murdered. Involuntarily, Gail shuddered at the horrible thought. She lowered her face and slowly shook her head in dismay.

"I—I—I know nothing of the grandfather. I worked for the family as tutor and companion to the children. I have never met the grandfather. I don't know him at all."

Boutari felt his annoyance growing again. *Nothing— nothing was going right.*

"But he loves the boy, does he not?" he demanded in exasperation.

Gail lifted her head and looked at Boutari as the tears gathered in her eyes and ran down her cheeks.

"You killed them, didn't you? You killed them all— and you're going to kill us, too. I know it now. We will never go home. You're going to kill us, too," she said in a terrified whisper.

Boutari slapped his boot with the whisk. *This woman—the stupid cow, she is no help at all.*

Boutari looked to Commander Yagmour and spoke again in Arabic: "Take her away, and see that she and the boy are taken to the quarters as I have instructed."

Yagmour returned a look to Boutari that bordered on becoming a sneer.

"As you order, Colonel," he said as he rose to his feet.

Taking Gail by the elbow, he guided her from the chair.

"Come with me," he said in English.

The two departed and left Boutari seated at the table, flailing the whisk and fingering his mustache. And as he listened to the fading footsteps of the sobbing woman, he realized that he was more concerned than ever.

CHAPTER 18

"YOU MUST CHANGE YOUR *TAGELMUST* and robes and wear the colors of the Imouhar," said Amayaz as we stood outside my tent. "What you have on will attract rather than deflect attention. People will ask what tribe you belong to, and you will have no good answer to give. And do not be concerned with the color of your eyes. Blue eyes are found among many of the northern Imouhar. It is not common, but it is nothing strange."

He was correct on both counts.

"As you say, good sir. I am in your hands," I remarked.

Amayaz sent a boy to bring me new clothes. While waiting, I unwound my *cheche* and removed my djelaba. When the boy returned, I pulled on the new robes. Amayaz wrapped my head with the *tagelmust*, then took off his own, showed me how to do it, and had me remove mine and put it on myself until I could make the wrap with ease.

That Amayaz would remove his *tagelmust* outside the privacy of his own tent is something to remark upon. A Tuareg will usually never remove his veil in front of another person unless it is a family member or someone he feels very close to. I took his act as a mark of friendship.

That settled, we turned our attention to the bike.

"I think you should drive the machine, at least in the daylight hours. It is important that you know how to operate the device, in case something should happen to me," I said to Amayaz.

He looked from me to the bike and to me again. And when our eyes met, his had the light of pleasure and thanks within them.

"I would like that," he said quietly. "I would like that very much."

I got on the bike and walked him through how to crank it up. Next I showed him how to operate the throttle and the brakes, and then I asked him to watch as I drove around him in a circle. I then bade him climb aboard behind me so that we could retreat to a practice ground free of prying eyes and wagging tongues. Farther up the wadi we found a good spot with varied terrain to put both bike and novice driver through their paces.

Amayaz was a natural, and within thirty minutes he had mastered the machine. He was extremely impressed with the Rokon's climbing ability and its ease of operation. And fortunately, he was a mature man who didn't have the adolescent's need for unnecessary and dangerous speed.

We returned to camp and made ready for our trip. I called for Terry, Istvan, and András to join us at my tent. I asked Amayaz if he would send a boy to politely inquire if Sheikh Talmun could join us. When we were all gathered and tea was served, we went over last-minute details.

"We'll spend tomorrow and part of the next night in and around the town," I said as I motioned to the map laid out on the ground.

"If we can grab someone who has access to the fort, maybe one of the militia men, all the better."

"How long before we should think of looking for you, if you fail to return?" asked Terry.

"Give us forty-eight hours. If you haven't had word from us by then, move to this location. . . ."

I pointed to a spot on the map. "This will be the emergency rally point. If we're not there, use your own discretion as to how to proceed."

"If we believe you have been captured or harmed in any way, we will attack the fort," said Sheikh Talmun.

I started to protest, but the sheikh held up a hand that indicated I should be silent.

"This was our war to begin with, not yours. If I believe it necessary, I will launch an immediate attack."

I nodded my acknowledgment to the sheikh and turned to Terry. "If an attack is precipitated, do all you can to fulfill our original mission. You may be able to salvage something."

"Right, mate," was all he said.

"If, during the reconnaissance, I detect something that makes me believe the hit should be moved up, and I'm unable to return to this location, Terry, move forward with an emergency assault team and"—I turned to the sheikh—"Lord Talmun, please follow on as swiftly as you can with the remainder of your men."

"It will be as you say," said the old warrior.

I looked to my comrades.

"If things go completely to hell—Terry—Istvan— saddle up and clear out."

I turned again to Sheikh Talmun.

"If we are unsuccessful and have to leave, all the equipment—guns, ammunition, everything—belongs to you. It is our gift for having brought unsought trouble to the door of your tent."

The sheikh made a motion of dismissal with his hand.

"We had this trouble before you arrived. You have brought nothing but the pleasure of renewed friendship. We have a score to settle with this jackal of a false Mahdi. If you are killed or harmed, I will add the tally to the list of his debt. We will avenge you as one of our own."

Amayaz looked to the sky and then to me. "We have talked enough, and this talk of what to do in case of failure bores me. When Amayaz sets out on a task, he does not fail. It is time that we left."

I nodded in agreement.

"Let us do so," I said as I got to my feet.

Everyone followed us to where the bike was parked near the side of the tent. Amayaz slung his rifle over his shoulder, took his seat on the machine, and cranked it up. I made a last-second check of the trailer and its load, slung my SKS over my shoulder, and took my place behind Amayaz.

"*Yah lah*," I said so that Amayaz could hear.

"*Bismillah,*" he replied as he twisted the throttle.

I felt the bike tremble as Amayaz applied power, I picked up my feet, and we were on our way. We had a rugged trip ahead of us, and I could tell already this backseat perch was going to get mighty uncomfortable.

Ah, what the hell, I thought. *Nobody ever said it was going to be easy—and if it were, then any fool could do it.*

We made steady, if slow, progress. Amayaz took us by way of an old and seldom-used winding path that was little more than a faint animal trail. By this route, he told me, we were unlikely to meet any other travelers. Once the sun went down, we were able to take a more usable track that allowed us to keep a better check of position.

During the night we switched off driving duty about every hour. Driving under blackout is very fatiguing, but we couldn't chance showing a light. The desert has eyes, and we didn't want to show ourselves until we stepped into town.

Amayaz had an unerring sense of location and direction. I kept track of our orientation by the stars and frequent checks with my GPS and knew that we were headed the right way. At two o'clock we made a halt under the brow of a slight rise, where we climbed off for a pit stop and to stretch our cramped limbs.

When we set out again, the night air was crisp, and the quarter moon cast a cool, pale glow across the landscape. We made excellent time, and at half past four, Amayaz said it was time to find a place to cache our bike and continue in to town on foot.

We found a narrow wash in a patch of ruggedly folded terrain, where we tucked in the bike and trailer and covered them with a camouflage cloth. I took a GPS reading of the spot so that I had the exact location.

The last items we put aside were our rifles. These we laid on the top of the covered equipment so that we could snatch them up quickly if needed. We loaded our pistols and positioned them where we could best grab them from beneath our robes. Then we moved out.

The only sound in the vast silence of the desert night was the slight crunching of our footsteps and the muted purr of our individual breaths. When we topped the next bit of high ground, Amayaz pointed out to me the faint glow of light from the town. It wasn't far now, and I began to feel a sense of anticipation building in my chest.

What will we find there? I wondered.

When we were several kilometers out, we halted to plan the rest of our approach.

"We must get close, unseen, then come into town by

the regular road," said Amayaz. "If questioned, we can say that our camel went lame, and we had to leave him behind."

"Will you inquire about your men while we are here?" I asked.

"If I can do so without drawing attention from the fort. I don't want to show my hand before it is necessary," he said. "I will ask about horses for sale and hint that we have money—but not on us. The merchants will believe we are smugglers of contraband goods and hope for some of our later business. I don't know why, but they always think that of our people."

I merely nodded and made no comment.

"Is there no one to provide assistance here? No man you can trust?" I asked.

"We will see," said Amayaz in a cryptic manner.

I took that to mean that he wasn't sure and was perhaps worried about someone in particular.

We entered the town just as the eastern horizon showed the gray sliver of a new dawn. And as the call to prayer echoed through the dusty streets, we stepped cautiously into the lair of the enemy.

CHAPTER 19

AMAYAZ LED US THROUGH A LABYRINTH of alleyways and narrowly winding streets. The ancient mud-brick buildings looming over our heads seemed to cast a brooding sensation of gloom over our passage. I tried to keep track of the numerous turns and corners but soon gave up the attempt and decided that if we separated and I had to make a run for it, I would just make my way in the general direction of east until I cleared the town.

At last we turned into an alley so narrow that we had to walk sideways to slide between the two buildings. This brought us into a small courtyard. We halted here, pressing ourselves against the cold wall while we listened for a couple of minutes down the alleyway we had just traversed.

Satisfied that no one was tailing behind us, Amayaz stepped to the other side of the courtyard and opened a cleverly concealed door. He looked over his shoulder, motioned for silence, and that I should follow. I glanced once more at the mouth of the alley, and when I turned again, my companion was disappearing into the doorway.

As I stepped into the portal, Amayaz stood waiting in the dark recesses of what seemed a tunnel. He pushed me gently forward, then turned and closed the door. The blackness within was now complete. I felt Amayaz take my hand, and with a slight tug, he urged me along with him.

I counted the steps as we groped our way forward. When I had ticked off twenty-two paces, Amayaz halted, and I heard four distinct raps on a wooden surface, followed by three more taps in a different cadence. There was a pause of a few seconds. Then a door opened before us, and we entered a windowless, low-ceilinged, smoke-darkened room, lit only by a single candle.

A withered, humpbacked crone closed the door behind us and then motioned that we should follow her. A cane in one hand and a lantern in the other, the old woman lurched along with a crabbed and halting shuffle that was painful to watch.

I'm sure I've never seen another human being who looked so old but was still able to move about under her own power. Every few steps she would turn to look at us as though she expected to find that we had disappeared. Finally, at the end of the corridor, she opened a door, and with a gesture of her cane, she indicated that we should go in.

The room we entered was richly and lavishly decorated in the North African/Arab style. Oil lamps cast a golden light that threw soft shadows throughout the room. A beautifully woven, elaborately designed wool carpet covered the floor. Sofa-like cushions were arrayed around the walls, and scattered here and there about the room were low wooden tables made of beautifully carved wood.

The high, arched ceiling was painted beautifully with the stars and constellations of the heavens that seemed to sparkle and wink in the yellow light of the lamps. On two walls intricate abstract designs of many colors had been worked into the plaster. In the far corner, a small fireplace held a charcoal fire that gave the room a warm glow. We settled ourselves on the comfortably uphol-stered cushions.

Amayaz dropped the veil from his face and gave me a knowing smile.

"The home of a friend. We will be safe here and can gain much knowledge of the comings and goings of the people from the fort," he said.

Before I could reply, the door opened, and a woman entered. She went to Amayaz, who stood and took the woman's hands in his. I got to my feet as the two ex-changed words of greeting. Then they turned to me, and Amayaz, with a delighted twinkle in his eyes, introduced me to the woman as Rashid of the North. The woman, he introduced as Rahab.

She was a very tall, darkly hued woman. The makeup she wore drew the gaze of the beholder deep within liq-uid eyes that were black as night. Her shapely nose poised over full and luscious lips that were slightly parted in a welcome smile, a smile that lifted and accen-tuated the delightful plumpness of her cheeks.

She was dressed in ocher colored silk robes, with a purple silk covering over raven hair that glimmered with an electric sheen. A necklace of gold coins, arranged in the several rows of an inverted pyramid, was arrayed about her long and elegant neck. The bottommost coin of the necklace was nestled in the hollow of her delicate throat.

Multiple gold-band bracelets jingled musically on her wrists, and her hands were tattooed with fantastically alluring patterns that were complemented by the color of her nails. On her feet she wore sandals wrought of worked silver and Moroccan leather. A perfume of gardenias lightly scented the air about her.

Never in my life had I beheld a woman of such beauty. I stood like a man turned to a pillar of salt and drank her in with my eyes. After several seconds I realized I had been holding my breath. When I had regained my senses, I inclined my head in a bow and placed my hand over my heart.

"Salam aleikum," I breathed.

"Al-hamdulillah," she returned with slightly downcast eyes.

Her voice, in that one word, was like the sigh of an angel. And then, looking up, she gave me a smile that I felt to the uttermost depths of my loins.

Good God a'mighty! I've never beheld such a beautiful woman. Yeah, you get it. I was hammered, and I knew it. I took a step back and tried to regain my composure.

Rahab gestured us to sit, and turning, spoke softly to someone just outside the door. Two serving girls entered with trays of food and pots of steaming coffee and hot milk. I settled back on the cushions, and as Rahab directed the efforts of the servants, I worked at coming down to earth once again.

With an effort, I tore my gaze from the woman and stole a glance at Amayaz. The look he returned made it obvious that he was enjoying the spectacle of my reaction.

When the food and drink had been arrayed before us, Rahab dismissed the girls with a flutter of a hand and turned to us with a tinkling of her gold bracelets.

"I will leave you alone so that you may refresh yourselves in peace. Should you or your friend need anything at all, Lord Amayaz, you need but call; a servant will be at your door at all times. Now eat and rest in the safety of my poor and humble house."

She bowed and then backed from the room, gently closing the door as she slipped from view. Again, I realized I had been holding my breath.

I looked to my companion, who was reaching for the bread and a pot of honey. I poured coffee for us both, and we ate in silence for some few minutes. At last, when we reached a break in our repast, I refilled the coffee cups and finally asked the first question.

"Amayaz, my friend, who is this woman, Rahab?"

Amayaz blew across the rim of his cup and held my eyes with his as he took a long sip. Putting down the cup, he tore off a piece of bread and drizzled it with honey and cinnamon.

As he brought the bread to his mouth, he paused momentarily and said, "She is an ally, Lord Rashid, a friend of some years. She owns this establishment."

He closed his mouth over the bread and chewed his food with evident pleasure. But the look on his face was enigmatic, as though waiting for me to reach a conclusion.

I took a piece of bread also, and as I chewed, I thought.

This establishment? What is this place that she . . . ? Of course, that's it. In Spanish we would call it una casa de citas. *But how does that translate? How do I say it in this language?*

"Lord Amayaz, would it be correct to call this place an 'inn of pleasurable encounters'?" I asked.

He took a sip of coffee and then answered, "Yes, that would be the correct term."

A cathouse, I thought in good old American vernacular. Or more properly, given the setting: a bordello.

"You say she is a friend, one of many years. I take it she is worthy of your trust?"

He tore open a blood orange and handed me half. We ate as I awaited his answer.

Finished with our meal at last, Amayaz wiped his hands on a cloth, leaned back against the cushions, and spoke.

"She was captured—she and her mother, along with some other women, and an entire caravan—many years ago."

"Captured by whom, Lord Amayaz?"

"By my father," he replied.

"And then?" I asked, leaning forward with fascination.

"The mother, an Egyptian, was renowned as a woman of, shall we say, entertaining talents. She was traveling to another city to open a new establishment when my father intercepted the caravan crossing our territory without permission.

"After exacting justice upon the trespassers who led the caravan, he brought the woman and her companions here and helped her establish her business. Upon the death of the mother, Rahab assumed the ownership."

"The connection, I take it, has been to the mutual satisfaction of both parties?" I asked.

"Yes," he replied. "My father has retained a percentage of the business and has found it a good place to invest monies from time to time. Much gossip of a commercial nature takes place within the walls of this house, and much of that gossip makes its way to our ears. When we profit by these items of knowledge, Rahab profits also. It has been most satisfactory for all concerned."

I lifted the coffeepot from its nest of charcoal and refilled our cups.

I took a sip and then said to Amayaz, "I should think that from time to time, the soldiers of the fort seek solace and entertainment within these friendly walls."

"When they have money," he replied.

"And one would think that perhaps they, too, gossip about matters within the fort."

"Alas, too often; it is the failing of men everywhere. I can only presume it is so with these soldiers as well," he said with a shake of his head and a slight frown at the thought of such indiscretion by frail men.

Another thought came to me, one from a previous conversation.

"And when you told me there was no man in this town in whom you had confidence—that was a true statement, was it not?

He smiled again and said, "As I told you, in all truthfulness, there is no *man* that I trust here—and only one woman."

He then wrapped a blanket around his shoulders and stretched out on the cushions.

"But let us sleep for a few hours. Afterward we will speak with Rahab and then see what we may see."

I rolled up in a blanket myself and heard only a few snores from my guide before I, too, was comfortably asleep, but not so comfortably that my hand strayed from my pistol.

CHAPTER 20

RAHAB WAS NOT ABOUT WHEN WE awoke, and her servants claimed not to know her whereabouts. So, leaving word that we would return, we set forth to spy out the town.

We ambled through the marketplace, fingering goods and casually haggling over the price of things we had no intention of buying. The mood of the market, in fact the mood of the whole town, was subdued and fearful. The merchants and other people we spoke with glanced about suspiciously as though trying to see if they were being overheard. Twice we saw a gendarme patrol of two policemen swagger past, and as they did so, everyone around came to a watchful halt, and if talking, lowered their voices.

We took our time as we casually strolled through the town. I wanted to get my eyes on the fort, but I also wanted a feel for the layout of the town and to determine in which general direction the streets and blocks were aligned.

Then we turned a corner, and at the end of a narrow street, I could see a segment of the mud-brick walls of the fort. It appeared that what was in view was a side portion of the structure, and as we came closer, that proved to be true.

As we came to the end of the street and looked up at the walls, I took a mental measurement and calculated their height to be about twenty feet. We walked for a bit in one direction so that I could gauge the length on this side and then retraced our steps so that we could see the place from the front and get a look at the main entrance.

We came near the intersection of a wide street that seemed to be the main thoroughfare for the town. I was watching out for traffic as we crossed, trying to avoid being run down, when Amayaz stopped dead in the middle of the street. I heard him suck air through his teeth with an explosive gasp.

An overloaded truck, horn blaring madly, careened wildly by, missing us by mere inches. I grabbed Amayaz by the elbow and dragged his resisting body out of traffic before we could be run down by another truck. When we reached the safety of the corner, I looked toward where Amayaz had his eyes fixed and saw what had stricken him so.

Bodies. The corpses of six men, in varying stages of decay, hung on crosses dangled by rope from the top of the fort wall. Three and three, they were arrayed on either side of the massive iron and wooden gates. Those grisly remains were a warning for everyone in the town to see and to heed. The message was very clear: *Obey or die.*

Neither of us said anything as we walked on the far side of the street that ran parallel to that awful wall. There were few pedestrians here, and in the traffic that hurried by, not one driver or passenger lifted their eyes to the gruesome scene. But not one person, either, could fail to sense the horrific presence of those poor men who had been so cruelly tortured to death.

We walked with the stunned and shuffling pace of men at a funeral, and I guess in reality that is what we were. We came to the next corner and continued for a bit, as I wanted to take a look at the next sidewall of the fort and get an estimation of its length and also to see if there was another entrance on that side. About a hundred feet from the corner was what looked like a narrow door set into the wall. I made a mental note of its location for the map I would later draw.

We then turned our backs on that foul place and made our way slowly back to the house of Rahab, two men sickened by the sight they had beheld.

"They were men from my tribe, good men, men I knew quite well," he said, with a calm voice but a flaming glare in his eyes.

Lost in his thoughts and in grief for his friends, Amayaz stared at the wall and shook his head. There was nothing I could say that would help matters, so I remained silent.

After a bit he looked at me and spoke again.

"This interloper, he has pronounced his own doom. We were wrong to let him go on here for this long. We should have exterminated this nest of vermin well before now."

"All I want is the boy," I said. "And if in gaining his return we can help you in your fight, I will do everything in my power to assist."

Amayaz reached over and put his hand on my forearm.

"Thank you," he said in a soft voice.

I went to the door, and summoning a servant, sent her for paper and pens. The materials arrived, along with a samovar of tea and a plate of pastries. Amayaz and I spread the sheets of paper on the floor and were busy sketching our maps when there was a knock on the door, and Rahab made her entrance.

"You have seen?" she asked after she had taken a seat.

"Yes," replied Amayaz.

"I would have told you earlier, but you needed to see with your own eyes what this man has done," she said in a sorrowful voice. "And those are only the most visible depredations he has committed. Many other innocent people are missing, supposedly held in the torture cells of the fort. His men conduct themselves as ravenous animals. They brutalize all they encounter."

She paused and touched a hand to her cheek, a vacant look in her eyes, as though recalling a bad memory.

"How long has this been going on?" I asked.

Her troubled face cleared as she came back to the moment, and the light of her incredible beauty shone forth once again.

"Six—no, seven months. Two months ago, the conduct of the soldiers became so intolerably destructive that I no longer could allow them to enter here. So I took to sending a weekly contingent of women to the fort. Even with that, the behavior of the soldiers has become so outrageous that I've had to pay my girls extra just to go there."

I felt an electric jolt course up my spine.

"Have you, yourself, Lady Rahab, been within the walls of the fort?" I asked.

"On many occasions," she said. "I have had to conduct the business end of matters with the commander, a man called Boutari—a crude and lowborn Sudanese."

She spat the last part out with a flash of vehemence.

"Have you heard of foreigners held within the fort? Foreign captives?" I asked.

She contemplated a second before she spoke. "It is said by the soldiers that they hold many captives. I am told there are a number of Lebanese who were captured from several places to the south."

Yes, I thought. *That would make sense. The man is running a full-fledged hostage/ransom business. Africa is full of expatriate Lebanese traders and merchants who are always prey for thieves and hostage-takers.* But that wasn't my concern now.

"Yes, I understand, but what I mean are *foreign* captives—?"

I grabbled in my mind for the word I sought.

Is it Qawadji*? No, that's the word in Saudi Arabia. What do they say here? Ah yes, there it is."*

"*Nasranis,* Lady Rahab. Have you heard of any *Nasrani* captives?" I asked.

She nodded her comprehension.

"It has been whispered that two new prisoners were brought in a week ago: a European woman and an Arab boy. But if this is true, no one has seen them since they arrived."

I could feel the electricity again, and I pressed forward. Sliding a large sheet of paper and a pen toward her, I asked, "Lady Rahab, could you draw a picture of what you were able to see inside the fort?"

She picked up the pen and looked at it as though trying to make up her mind about something. She then turned to Amayaz with a searching look.

"If I assist you in all you ask, will you do something for me?" she inquired in a businesslike voice.

"If within my power to give, it shall be yours," he said.

"Drive these evil men from this place. Kill the ones who stand and resist, and cleanse us of the filth they have visited upon us," she hissed with a feline fury.

Amayaz lifted his right hand as though taking a pledge.

"It is my intention to do just that; and do it I will— *Inshallah.*"

"Inshallah," we said, both the woman and I, in response to Amayaz's oath.

With that, Rahab leaned over the paper and drew a detailed sketch of the interior of the fort. When, with our prodding, she had sketched all she could remember, she called in some of the other women who had been inside those forbidding walls, and they were able to fill in most of the voids of the chart.

Before the women were allowed to leave, Rahab swore them to a bloodcurdling oath, with dire warnings of what would happen to them should they reveal to anyone the presence of Amayaz or myself or of our interest in the fort.

When we were alone again, Amayaz and I sat and looked at our maps, both the one of the interior and my sketch of the outside perimeter.

"There are unknown areas within our map of the interior of the fort, but that can also tell us much," I said, as I pointed out the blank places on the paper.

"Unseen places are forbidden places. Perhaps this is where the important captives are held," said Amayaz, looking up from the map.

"We must return to camp tonight," I said as I picked up one of the papers. "But I want to make a circuit of the exterior of the fort before we leave. We have yet to get a look at two of the sides."

"Yes," he replied. "We must search out hidden and covered approaches to the walls and also check the vigilance of the guards."

"What," I asked, "do you think the people of the town will do when we attack? Will they assist the garrison of the fort? Will they attack us in the rear?"

Amayaz snorted. "They will cower in their homes until the last shot is fired, then creep out to cheer the victor and declare their allegiance—to whoever has won."

But there was one other question I had, and though it had nothing to do with my own mission, I wanted to hear my comrade's thought on the matter.

"And you, Lord Amayaz, what will you and your men do to the town, once the fort is taken?" I asked with a sober voice as I looked into the eye of my comrade.

Amayaz looked at me steadily before answering. "We are not the bloodthirsty wolves our enemies make us out to be. And the town, Lord Rashid, is not our enemy. These people have been visited by a plague. We will provide the cure to the disease from which they suffer, and the town will become healthy once again. The well-being of the town is necessary to the well-being of my tribe. Thus it has ever been, and thus it will be again."

I bowed my head in answer to these words.

"I am gladdened," I said, "to hear this from your own lips. I wanted no innocent blood on my hands."

"And there will be none," he replied. "This, I can guarantee."

We then returned to our charts and discussed the reconnaissance we would undertake when the night was full upon us.

CHAPTER 21

DESERT TOWNS AND VILLAGES COME
to life after sundown. People stroll about, shop, and entertain themselves by taking part in the bustle of community life. Men sit in coffee shops where they smoke, drink endless cups of coffee and tea, and talk until late into the night.

Families walk with children in hand, taking in the same familiar sights and sounds as they did the night before and the night before that. Little boys, like boys everywhere, run about, playing games of their own contrivance and peppering the night air with happy yelps.

Older boys—teenagers and the unmarried twenty-somethings walk together in small groups, talking quietly and hoping to catch a glimpse of a lovely face. The sedate yet unspoken flirting, conducted with fleeting and surreptitious but nonetheless longing glances, makes the air, at times, seem faintly electric.

But here, there was a subdued quality to the street

life. The people spoke in strangely quiet voices, and the parents kept their children close. When a pair of policemen walked through the marketplace, the people cast their eyes to the ground, lowered their voices, and parted to allow the swaggering bullies to pass. No one ever forgot the bodies at the entrance to the fort.

Amayaz and I strolled the same streets we had ambled earlier in the day and took in the feel of the night. I looked for positioning of the few streetlights, and as we made our way closer to the fort, I made a mental note of which ones to knock out. When we were two blocks from that forbidding edifice, we stopped at a sidewalk coffee shop.

We ordered tea and a water pipe from the owner, who, though he looked at us in an inquiring manner, asked no questions of us. The other patrons sitting nearby gave us a few sidelong glances and put their heads together in quiet speculation as to who these two strange Tuaregs might be. As befitted two desert nomads come to town, Amayaz and I smoked our pipe, sat quietly, and ignored our neighbors.

Within a short period of time, we became part of the background scenery, and the other boulevardiers, forgetting our presence, resumed their previous discourse. Conversation was buzzing in a low hum when suddenly an abrupt silence descended on the place. Amayaz and I had positioned ourselves so that we could look across one another, and thus see in both directions, up and down the sidewalk. I saw Ayamaz's eyes fixed on the sidewalk behind me, and I turned in my chair just as he stood and addressed the two approaching "policemen."

"Esteemed guardians of the public," he said, with a flourish of the hands. "Will you do my friend and me the honor of joining us in a pipe and a cup of refreshment?"

The two young militiamen looked at one another and then back again at Amayaz. I could see they were trying to make up their minds as to whether it was a serious invitation or if this nomad was indeed mad.

Amayaz indicated the two empty chairs at our table and asked again, "Would you not rest a moment with friends? I have spent many a pleasant hour in conversation and conducting business with your famed commander. It would be our pleasure to host two of his brave soldiers."

They seemed to be leaning toward accepting, but at the mention of their commander, a resistance came over them, and they unconsciously withdrew a step. The older of the two spoke, and his accent confirmed my belief that these two were Algerian.

"Sir, we thank you for your invitation, but we are under orders to return to our barracks at the end of our shift of duty." He looked at his watch. "And as that time befalls us in just a few minutes, I must beg your indulgence and depart."

Amayaz stepped closer to the boys, as boys they were, for at most, they were only in their late teens or early twenties. He reached beneath his robes and stretched forth his hand.

"Then here," he said, as he placed a few bills in the hand of the policeman. "I know a soldier's pay is small, and it is lonely away from the fires of ones' own people."

The militiamen gawked at the money before the one whose hand was full stuffed the cash into a pocket.

"Thank you, sir. You have been most kind, and I hope to have the good fortune to see you and your friend again in the near future. You are a generous man and one kind unto strangers," he said with a smile at this unexpected good fortune.

Amayaz fixed the young man with a smile of his own.

"Allah commands us to be kind to the wayfarer that

we meet in life's pathways. *Ba'sallamah*," he said with a slight bow.

"*Ba'sallamah*," said the two as they turned and hurried away.

We sat down again and picked up our pipes. I could feel the eyes of the other patrons on my back. They must have thought us crazy to have spoken to those two and crazier still to issue an invitation to sit down.

"They had seen us earlier," Amayaz said in explanation as he took a puff on his pipe. "And I think they had made up their minds to take us to the fort. I hoped a friendly word would dissuade them from that thought, as I did not wish to kill them—at least, not yet."

I smiled and nodded as I took a pull on the pipe. When Amayaz stood up, I had seen the faint outline of his pistol beneath his robes, and I had put my hand on my own while I sat at the table and waited to see which way things were developing.

I had nothing but admiration for the way Amayaz had handled the encounter. Initiative and fast thinking are two marks of an excellent leader. Amayaz had those and other qualities besides in great abundance.

We stayed at the café for another hour or so before paying the bill and moving on. I think the proprietor felt nothing but relief when we finally thanked him for his hospitality. But I don't think he was exactly pleased when Amayaz promised that he would recommend to all his kinsmen that they visit his establishment whenever they came to town.

We walked in the general direction of the fort before turning down a darkened side street. The residents of the area were locked behind the walls of their houses, and the street was deserted.

"Let us part here," said Amayaz. "I have something I must do in another part of town, and I think only one of us should go on the errand you have need of fulfilling."

"I am in agreement," I responded. "Rather than return to the lodgings of our host, I think it best to meet where we halted before entering town."

"My thoughts also," he said.

I checked my watch. "Then let us find one another at that spot three hours before the rising of the sun."

"It shall be so," he said as he took my hand briefly before turning and retreating into the night.

I watched him disappear and then, taking my bearings, set out to take a look around the walls of the fort. I wanted to get a gander at the back of the fortress and also assess the state of security around the perimeter.

The militiamen I had seen earlier in the day had been positioned in static posts atop the walls, at the corners, and also at the front gate. They had been posted singly rather than in pairs. And from what I had seen from my furtive glances, they seemed bored out of their skins. With luck, that same attitude prevailed at night also.

I came out on the main street about two blocks from the corner of the fort. It was an area of town that had once been used as the animal market. Empty stalls and low scattered huts lay sprinkled across the area. And the place still carried the strong odor of the great multitudes of sheep, goats, camels, and donkeys.

I walked along the outer edge of the market, and when I had passed it completely, continued out into the desert until I was enveloped by the darkness. I would sit here quietly, listening and thinking, and wait until my night vision had gathered its full strength.

CHAPTER 22

OUR EYES WORK DIFFERENTLY AT night than they do during the day or when we are under artificial illumination. The rod cells of the retina are the ones that give us our vision at night, and these take a bit of time and adjustment before they come fully into play. And since these cells are found around the outer edge of the retina, we have the phenomenon that when looking at something at night, in order to see it best, we should look off to its side, rather than straight at it.

I'm about the same as most people in that it takes roughly thirty minutes for my eyes to adapt to the darkness. And while I waited, I also let my ears become attuned to the surroundings. It is amazing what you can sense when you are still and let your mind clear itself and become a receptor of sensory input, without the clutter of human society's noise and commotion.

As my eyes started to make out more and more images, I was able to see a faint haze in the sky and could detect a slight reflected glow from the lights of the town. Somewhere, off toward the northern hills, far in the distance, the pining *yip-yip-yip* of a prowling jackal was heard. Now it was time to begin. A slight breeze moved across the desert as I got to my feet and moved toward the distant black line of the fortress walls.

When walking stealthily, the worst thing you can do is try to sneak. You know what I mean: that exaggerated tiptoeing stance, with shoulders hunched over, bent forward at the waist, arms held out to the sides like a pair of drooping wings.

First thing, if anyone sees you like that, they know you're up to something. Secondly, you're off balance. If you have to stop suddenly, you'll fall on your ass. And more importantly than the first two, you're not quiet.

No, to walk quietly and cautiously at night you should walk like a girl. Put one foot forward directly in front of the other, just the way a runway model walks. Also plant each step so that the entire foot touches the ground at once; no heel and then toe, but place the whole foot lightly on the ground.

This will do several things. You have great balance. And you can feel something under the foot before you put your weight on it and make an inadvertent and unwanted noise. If you have to suddenly stop in your tracks, you merely lower the foot and freeze. It is also extremely quiet. Walking in this manner, I can cross a gravel parking lot and make little more sound than if I were walking across a grassy lawn.

Another point of reconnaissance field craft: When approaching a point at night or in the day, walk straight toward it and never approach from a parallel track. By approaching head-on, an observer has a more difficult time detecting your movement. Our eyes are geared to see lateral movement with great ease. That's the reason we are often startled by slight movements detected in our peripheral vision. It's a protective reflex.

So I would walk straight in, take a look at a certain section, then back away and come in again, all along the perimeter of the fort. It would take a while, but I had several hours.

As I closed in, I would take ten or twelve steps and then stop and listen a few seconds. I was aiming to approach the wall at about the midway point, just a little away from the side entrance I had seen earlier in the day.

The walls of the fort were beginning to appear higher now, as I got closer. I had slowed down and was listening twice as long as I was walking. The one thing I could not afford was to stumble over a foot patrol as it made its rounds about the perimeter. Then the breeze shifted slightly, and I caught an odd smell. No mistaking that odor: It was a whiff of hashish.

I slowly lowered myself to my knees and pointed my nose into the wind. The smell slipped away as the wind died, but then it drifted back to me again. I had the wind line now. I got to my feet and edged forward a step at a time. Somewhere up ahead, someone was having a toke, and I had to see who that was. Hashish is a communal repast, something you share with others, and I needed to determine how many people might be out here and who they were.

I continued to slide forward, a tentative step at a time. My route took me down into a very shallow wash, and as I came up the other side, I heard the sound of a voice. I slithered up the edge of the ditch, took to my knees again, and then sat back on my heels to look and listen.

There, thirty feet ahead, were two men. They were lounging on the ground, heads together and murmuring in low voices. I saw the flare of a lighted ember glow as air was pulled through a pipe, and then I saw the movement of an arm as the pipe was passed by one man to the other. He released a cloud of smoke as he exhaled, and then I was bathed by the pungent odor of North Africa hashish.

I sat and watched, trying to determine who these two were and why they were here. Then I saw the rifles on the ground and realized they were soldiers who had slipped out of the fort for a little relaxation.

One of the soldiers lurched to his feet and took a few unsteady steps in my direction. I held my breath. I had no intention of shooting them. Instead, if detected, I would run away. But the soldier stopped, and stooping to his knees, he undid his fly and took a whiz.

North Africans and Arabs almost always kneel when they take a leak outside. They say they do this so they won't drill holes in the ground and let the evil spirits that live beneath the surface of the desert escape. But I think it's so they don't splatter their feet.

When he finished his business, the soldier got to his feet, and as he turned in profile, I recognized him as one of the policemen we spoke with at the café.

Well, I thought, *at least they put to good use the money Amayaz had given them.*

I waited until they finished their outing and then watched as they returned to the fort, where they entered through the side entrance I had seen that day. The door was either unguarded or these guys had a key. Either way, it was noteworthy. It also told me there was probably no one watching outside the fort at night. And if you don't patrol your area with vigor and alacrity, you don't control the surrounding terrain.

I continued around the perimeter of the fort and found the same condition on all sides. Lights were in place at various points along the wall but with seemingly no rhyme or reason as to their positioning. The guards at those points stood directly beneath the pool of light where they made easy targets of themselves. In the back wall was a double gate, wide enough for a vehicle to pass through. It was locked from within but with no sign of guards.

As I circled the fort, I would come in close at various intervals, stand well out in the darkness, and throw stones at the tops of the walls. If anyone was there at all, they were fast asleep.

The only guards I could find along the entire length of the wall were those posted under the lights and at the main gate at the front of the fort. It wasn't a perfect situation, but it was better than I had hoped for.

I checked my watch. It was nearing our rendezvous time, so I angled away from the fort and made a wide circuit of the town. As I approached the spot where we had cached the bike, I stopped and made the mournful call of the nighthawk. The song was answered, and I soon found Amayaz waiting for me.

"I'll drive," he said. "I think you must be very tired."

He was right. The nervous strain of my walkabout had pulled the energy out of me. I put a blanket down on the equipment in the trailer, curled up on top of the load, and was soon rocked to sleep as we trundled our way back across the desert. At the midway point, just as the day was dawning, we stopped and changed places. Amayaz slept soundly until I aroused him just outside the entrance to the wadi.

CHAPTER 23

ROOSTY, TERRY, AND I SAT AT THE entrance to my tent as they filled me in on what had taken place during my absence.

"We ran the boys through a basic proficiency test with the rifles," Terry said. "Some are pretty good. Some are barely okay. And some are downright untrainable."

"How many did you take a look at?" I asked.

Terry consulted a small notebook.

"Eighty-six with the rifle," he replied.

"And twelve with the machine guns," said Roosty.

Roosty was a master machine gunner and a superb trainer. And in a heavy fight, nothing is more important than the machine guns.

"How were they?" I asked.

Roosty scratched the back of his neck. "Four of them will make good gunners. Four others will make decent assistant gunners. The others can be ammo bearers."

"Any of them afraid of the gun?" I inquired.

"No," Roosty answered. "Just the opposite problem—they all want to be gunners."

"We will probably need only two machine guns for the hit. And I'll want you to keep a tight hand on them—literally within arm's reach," I said.

"You know how inexperienced gun crews act in a fight; once they start shooting, they get so excited they forget everything except how to hold down the trigger. I'll need you to make sure to lift and shift fires when the signals are given. Otherwise, they'll shoot anything they see—including us."

Roosty gave me a gap-toothed grin.

"You still upset about what happened that time in Mozambique?" he asked with a grin.

"Yeah," I replied. "And I know you are, too. And neither of us wants a repeat of that little experience."

He was referring to an incident we had when our own native troops kept us pinned down in a ditch for half an hour. It was only when they ran out of ammunition that we were able to get it across to them we were friendlies.

At that moment Istvan and András joined us. I pointed to the hand-drawn maps spread out before us on the ground and quickly filled them in on what we had found in town and the status, as we knew it, of matters inside the fort.

They studied the maps as I spoke, and Istvan began to slowly shake his head as I briefed the situation.

"A very difficult task," he said when I had finished. "An attack against a fortified position is always problematic, even when the defenders are less than vigilant."

He rubbed his chin as he looked at the sketch of the fort once more before continuing. "By its very nature, the defense has the strength of inertia. It requires an overwhelming force on the part of the attacker to break that type of strength. The accepted tactical standard, I believe, is a force advantage of four to one. And from what you have said, you do not have such force at your disposal."

"That is true, my friend, but only if you confront your opponent where he is strongest. And I have not the slightest intention of doing that," I replied in an offhand manner.

He gave me a quizzical look.

"We will open our assault on the side of the fort he has left undefended," I said.

Terry looked at me as though I were speaking gibberish. "Granted, that may not be the Queen's Own Rifles defending the place, but those twenty-foot walls were built by the French to keep out the Tuaregs and other such riffraff—and they've served that function pretty well for the last hundred years," he said, his eyebrows dancing like a pair of ballerinas.

"Kennesaw, you old sod, we hit those walls head-on with this lot, and we're going to lose a lot of men. Not to mention maybe some of us as well."

"But we ain't gonna hit 'em head-on; leastways, not with the first whack," I said in my best north Georgia twang.

"Well, mate, unless you tunnel underneath, and that might take some time, I don't see what choice you have," he said, a tone of exasperation in his voice.

"Why, boy, they ain't no choice to be made 'bout it at all. Somebody's jus' gonna flang them gates wide open up fer us," I said, laying it on thick.

Terry started to reply, but Istvan's sudden laughter cut him off. As I looked from Terry to Istvan, András also began to chuckle as well.

"Of course," said Istvan. "The undefended side. It is so obvious, is it not?"

"Well, if it's so obvious, pray enlighten this poor dolt here, if you will," Terry barked as he poked himself in the chest with a thumb.

Istvan ignored Terry and looked at me with an amused smile. "How many do you intend to take with you?" he asked.

"There will be eight of us," I replied.

"Eight?" Istvan queried. "You don't have that many qualified men."

"I only need one," I replied. "The remainder will be made up of our allies. Besides, I can't equip more than eight. You know that yourself."

"I don't think you will have the time necessary to train them properly," he said.

Terry was watching us like we were engaged in a Ping-Pong match.

"What? What?" he said as his head whipped back and forth from me to Istvan.

Ignoring Terry, I gave my attention to Istvan.

"I will give them ground training only. The first time they do it will be for real—we all know the second time is harder than the first. All I need are brave men. And the tribe will sing of their bravery for a hundred years to come," I said.

"It is brilliant," replied Istvan.

"No," I said, "it is merely necessary. Now, my friend, if you will get the plane ready, I want to take Sheikh Talmun and some of the elders for a ride. And we will use the flight as an opportunity to make a demonstration."

"The plane will be ready in fifteen minutes," said Istvan, as he and András got to their feet.

"Will you please, in the name of all that's holy, tell me *what* you two are talking about?" asked Terry with decided irritation in his voice.

"Come with me, Terry. I need to speak with the sheikh," I said as I got to my feet and brushed off my rear end. "You're going to like this."

"I'd better," he said as we ambled over to the sheikh's headquarters tent.

He turned and gave me an inquiring look, and I'll swear, I thought his eyebrows were about to take flight.

CHAPTER 24

I CLOSED THE DOOR TO THE PLANE and over the intercom gave Istvan the all-okay. Terry checked the belts on our passengers a second time. The four old chieftains who had constituted the faux jury when I had arrived in camp, along with Sheikh Talmun and Amayaz, were seated on the floor of the forward cargo area. András had rigged safety belts for each of them, and these were fastened to the ringbolts set in the floor of the fuselage.

As the engine roared to life, the plane quivered like a dog shaking off a dousing of cold rainwater. Our passengers gave me a nervous look, which I returned with a confident smile. This was a first for these men. In fact, no member of the tribe had ever been up in a plane. I wanted this to be a memorable experience. I also had an additional agenda. I hoped to induce a certain degree of envy in some of the other tribesmen.

Istvan released the brakes, and we started to roll. As

we taxied the short distance to our hand-cleared runway, the men sitting nervously on the floor felt every bump and jolt of the primitive airstrip. I gave them another smile of reassurance.

In readiness for takeoff, I knelt and grabbed a firm hold of one of the exposed ribs of the fuselage. From his perch up in the cockpit, Istvan shoved the throttle forward, and the engine threw its one thousand horses of power to the spinning propeller blades. We were on our way.

The tail came up, and now we rapidly gained speed. The dust cloud we kicked up in our wake was absolutely biblical. As the four wings gained a grip on the air that rushed faster and faster over their upper surfaces, the plane became light on its wheels, and then, with a sudden bounce, we were airborne.

The jolting violent shaking of the takeoff run was soon replaced by a smooth and easy movement as the plane took now to its natural element. Istvan pulled back the power just a bit and brought us into a steady climb.

I stood and looked at the men seated on the floor. They returned my look with brave aplomb, but I think it was only with the supreme effort of stoic courage on their part.

Terry shouted to me, and I turned to where he stood at the rear of the cargo area.

"Come on," he gestured to me. "Time to get suited up."

I joined him at his station and gave him a hand as he got into his harness, and then he did the same for me.

András came down from the cockpit and plugged his headset into the jack near the cargo door. He put a hand to one of the earphones and listened intently for a few seconds before looking out the nearby window and then turning to face me.

"Ready?" he asked.

I had just finished checking Terry's equipment. I gave him a thumbs-up.

"Ready," I said.

András stooped to the floor of the fuselage and snapped the end of his safety line to a ring in the floor. I motioned to Terry to hand me his line, and then snapped both his and mine to another floor ring. András checked the anchor points of the rings, gave me a nod, and then turned and opened the door to the plane.

Eighty knots of wind swirled in through the open door. I looked to the startled men seated forward of us and gave them a smile and a reassuring gesture.

"Do not worry," I called out above the howling wind pouring through the open door. "Everything is all right."

I then leaned over to András and lifted one of his earpieces.

"As soon as you get the door closed, get our friends on their feet and at the windows. I want them to know exactly what happened."

"Yeah," he yelled back at me.

I then stepped to the doorway, took a good grip on the frame, and leaned outside. The rushing power of the air tried to pull me from the plane, but I hung on to the doorframe with firm determination. On the ground, forward of the nose of the plane and two thousand feet below, I could see the entire assembled tribe standing in a mass. Roosty was the ground wrangler, and I was sure he had his hands full trying to keep the crowd in control.

I fixed my eyes on the ground at a point about one hundred meters away from the spectators on the ground. I watched as that spot on the earth slid steadily toward us, and as it disappeared under the wing, I pulled myself back inside the plane, turned to Terry who stood just behind me, and pointed to the aft edge of the open door.

"Stand in the door," I yelled.

Terry stepped to the edge of the door, took a good

grip on the doorframe, and hung his toes out into space. I leaned my head out and looked at the ground.

There's the spot now, just below the belly of the plane.

I smacked Terry on the backside. "Go!" I yelled.

Terry sprang straight out and was lost to view. I quickly glanced back at the passengers and saw the startled and horrified looks on their faces. I held my hand up and waved in a reassuring manner.

"It is all right," I shouted before turning to the door and leaping out into the waiting atmosphere.

As I cleared the door of the plane, I tucked my chin in my chest, my elbows to my side, pressed my knees tightly together, and counted.

One thousand—two thousand—three thou . . . and then I felt the parachute blossom open and grab air. I gave the canopy over my head a quick but thorough scan.

All okay. No unwanted holes, no lines out of place.

I then looked around to find Terry. He was off to my left and about one hundred feet lower than me. I pulled the left riser of the parachute down to my chest and inclined in his direction. He looked up and gave me a wave and a shout.

"Watch where you're going, mate. I don't need you fouling my canopy," he called.

"Just make sure you don't break a leg. I don't want you embarrassing us in front of our friends."

Terry replied with a wicked grin and a single-finger salute.

I had almost forgotten what a peaceful but at the same time exhilarating experience this was. I looked to the crowd below, picked out my landing spot, and watched as, slowly at first and then with a surprising burst of speed, the ground came rushing up to meet me.

I let my feet and legs go slack, pressed my knees solidly together, and then, with a rolling collapse of my body, I hit the ground with a solid jolt.

Before I could get to my feet, I was covered in a mass of shouting, laughing, back-pounding humanity. A multitude of hands picked me up and shook me like a rag doll. I could hear Roosty shouting above the fray, trying to get the people to release Terry and me from their collective grip of exaltation, but it was to no avail.

The men whooped and shouted at the scene they had just beheld. The women ululated their excitement in shrill warbling tones, while the boys and young men literally danced with joy.

This is better than the county fair, I thought as I was finally able to stand on my own feet once again. *I don't think I'll have any trouble at all when I ask for volunteers to parachute with me into the fort.*

Many willing and helpful hands vied to help me as I gathered up my parachute and stuffed it into the kit bag. But when I tried to sling it over my shoulder, several young men grabbed it and took turns carrying the unwieldy bundle over their heads.

The returning plane was on final approach now. So, like a pair of Pied Pipers, Terry and I led the people away from the airstrip, where we could all watch the landing in safety.

When the bird touched down and taxied to a stop, the tribe surged forward to greet the passengers with great and loud exuberance. András and Amayaz hopped down and gave a hand to the old men as they emerged. Everyone was shouting and trying to talk at the same time. People touched and petted the plane as though it were a live animal, while others pointed to the sky and pantomimed the parachute drop.

Sheikh Talmun and the elders stood by the door of the plane and told excitedly of their experience. Sheikh Moghal, the old one-eyed chieftain, pointed to inside the plane and then to the outside, as he gave his impression of the flight and what it was like to see the two crazy men jump from the plane.

I looked over the heads of the animated crowd and wondered at it all. Here was a people who lived without any of the things of life we, in the *civilized world*, think of as necessities. They have no permanent homes, no running water, no electricity, no central heat and air, no refrigeration, and practically no medical care.

If their children get sick, they either heal on their own or they die. If the springs and wells they depend on fail, their flocks die and the people suffer.

Governments, by their very nature, lust for control over people. And because they are under the control of no one, the Tuaregs are hated and feared by the national governments that claim the desert regions they inhabit.

But when those governments attempt to restrict the Tuaregs in their movements and herd them into settlements, the Tuaregs fight, and they fight hard. There have been Tuareg uprisings since the time of the French colonial administrations. There is a current conflict in the nearby nation of Niger, where the government is trying to steal Tuareg land and give it to a uranium mining company. But through it all, these desert wanderers have managed to persist.

They are some of the most wonderful and honorable people I have ever known, I thought as I watched them now. *I hope they last for another thousand years.* And with that thought, I knew I envied them.

I envied them their knowledge of who they are and what they are. I envied their sense of self. I envied their sense of place in the universe. Because in comparison, I could only wonder who and what I am and felt that I am a man adrift, without rudder or compass.

The crowd shoved me toward the plane. As I neared

the door, Sheikh Moghal grabbed me by the arms and laughed.

"This has been the greatest gift of my life," he shouted, sending spittle flying through the air.

"As a boy, herding my father's goats, I would watch the eagle hunt and dream of soaring like that brave bird. And now that I have done it, I can go to my grave knowing I have missed nothing in life. Thank you, thank you for this grand gift."

"I'm glad I could provide you the experience," I said. "I hope it was not too frightening."

"No, it was not frightening at all, not even when I thought you and your friend had jumped to your deaths," he said. "But that is something I think I will leave to the young men to try."

His toothless smile wrinkled his entire face.

The old man took me by the arm, and we led the way back into camp. As we walked, I told him that I would need some of his bravest warriors to join me in a parachute jump when we made our attack. He assured me there would be no shortage of willing young men and that he would personally help me select the best and bravest.

While food was being prepared, Amayaz and I gave the chiefs a briefing of our general plan of attack and of the task that lay before us. I then solicited the help of the elders in configuring our force. I wanted to hit the fort with a company of eighty men. Amayaz would be the commander.

The overall group would be configured in three different elements, each led by its own lieutenant. One element, at the moment the attack was sprung, would sweep through town and take it under control. The other two elements would be in position to launch the assault on the fort.

I would take charge of the airborne squad. We would

initiate the attack by parachuting into the fort and throwing open the main gates. The main force would then stream in and overwhelm the defenders, thus allowing Roosty, Terry, and me to make a rapid search for the boy. The plane would circle overhead with András in the door manning a machine gun and providing fire support for us as we made the attack.

When the boy was found, the plane would land on a stretch of road just outside of town. From there, my group would evacuate, leaving the Imouhar force in charge of the fort and the town. All supplies, arms, ammunition, and equipment would remain in the hands of the Imouhar.

"And," Sheikh Talmun pointed out, "any loot found inside the fort will belong to us, also."

"That, sir, is for your men and no one else. It is the uncontested prize of the victor," I replied.

"And what is your thought, should we take this man, Boutari, alive?" he asked with a querying look. "It is my experience that commanders are seldom killed in a fight, only soldiers."

"I think, wise sheikh, that he should receive the justice of your people—and that is something that is up to you and the other men of mature and learned judgment."

"Yes, justice is all we seek. Justice for the wrongs we have suffered, and nothing more," he said with satisfaction in his voice.

"I think, then, that we should next form our force into its various elements and rehearse our actions. A night attack is always a hazardous enterprise, and a thorough preparation will do much to insure a rapid victory," I said as I looked around to those assembled.

"We attack tomorrow night, is that your plan?" asked the sheikh.

"With your permission, and if it pleases you and your people," I said. "I am here merely to assist."

Sheikh Talmun put his hand on my shoulder. "It pleases me greatly," he said. "Tomorrow night, we attack."

Just then, Sheikh Talmun's wife and several other women arrived with platters of bread, dates, and cheese.

At the sight of his young wife, the old sheikh clapped his hands with delight.

"But first let us eat," he said. "War is not to be made on an empty stomach."

My own stomach growled as the heaping platters were set before us, and I realized that I hadn't eaten since yesterday. We attacked the food with the relish of hungry men.

CHAPTER 25

GAIL SAT AND THOUGHT AND TRIED to determine what she must do next. The move to new quarters had brought a great improvement in the treatment of Abdullah and her. But it had also brought her an understanding of just how dire the situation was.

Wicker-covered openings high in the walls allowed for the circulation of air between the rooms in the interior of the fort. They also allowed Gail to overhear the violent arguments in the next room between the two men who had hauled her in earlier.

She was stunned to the core by what she had overheard. As bad as her situation had been up to now, she had not had the slightest idea as to the depths and layers of horror and intrigue that had brought her to this place.

That poor family, she thought. *Slaughtered for such a vile reason. And now the inevitable falling-out of thieves. But it also explains the secretive man who had visited the young emir on those several occasions before the attack on the yacht.*

Gail looked down at the boy sitting next to her on the cot; his knees were drawn to his chin and his arms wrapped tightly around his legs. He rocked slightly, back and forth, and hummed a droning, monotonous tune. His blank eyes were fixed on the far wall, but the boy himself was somewhere far away. Gail put an arm around his small shoulders.

"We will be all right, Abutti," she whispered and then kissed the crown of his head. "I promise."

She held him next to her for several minutes and then got up and paced the room.

I must get away. I must escape, she thought. *But how? And if I can get out of here, will I find help outside?*

Last night she had heard feminine giggles and the lewd laughter of men passing in the hallway outside. And later, from somewhere farther down the hall, she had heard the raucous sounds of animated male voices and shrieking women. It had sounded like a party of carnal and epic proportions.

Maybe, she thought, *if that sort of thing were repeated, it would give me the opportunity to slip out of here. But first, I have to get out of this room.*

Gail went to the door and studied it closely. It had been opened when she and the boy were led here from their cell and also when the old woman brought their food. It was a massive affair made of solid wood and looked like it would survive the charge of a rhinoceros.

Gail knelt down and looked at the lock. It was an old-fashioned box lock, like the ones in her grandmother's Victorian-era house. She closed one eye and peeked in at the slot for the key. No light came through; it was blocked. That meant the key was in the lock.

She then lay on the floor and looked underneath the

door. There was a gap of about a quarter of an inch between the floor and the bottom of the door. Gail got to her feet and began to cross the room. Her eyes searched from wall to wall and from floor to ceiling.

What is in here that I can use? she thought as she paced back and forth. Her mattress on the floor was no use. She stopped and looked at the boy, who still sat rocking and humming on the cot. A sudden thought hit her.

"Abutti, darling. Get up a second and let me look at something," she said.

The boy did not look up but continued as before. Gail knelt down and lifted the boy's chin in her hand. Their eyes met.

"Abutti, I need your help, love. I need you to sit on the floor for a moment."

The boy made no response, but neither did he resist as she lifted him from the bed and sat him on the floor nearby.

"Let there be something—anything," she said under her breath as she removed the blanket and the sheets from the bed and then slid the mattress to the floor.

"Yes," she said to herself as she looked down at the latticework of thin metal strips, mounted by coiled springs that were attached to the frame of the bed. "This will do perfectly."

She went to work and quickly popped one of the springs from its attaching hole in the frame. With quick hands and nimble fingers, she unclipped the strip from the spring and disconnected it from the other side of the bed frame. She then pulled the mattress back into place and hurriedly replaced the sheets and the blanket.

She looked around the room for a place to hide the precious tool. "Where—where will it be safe?" she muttered as she looked all about.

Then a smile came on her face as she saw the perfect

spot. *What better place than there, right where it came from?* she thought, as she stepped back to the bed and shoved the metal strip under the mattress. She then took the boy by the hand, led him back to his place on the bed, and sat next to him.

"Abutti, I need something small and pointed," she said almost absentmindedly, more to herself than to the boy. "I need a pin."

She felt the boy touch her on the belly. She looked down and saw his finger pointed at her midsection.

"I don't think that's it," she laughed, as she put her arm back around the boy.

But he looked her in the eye, then at her waist, and put his finger on her belt buckle.

"Here," he said in a small voice.

She looked at the place he had planted his finger. He was raking his fingernail across the metal pin of the buckle that fitted in the hole of the belt.

Yes, that's it.

Gail leaned over and kissed the boy on the head again.

"Oh, Abutti. You are such a clever boy," she said with warmth in her voice.

The child looked at her and smiled; it was the first smile she had seen since they had been captured. Gail felt the tears begin to well in her eyes.

Maybe, just maybe, he is beginning to come back to life, she thought. *Now, if we can just hang on until an opportunity presents itself. Oh, I hope I can be brave.*

CHAPTER 26

AT THE MOUTH OF THE WADI, ON THE far end of our make-do airstrip, Terry, Roosty, and I scratched a full-size outline of the fort in the sand and dirt. Amayaz and the tribal elders watched with confused amusement at first. But when we walked them along the contours of the mock-up and pointed out the exterior walls and the interior layout, they grasped the idea with enthusiasm.

Amayaz sent two boys running back to camp for tent poles, and when they arrived, he put these in place to replicate the gates and the corners of the fort. We then used stones from the dry wash to outline the rooms of the interior and the corners of the fort. After that, we marked the town streets around the fort and the area of the animal market grounds.

Amayaz and I stood and looked at the layout of our target. We then backed away and determined the approach routes by which Amayaz would bring his men into position.

"Lord Amayaz," I said as I pointed out the location of the main gate. "When the gates are thrown open, it is vitally important that your most valiant and reliable men are the first to come through. The fight, I think, will be decided at that point."

Amayaz looked me resolutely in the eye. "I am leading that group in person. When the gates are breached, I will be the first man you see."

"I could not ask for better," I said. "Now, let's you and I walk through and talk about our actions before we bring the men down here to show them what we intend to do. Time is short, and it is much easier if you and I eliminate tactical problems before involving the men."

I waved to Terry and Roosty, who were walking the perimeter of the fort and looking at possible fields of fire, and beckoned them over.

"Guys," I said when they had joined us. "I've been thinking. . . ."

"Aye, that's a first, that," quipped Terry.

"Thanks, Terry," I said, giving him the old stink eye. "Bear with me a bit, if you don't mind."

I continued, "Lord Amayaz is leading the attack at the main gate. I need you, Terry, to take charge of the second wave and lead the attack on the barracks area of the fort. Roosty, I want you to take charge of the fire support element outside the fort, and if things get sticky and we get bogged down, then you come in with your men as a counterpunch. If the attack goes well, meet Terry and me at the corner of the headquarters building."

"You don't want me on the jump?" Terry asked.

"I can't put all our eggs in one basket. I want you and Roosty on the outside coming in," I said. "That way, if things go amiss, one of us, at least, will be in position to take charge and pull the fat out of the fire. Remember, *our mission* is to get the boy and get the hell out of here."

"Just wanted that made clear, mate," said Terry with a grin. "Because I didn't particularly relish the idea of jumping into that place in the middle of the night anyway. As me dear old mum used to tell me, 'Terry, me lad, you can always parachute in, but you sure as hell can't parachute back out again.'"

"Sounds to me like your mother was something of a tactical genius," I replied.

"Mother Wagstaff, she didn't raise no fools," Terry said with a solemn shake of the head.

"Then she must have adopted you at a late age," roared Roosty with a huge laugh.

I joined in the laugh. Terry gave us an admonishing look and pressed his lips together as though viewing two wayward children.

"Comedians," was all he said.

We got back to work. I asked Amayaz if he could assemble his men so that we could rehearse our actions for the attack on the fort. I went with him back to camp, as I also wanted a word with Istvan and András.

As we walked, we discussed the upcoming operation in ever-increasing detail. As an experienced leader, Amayaz knew that combat preparations are never complete, no matter how hard you have tried. At most, you prepare for the worst and hope for the best.

But I also know this: Even a poor plan, forcefully executed, stands a good chance of success. It is always a question of who holds the initiative and who is forced to react. Until now, we had been on the side of reaction. But when we launched the attack, we would be the ones calling the tune, and the other side would have to dance to our music.

It took a while, but we finally got the attack force assembled and at the rehearsal site. Everyone was outfitted with his weapon and equipment, minus ammunition. That would be issued just before departure.

At first it felt as though we were in the grip of complete anarchy. The men milled around in clan and family groups, and it seemed at times as though we were doomed to an interminable debate on how best to proceed. But these were not men to be ordered lightly about. Amayaz let them talk, and everyone had their say. At length, when every man had expressed his opinion, we got down to the plan for the operation.

It was like the first rehearsal for a large-scale open-air play. Amayaz took the leaders of the various elements and posted them at their respective assault positions—the spot from which they would begin the attack. The men sat in a wide semicircle so they could observe.

Amayaz then walked the perimeter of the fort and pointed out the gates, the corners, and the height of the walls. Next he had the men join their commanders in their positions and spread them out in the imaginary streets and buildings of the town, from which the attack would commence.

He had each group look at the location of the other elements and consider the direction of their fire. The last thing we wanted was a case of confusion that caused one friendly element to fire on another. Finally, when everyone was in position and the many new questions had been answered, it was time to walk through the attack. There is no point in a rehearsal more important than this one. This is where timing and coordination are worked out, with everyone getting to see how his movement and action affects the entire operation.

We were set. I was standing way off to the side. Amayaz lifted his arm and pointed to me. I then spread my arms as though I had wings. The men followed my progress with laughter, as I flew to the fort, where I simulated parachuting into the interior of the compound.

I then ran to the portal, firing pretend rounds at the pretend gate guards. As I threw open the gates to the fort, the attack force made a mad dash forward. Most of the men completely ignored the gate outlined with tent poles and came surging wildly across the outline of the imaginary walls, shouting war cries and brandishing their weapons menacingly as they came.

It took Amayaz several minutes to get his men back under control and to point out that the real walls of the fort would not allow such an easy passage. To demonstrate, he had everyone line up and walk through the space designated to simulate the gates of the fort. Once everyone was familiar with the concept, we tried it again.

The second time went more smoothly. The third time we ran it, the men were starting to get into the idea and became quite enthusiastic. Soon they started to operate as a whole rather than as a collection of individuals. I saw men pointing out angles of fire to one another and critiquing each other as to when and where to move.

Now we were ready to add the next step of the assault, where we would sweep the interior of the fort and make the attack on the barracks buildings. This was the point at which Terry, Roosty, and I would penetrate the headquarters area and make our search for the boy. We had just turned to go back to our start positions when—*BLAM!*

A shot rang out. And a man fell to the ground.

At the sound of the shot, everyone froze for a split second and then surged to where the fallen man lay on the ground. I pushed my way through the crowd and arrived where the man lay just as Amayaz arrived.

The man was on his side, grasping the top of his right thigh and grimacing in pain. When Amayaz asked him where he was hit, the man nodded to where his hands clenched his leg. While Amayaz and I rolled the man onto his back and opened up his robes, the crowd started to rumble and mutter. It was a dangerous sound.

Roosty and Terry came running over. They took a look and wasted no time swinging into action.

"Roosty, come with me. You get the bike and its trailer to carry the man back to camp, and I'll get the medical kit," Terry said as soon as he saw the man.

"Right," Roosty replied.

They pushed their way back though the crowd and were gone before I could respond.

I looked at the wound on the man's thigh. On the back of his leg, set in the middle of a large bruise, was a small black dot about the diameter of a pencil. On the opposite side of the leg and just above the back of his knee was the exit wound. Three strips of skin made an ugly, ragged mouth where the bullet had exited.

Blood was just beginning to seep from the wound. I tore two swaths of cloth from my djelaba and used these to make temporary bandages. As I bound the wound, I checked the thigh for signs that the bullet had hit the femur or the femoral artery. Either of these is a terrible situation, but it looked as though the bullet had missed both and had passed through without touching bone or artery. The man still had his color about him, and though excited, he didn't appear to be going into shock.

As bad as it was, it could have been much worse. We then got him on his back with his feet elevated and waited for Roosty to return with the Rokon and the trailer. While we waited for the make-do ambulance to arrive, Amayaz turned to the gathered men and asked the one question that screamed for an answer.

"Who did it?" he asked in a voice of authority.

The crowd parted and the murmuring subsided as a young man stepped forward. All eyes were on the man as he stood quietly and faced Amayaz. He looked around at the gathered tribe of warriors and then once again to Amayaz.

"It was me," he said in a calm voice.

Amayaz said nothing for several seconds. The men arrayed in a circle all around the two also held their silence.

Amayaz took two steps forward and stopped directly in front of the man.

"Give me your gun," he said.

The man had his rifle slung muzzle down over his right shoulder. He stood still for a second, then slowly took the rifle from his shoulder and held it with two hands in front of his chest.

Amayaz said nothing further but held out his hand. The man hesitated, then stepped forward and placed the weapon in Amayaz's outstretched hand. Amayaz pointed the muzzle to the ground, grabbed the bolt, and jacked four more rounds out of the magazine. He then inspected the rifle to make sure that it was now empty.

The man turned, and as he walked away toward camp, the crowd of men silently parted to let him pass, closing behind him once he had gone by.

I was mortified at this turn of events.

Oh hell, I thought. *This is the sort of thing that can wreck the entire operation. A grudge shooting—an old blood feud finally acted on—the culmination of an argument or a long-standing slight of some kind. Now everyone will fall back to family and clan associations and take sides. Before you know it, we'll have a war right here. It's all going to fall apart.*

Just then Roosty arrived with the bike. Willing hands lifted the man onto the trailer and made him as comfortable as possible. Terry checked the bandages and said they would do for the moment. As the wounded man was settled into position on the trailer, he looked to Amayaz and took him by the hand.

"Tell Malikan I know it was an accident. Tell him I am not angry, but I will expect him to provide for my family until I am better," the man said between teeth

gritted in pain. "Also tell him he owes me a donkey—
that will be sufficient payment for shooting me, and I
will hold him no animosity."

"It will be as you say," Amayaz said as he gave the
man a pat on the shoulder.

I motioned to Roosty, who slowly and gently put the
bike in motion and headed for the camp.

"I will have the man flown to Tamanrasset, where he
can be seen by a doctor," I said to Amayaz, as the bike
pulled away.

"That is not necessary," replied Amayaz. "He will be
treated here, and when we have taken the town, we will
bring him to a doctor there."

"But the wound may become infected," I said.

"The bullet went completely through, and there is no
broken bone. I have seen men recover from much worse.
Our healer will clean the wound, and he will be all
right."

Amayaz clapped me on the shoulder. "Don't worry
so much about small things such as this; it brings bad
luck."

"But the wounded man, he will hold no grudge
against the other?" I asked.

Amayaz shook his head, "The two men are cousins
and best friends. And you heard the words of Salwarsh,
the man who was shot. He has forgiven already. The
shooting was an accident. Stupid, yes, but still an accident. These things happen."

Bending to the ground, I scooped up a palm full of
sand and cleaned the blood from my hands. I was sorry
the man was hurt, but at the same time, I was very relieved that the incident had not damaged our cohesive-
ness. For a minute there, I thought it was all about to
collapse. But we were still in business.

Amayaz clapped his hands loudly, and the crowd
gave him their attention.

"Now, let us finish our preparations," he called. "We have serious business to attend to, and great vengeance to exact."

The men shouted their agreement, and we took up our rehearsals once again. The accidental shooting may have had some positive effect after all. Because from then forward, the joking and laxity was gone for good, and every man seemed fully intent on properly executing his part of the overall scheme.

Before long, Roosty and Terry returned and gave a good report of the shooting victim's status. After that, we made two full daylight rehearsals that went very well.

As it was now the heat of the day, we decided to break until the evening, when we would do another walk-through at last light and then conduct a full-scale night rehearsal. We would then get a good night's sleep. For in the morning, well before daylight, we would set out on the trek to town. God willing, tomorrow night, we would launch our attack. And God willing, all would go well—*Inshallah*.

CHAPTER 27

I ROLLED OUT OF MY BLANKET AND shuffled to the front of the tent, where I threw back the flap, stood in the chill of the very early morning, and wrapped my *tagelmust* around my head. Terry and Roosty soon followed, and as my comrades walked out into the desert to attend the call of nature, I knelt at the fire pit and blew on the embers that lay nestled in their bed of ash.

When a small tongue of flame licked upward, where it danced silently in the pool of its own light, I added a few more dried camel droppings and slowly coaxed the fire to assuming a useful size.

My friends returned just as I added water to a copper kettle and settled it on the rock stand of the fire. While Terry and Roosty got the makings ready for tea, I stepped off into the darkness and took care of my own needs. When I came back into the light of the fire, the kettle was bubbling a cheery tune, and Terry was shaking tea leaves into the pot.

A young boy soon arrived with bread, dates, honey, and camel's milk. Roosty and I held out our cups as Terry poured the steaming and aromatic liquid. We sat in silence for a while, blowing across the rims of our cups and taking cautious sips, reaching now and then for bread and honey.

All around us, the lights of other fires flickered to life, driving the darkness back a few feet here and there, leaving the camp dotted with small islands of shimmering light and the fleeting passage of obscure and furtive-looking silhouettes. Out in the darkness, the camels of the gathered herd muttered and groaned their protests as the herding boys moved among them and readied the animals for the coming trek.

I looked at my friends seated across the flames and thought of what lay ahead of us. Tomorrow morning at this time, we would know something that was hidden from us now. But what that could possibly be was known at this moment only to the gods of chance. Success, failure, life, death: These all lay out there, just over the horizon of the near future, each awaiting its own opportunity of expression and power over man.

I leaned back and looked at the sky. The stars seemed to shimmer with an extra intensity that made them look to be just slightly beyond the reach of an outstretched hand. These are the moments, just prior to setting out on an act that puts life at hazard, when I can taste the sweetness of life in a fullness that is almost overwhelming.

Twenty-four hours from now, when the earth has made one full rotation on its axis, I may no longer be counted among the living. But if that is to be, I will savor each and every second of this day, and if I'm still here tomorrow—why, so much the better.

Putting down my cup, I stood, fastened my equipment belt around my waist, and shouldered my rifle.

"Time to get this circus on the road," I said to my mates.

"We'll get the rest of the gear bundled and loaded. Don't want our hosts to think us laggard," said Terry as he got to his feet and lit the first cigar of the day.

"I'll see to our animals," Roosty said as he rose and then walked quietly into the darkness.

I walked through the awakening camp to the tent of Sheikh Talmun. There I found the sheikh and the other elders of the tribe, along with Amayaz and his lieutenants.

The sheikh looked up as I approached and hailed me with the greeting of the morning.

"*Sabal'al heir,*" he said in a cheerful voice.

"*Sabal'nur,*" I replied, as I took a seat at the fire.

"We were just discussing the final points of the attack," said the sheikh.

"The tribal council and I will follow in two days from now. From there we will send a delegation to the capital to present the reasons for the action we were forced to take."

"I think that is a wise idea. And perhaps the government will allow you to have a voice in the selection of the next regional council," I offered in reply.

"One never knows what a government will do," he said. "They are as capricious as the weather and as fickle as a woman. But a wise man realizes he must live with all three."

Amayaz stood and bowed in the direction of the sheikh and the other elders.

"If you fathers will give us your blessing, I desire to set forth."

Sheikh Talmun got to his feet and lifted his arm in benediction. "Go with the blessings of our people. And may the youth of our tribe bring us victory and justice. *Bismillah.*"

And the other older men intoned, *"Bismillah."*

Amayaz bowed once again.

"We go," he said and then turned to join his men.

We took our leave of the tribal leaders, and as we walked through the camp, the fighting men joined us as though called by an unheard signal. From among the tents, they came first as individuals, then rivulets, and then in streams, until when at last we arrived where the camel herd was held in readiness, we were the field force of the Imouhar.

I found Roosty and Terry waiting near the head of the vast herd. Roosty held two camels by their nose reins. When I approached, he handed me the reins of a tall gray mare.

Terry waited astride the Rokon. Earlier he had made it clear that he hated camels and that the sentiment was a mutual one. The rest of us could ride flesh and bone, he said, but he would ride iron and rubber.

Amayaz made no speech to his men. Instead, he brought his camel to its knees and swung himself into the saddle. The groaning protest of the animal was the signal to everyone else to mount. And the dark plain was filled with the sounds of men giving commands to their animals and the camels responding in their own language.

I climbed astride the mare, touched her flank with my riding stick, and was rocked first backward and then forward as she got to her feet. Amayaz was only a few feet away, and I could just make out his silhouette. I saw him turn in his saddle to look at the indistinct forest of camels and men spread behind us in the darkness. Then with a low "Hut, hut" spoken to his camel, we set forth.

The entire group seemed to move as one organism. We rode first in a long line of two or three camels abreast, until we had passed the defile at the mouth of the wadi. Upon reaching the valley, the formation became wider and more compact, as the camels sought the company of their own kind. I looked to my left and saw the dark outline of Terry and the bike as he patrolled along the flank.

No one spoke a word as we rode silently through the darkened desert. The feet of the camels made soft and muffled padding sounds as they paced along with the rhythmic and rolling motion peculiar to their gait. As the land rose and fell beneath the feet of my camel, I thought how similar it felt to being on board *Miss Rosalie*, making a blacked-out night passage on an ocean lightly animated by the low, slow swells of deep water and steady winds.

I felt the rising and falling of the land beneath our feet and listened to the faint tinkle and jingle of equipment carried by the men around me. We moved like ghosts across a deserted landscape that was lit so very faintly by the chill, pinpoint lights of the stars above. I pulled the veil of my *tagelmust* firmly about my face and neck to counter the cold breeze of our passage.

As a camel strides along, it moves both legs on one side of its body, and then the legs of the other side. This gives it a smooth rolling motion that is easy on the animal and also easy on the rider. It is this type of gait that allows a camel to strike a speed and keep it up for hours on end, but would kill a horse.

As I rocked comfortably in the saddle, I imagined other rides such as this, carried out by the ancestors of these men, time and time again over the centuries. The French were always astounded at the swiftness of the Tuaregs' movements and the great distances they could cover in such short periods of time. It has been said that a Tuareg raiding party could hit places a hundred miles apart within the space of twenty-four hours. We would have to cover more than sixty miles by sundown this evening.

As we descended into the plains of the valley, Amayaz set a pace that ate the miles. I felt the mare lengthen her stride, but still she was not even breathing hard. We held this pace for nearly two hours, until the sky began to lighten. And then, when man and animal could better see the footing beneath, the tempo was increased, and we fairly flew across the desert. We rode like this for another hour and then halted for a short break.

I tapped my mare on the shoulder and commanded her to kneel. She lowered herself to the ground with a groan and then, as I climbed from the saddle, she turned her head to look at me as though I were an alien being.

Roosty came over and joined me just as Terry puttered up on his bike. I walked around to loosen my hips, then bent and touched my toes to get the kinks out of my legs. As I bent over, I felt the Skorpion machine pistol swing freely under my clothing and then bump against my chest as I stood upright again. My hand drifted up to reassuringly touch the gun that lay hidden under the folds of my djelaba.

"A little saddle sore, are we?" asked Terry with a mocking laugh.

I took a few more steps and twisted my shoulders and hips in the attempt to limber my aching body.

"It's been a while since I've ridden. And it's not like getting back on a bicycle, that's for sure," I said as I rubbed my backside.

"Well, I can assure you that trying to keep up with these animals in the dark, while riding that thing is no walk in the park either," Terry said as he pointed to the Rokon,

"You two sound like a couple of old women," said Roosty. "My grandmother complains less on a march, and she's eighty-six years old."

"But she was born in a tent, mate, and crossed the deserts of Morocco by camel long before you were born.

Whereas *I* am an educated gentleman of culture and refinement," retorted Terry.

At that moment, Amayaz broke away from a group of his men and came to where we were standing.

"The scouts are ready to continue on," he said as he looked first to me and then to my comrades.

"That's our cue, lad," Terry said to Roosty.

"But no unnecessary risks, boys," I said before they turned to go. "Just put eyes on the target and establish a secure rally point outside of town."

Roosty touched the fingertips of his right hand to his forehead. "Aye," he said, then turned to mount his camel.

Terry climbed back aboard his bike and started the engine. "I'll see you lot at the relay site. Just don't get lost and leave it all to Roosty and me."

"Give me a test call once you're in position," I said as Terry adjusted his goggles.

"Soon as I get there, I'll shout at you," he said as he twisted the throttle and pulled away.

He and Roosty joined the group of men Amayaz had been speaking with. I watched as they set out at a fast pace. Forging ahead of the main body, they would serve as our guides as we approached the town. Terry was going to drop off at a small hill midway to the town and act as a radio relay between the scouts and the main body.

Part of Roosty's group would establish a camel holding place outside of town where the main element would dismount and proceed from there on foot. The rest of the group would slip into town at last light, where they would lay surveillance on the fort and advise us of any last-minute developments that might affect the attack plan.

The recon team had an extremely sensitive and delicate mission that called for great tactical maturity and a

sense of courageous caution. One misstep, and everything could be compromised. But there was no one better at this sort of thing than Roosty and Terry. And the
Imouhar scouts had been hand-selected by Amayaz and
the elders.

I looked skyward. The dawn of day had been tinged
with the color of blood, and in the few hours since, the
sky had taken on a metallic and brassy-looking sheen.
The faint and uncertain breeze that had risen from the
east was heavy with the feel of heat and static electricity.

Amayaz stood beside me, and he, too, was looking at
the sky.

"Will the storm arrive today?" I asked in a low voice.

"Yes," he replied. "The simoom comes—this afternoon—by nightfall, at the latest. It will be powerful."

He turned to look at me. "The plane will not fly tonight, my friend. We will have to think of another way
of getting into the fort."

"But we make the attack, yes?" I asked.

"The storm will provide us with excellent cover. The
townspeople will be in their homes, and the soldiers in
the fort will have their heads beneath their blankets.
Only madmen would be abroad at such a time." He
smiled.

"Then we will be able to get much closer to town before we must dismount," I said.

"Yes, that is so. The scouts will find a new place to
rendezvous and will leave a guide to bring us in," he
replied. "Now, let us refresh ourselves. I think I smell
tea."

Here and there men had huddled in small groups and
made fires for the brewing of tea. Amayaz and I joined
one group and were made welcome with banter and cups
of the delicious liquid.

As I drank, I thought about the coming storm. There
are two kinds of storms in the desert. One is the local-

ized storm that comes from a thundercloud. These are hit-or-miss, and you can see them from a great distance. They are exactly like a thunderstorm in the United States but with a notable difference. As the cold air falling from the towering cumulus cloud hits the ground, the outward rushing air picks up the loose soil and sand and spews it like a giant sandblasting machine.

As the galloping wall of dirt rages across the surface of the earth, the rain that pelts down either evaporates before it hits the ground, or as it passes through the heavy clouds of dust and dirt, it falls as mud.

I was once caught in one of these storms in a truck. When the storm had passed, the vehicle was completely covered in mud. The next day, when the dried mud had fallen off, I found the paint on one side of the truck had been scoured away by the initial blast of dirt and sand. You can imagine what happens to a man or animal caught unprotected in such a storm.

Then there is the other type of storm. This is the one of legend. It has many names and a few variations. The simoom, the name Amayaz had spoken, blows in for a day, or perhaps two, at the most. But it is nothing to take lightly. It can blot the sun, turning midday to twilight. It is well noted for the atmospheric electricity it generates. And men and animals are said to sometimes go mad as a result of its passage.

The worst of the massive storms is the harmattan. This is a system that can blanket half a continent and send African dust all the way to the Americas. The air of a harmattan can become so compressed that the temperature rises to over one hundred and thirty degrees. People and animals die as a result of heatstroke.

Hopefully Amayaz was correct when he pronounced the coming storm a simoom, rather than a harmattan. Otherwise, we might be in for a deadly experience even before making the attack. We went ahead and ate a hasty meal, because we would be unable to do so once the storm arrived.

Everyone, men and animals alike, could feel the approaching storm. As I ate, I cast my eyes about our congregation and saw men tossing furtive glances at the sky before returning their attention to the conversation of their comrades.

The camels, nestled on the ground, their legs tucked underneath their bodies, grumbled and growled despondently, as though they could already feel the grit and dust in their nostrils.

Amayaz gave word to load up and prepare to move out. I checked all my equipment and cinched tightly the straps to my saddlebags. Men adjusted their *tagelmusts*, rewrapping the veils across their face and neck. Many plugged the muzzles of their rifles with bits of cloth. When Amayaz took to the saddle, we all followed suit. With little commotion and within no time at all, we were mounted and on our way once again.

CHAPTER 28

AMAYAZ LED US ON AT A GRUELING pace. I sat deeper in the saddle and loosened the reins as my camel stretched out her neck and lengthened her steps. I let my body become an extension of hers and shifted my weight from side to side in unconscious rhythm with the coursing of the she-camel's tremendous stride.

We rode in a wide formation, watching the horizon the same as sailors watch for a storm at sea. This was a race, a race against time and against Mother Nature. We must eat the miles with a ferocious appetite, for once the storm overtook us, we would be slowed to a half-blind crawl.

I looked back over my shoulder, and in the northeast saw the first red tendrils, the first outriders of the storm, as it felt for us in the desert below. The temperature began to drop, and the color of the sky began to shift from the polished sheen of a brass bowl to the darker hue of copper and then to the hard red-gold of ancient bronze.

Relentlessly, we forged ahead. And as the afternoon darkened, our formation began to close in upon itself and become more compact, more dense, as though seeking the protection of our fellow beings.

I reached for my water bag and brought it to my mouth. As I tilted my head back to take a drink, I squinted at the sky, and through the gathering haze I could just make out the faint disk of the sun. It seemed tiny and more remote than ever, and that very word resonated in my mind: *remote.*

Many times I have been somewhere on the face of the earth and realized how far I was from the works of modern man. Deep in a jungle, I have looked up and seen a jetliner making its way to some distant city and remarked to myself that the plane and its passengers were only hours from their destination, whereas it may take me a month to get out of there. Or when in a storm at sea, I have looked at the boundless and eternal ocean and thought that should I go down, nothing would be there to mark my disappearance.

But here, on this desert, with an angry sky closing in on us, about to enfold our lonely band of men within the dusty breath of Mother Earth herself, I felt so far from the modern world that I could just as easily be living one thousand years in the past.

I would not trade this experience for an additional ten years of life, I thought as we surged over the undulating ground in a pounding rush toward destiny.

Something spoke to me to look back, and when I did, I saw it: a bulging, rolling, gray/brown/black wall, slithering over the horizon with the pulsing horizontal movements of a sidewinder rattlesnake. I rode to the side of Amayaz. As I came level with his knee, he glanced over at me, and without looking behind he announced, "It comes."

"Yes. Soon," I replied. "It is now within sight."

He nodded. "It will come over us at the same time we hear it."

"Do we slow our pace in anticipation?" I asked.

He shook his head. "No," he said. "When the storm strikes, it will dictate our pace. We close up in a tight formation so that the animals do not despair and no one becomes separated."

Amayaz turned in the saddle, lifted his arm, and waved his riding stick in the air. When the riders saw him, they began to close in on one another until we were jostling along in one compact mass of men and camels.

We were still making a great speed, and I thought that should a camel fall, the man and beast would be trampled to death by the many hundreds of feet. I took a tighter hold on the reins and dug my knees more firmly into the skirts of the saddle.

Suddenly the sky darkened. I looked above and saw the black rim of the leading edge of the storm as it rolled over our heads like the overarching crest of a wave crashing on a beach. Then we were hit by the solid mass and power of the storm.

The first blast of wind and dirt plowed into us with the fury of a dry hurricane and almost took me from the saddle. My own clothes beat viciously against me as they were flailed by the maliciously raging wind. I reached up to tuck the tail of my *tagelmust* deeper into the neck of my djelaba and then tighten the veil over my mouth and nose, leaving only the tiniest slit possible for my eyes.

Even with this, I could feel the grit as it found its way into my clothes, and I could taste the dirt that invaded my nose and mouth. I pulled my hands as deeply as I could into the arms of my robes and wished I had brought a pair of gloves.

As the storm howled over and through us, we were

reduced to a slow walking pace. The camels crowded in on one another, seeking the reassurance of their own kind as the atmosphere became more and more solid. We were riding shoulder to shoulder and head to tail.

As I peeked out from beneath narrowly slitted eyelids, I could just make out the image of the three or four nearest men. We groped along like this for hours: blind, but for the innate knowledge of the camel's feet and the intuitive feel of Amayaz for the drift of the land.

As we bumped one another in the thickening swirls and roaring clouds of dust, I felt as though as I was utterly alone in the world, shut off from contact with all other men. I retreated into the recesses of my mind and wandered among old and half-forgotten memories. And in that state, time seemed to have become suspended, and place had little meaning.

I realized we were standing still; for how long, I didn't know. I looked to my right and saw Amayaz. He leaned over and put a hand on my shoulder and his mouth near my ear.

"We are making a short halt to ensure that we have lost no one," he shouted in my ear. "In a storm such as this, a man sometimes wanders in his mind and becomes separated from the group. I will check with my commanders and return momentarily."

I nodded my head to show I understood as Amayaz turned his camel and disappeared into the curtains of dust.

Easy to wander in the mind, I thought. I had been lost to all contact for who knows how long. It was as though I had been locked in a closet. I checked my watch and then realized: *Terry—he's out there by himself.*

I took my radio from my saddle pouch and gave a call. It took several attempts before I got a reply.

"Right bloody weather we're having, mate. How're

things in your locale?" he deadpanned when we made contact.

"Have you been able to reach Istvan?" I asked.

"Yeah," he replied. "Mad Hungarian says you're on your own, mate. Not even he will fly with half the Sahara floating in the air. Says they've got the plane lashed down and well protected."

"Great. How are you holding out?" I shouted above the howl of the wind.

"Too breezy to brew up a tea but other than that, all right. Roosty sends that they are close to the outskirts of town and that with this blow we can walk right in with nobody knowing the bloody difference. Says to meet them on the north side of the old animal market grounds."

I checked my GPS and took a distance reading from my location to the town.

"I think we are only a couple of hours out, and probably an hour from you. Can you meet us en route, or do you want to try to link up at the rendezvous?" I asked.

"I'll see you in town. I'll have to feel my way carefully, and I don't think I could find a moving target in this soup," he replied.

"Roger that," I responded. "I'll keep my radio on until then."

Amayaz reappeared from the gloom.

"Everyone is here," he called. He looked about. "And I think the worst of the storm will soon be past."

I peered out from under the folds of my *tagelmust*. He was right. Though still raging wildly, I thought the wind had abated just the slightest bit.

"I have made radio contact," I said. "The scouts report they are approaching the town and wish us to meet them on the north side of the animal market."

"That is good. We can hold the animals there, and no

one will detect us tonight, for the storm will not completely pass until the morning."

He then raised himself in the saddle, gave a piercing
whistle, and nudged his camel into a walk. I touched my
mare with the riding stick, and we were off once again.

CHAPTER 29

WE HALTED THE MAIN BODY OF THE
troop in the mouth of a wadi on the north side of town.
Amayaz and I, along with two other men, went forward
to link up with Roosty and the scouts. The wind still
moaned, and the swirling dust, combined with the blackness of the night, barely allowed us to see our own feet.
Amayaz led, and we went in line, each man holding on
to the robe of the man before him. Cautiously, we felt
our way downward by following the banks of the dry
wash. We stopped when we reached a place where the
gravel of the wash hit the hardpan of the plain.

"We are near," said Amayaz.

I strained my eyes, and far in the distance I thought I
detected the pinpoint of a light, but it quickly disappeared. Then the wind slackened for a second, and I saw
it again: a dim light, haloed by the dirty atmosphere.

I touched Amayaz and pointed. "Look. A light."

The light went out, then came on again.

We moved forward again and had not made twenty steps when we ran into our comrades. The light that had looked miles away had been almost close enough to touch.

I saw a dark figure loom in the blackness, and I reached out to touch him. It was Terry. We all retreated to the wash and took what shelter we could find under the lip of the low bank.

"Roosty and the scouts are in town. Says the fort is locked up tight as Dick's hatband, and the good citizens of the town are all tucked safely in their beds," Terry reported.

"He left five men as guides here with me. They've been to the edge of town and can take you lot to the rally point where you'll find Roosty and his gang."

I checked my watch. It had taken us even longer than anticipated to get to the rendezvous. Though still severe, the storm was beginning to die down, and daylight was only a couple of hours away. It would take us at least an hour to get everyone in position to launch the attack. We had no time to waste.

I turned to Amayaz and put my mouth to his ear.

"Let us take the entire group to the edge of town and then split up from there. It will save us some time. I will go ahead of you and meet Roosty. I need to find a large truck. I will meet you at the end of the street nearest the gate. Have four men ready to get on the truck with me. When you are ready to commence the attack, have the machine guns fire at the corner towers; that will be my signal to go forward."

"Yes," he replied. "Let us get the men and move as quickly as we can. The storm will die when the sun comes up."

Terry gave us three of the guides, and we returned up the wadi to gather the men. It took some effort to get the attack force lined up in the three different elements, with every man in his proper position. We then headed down the wadi, each man holding on to the robes of the man in front of him. As we groped our way across the animal yards and toward the edge of town, it was literally a case of the blind leading the blind.

We finally came to a large mud-brick building that I remembered as being on the very outskirts of town. Roosty stepped out of the darkness with his other guides.

"We can go down the back streets to get in the attack positions," he said as he held me by the collar of my robe. "No one has moved in town, no one at all."

"Policemen in the town?" I asked.

"None. No one has moved from the fort, neither in nor out. They are all inside, and it is locked up tight. If there are guards in the towers, they have not shown themselves either," he responded.

Good. No enemy forces in town. We would not have to worry about covering our backs. Everyone could concentrate on the attack. But I had another query for Roosty.

"I need a large truck, at least a five-tonner. Have you seen one that we can grab?" I asked.

"I thought the same thing. I've found one a few blocks away. When we get the men moving to their locations, I'll show you," he said.

"Great," I replied. "One more minute with Amayaz, and we'll set out."

I found Amayaz giving last-minute instructions to his element leaders. The men were hunkered down under the lee side of the building. Even though the wind was diminishing by the minute, the dust still swirled heavily in the air. Amayaz saw me looking about.

"When the wind stops, the dust will persist for many hours, perhaps until midday. Do not worry; we will not be seen," he said.

"Are we ready to move?" I asked.

"Yes, we are ready. I will lead us to the dispersal point and then wait for you on the main street," he said.

"Roosty has found a truck. I will wait at the end of the street for you to open fire. Tell your men to stay out of the street until the truck has passed and follow only then. I won't be able to stop if any of them are in the street," I told him.

"Yes, I will tell them. Now we go. I will meet you inside the fort—*Inshallah*."

"*Inshallah,*" I replied.

Amayaz got the men on their feet, and with the silence of a band of deadly wraiths, they quickly disappeared into the darkness.

Roosty led, with me hanging on to the back of his robe, and Terry hanging on to mine. We felt our way down the wall of the building until coming to a gap. From there, Roosty took a heading, and I could hear him counting the steps as we crossed to the next building. We found an alleyway and followed that until it came to an intersection with a street, and then, in like manner, turning here and there, counting steps and keeping a hand on the sides of the buildings when we could, we finally arrived at a large open-sided shed.

"It is an old Renault," Roosty said as he led me to where the truck was parked. "Solid. Built like a tank."

We were at the tail end of the truck. I felt my way down the side toward the cab. The truck was a stake body with slatted wooden sides and an open bed for hauling freight and livestock. I went around to the front and felt for the bumper. *Perfect.* Constructed of heavy steel, it had been made for angry confrontations with other trucks but would do just as well for my purposes.

When I climbed into the cab, Terry opened the passenger door and joined me inside. The dust in the cab was so thick that even with the dome light on, I could barely see the windshield.

"Tires are okay," Terry said. "No flats."

I was under the dash feeling for the ignition. The starter on the old truck was a push button on the steering column, but I had to find the wires that let me circumvent the switch. I found the back of the switch and was feeling for the wires, when somewhere in town, a gunshot rang out.

Holy hell, I thought. *Some bonehead has fired an accidental shot.*

But the thought had not completely flashed across my mind when, in rapid succession, two other shots assailed the night, followed closely by the angry, snarling scream of a machine gun.

"They've kicked off the attack, the bleeding sods! Get this bastard fired up. We've got to get up there," Terry yelled.

Just then I found what I hoped were the correct wires. I touched them together and got sparks. As quickly as possible, I twisted the ends together and let them dangle under the dash. I sat up behind the wheel and pushed the button with my thumb. The starter spun, the engine lugged over, sputtered, and then coughed to life with a great, deep-throated rattling sound. The truck shook with the power of the old diesel engine.

"Roosty," I yelled out the window. "Get in. You have to show us the way."

"I'm here," he called.

And as I looked to the side, I saw he was in the cab and sitting next to Terry.

"Pull out and turn to the left, then we will take the second left. After that, the fort will be straight ahead," Roosty ordered.

The gunfire was generalized now. It crackled with the throbbing, pulsing sound of a close-range firefight. I reached into my robes, pulled out the little machine pistol, and let it dangle on my chest. I found the switch, threw on the lights, put the truck in gear, and wheeled us into the narrow street.

The headlights reflecting on the dust let me see for little more than a few feet in front of us. I hugged the walls of the buildings on the right to keep some perspective of where we were. Roosty was leaning forward with his nose almost on the windshield.

"Here! Turn here," he shouted, pointing to a gulf of darkness on our left.

I turned sharply, and the lights of the truck found the wall of another building as we entered the street. The sounds of the firefight were growing louder by the second. I accelerated as fast as I dared. We passed the intersection of another block.

"This is the final block," Roosty called. "The fort is straight ahead."

Just then, appearing as dim orbs in the thickness of the dust, I saw the lights above the gates of the fort. I switched off the headlights and slammed the pedal to the floor.

"We ain't stopping," I yelled over the roar of the engine. "It's too late now. We're going in."

As we hurtled past men firing wildly at the walls of the fort, I lay my forearm on the button in the center of the wheel and let the horn scream in a long, continuous blast. The pulsing muzzle flashes would light a shooter for a split second before the darkness swallowed him up again. There were so many shooters in the street that it looked like a plague of fireflies on a hot summer night.

I aimed the truck for the black spot between and underneath the lights on the wall. From the tower to our right, a red stream of tracer fire reached out for us, rending the air just above the cab of the truck.

Roosty fired his submachine gun toward the tower,

and the gun went silent. Then we were in the intersection of the streets and almost at the gates. In my peripheral vision I saw Terry put both hands on the dash and lean forward. Then, straight ahead, I saw the gates leap at us from the darkness. To the left, I caught a brief glimpse of one of the bodies dangling on the wall.

"Hang on!" I yelled.

And then, with a deafening scream of rending metal and the crash of splintering timber, we smashed through the gates like a runaway locomotive.

CHAPTER 30

GAIL WAS ALMOST FRANTIC FROM the effects of the storm. As it roared and growled in its fury, the room became filled with a choking dust. Abutti's asthma had flared, and the poor child gasped and labored for every breath. Gail pounded on the door and screamed for help, but no one came to her aid.

She had to do something or they would choke to death. She tore strips from her blanket and shoved these into the cracks underneath the door and over the ventilation grates to the next rooms, but nothing seemed to help. The chamber became so dust-filled that soon the one light in the room appeared so small and feeble that it seemed miles away.

Gail gathered the boy in her arms and pulled the blankets over them in an attempt to protect themselves from the invading dust and sand. She could taste the dirt in her mouth, feel it in her nostrils, hair, and ears, and it abraded her body in places she didn't wish to dwell on.

Held captive by murdering madmen, with a boy who was fighting for his every breath, not knowing what other horrors fate had in store, Gail had never in her life felt more helpless and despondent.

If I were alone, she thought, *I would end this; I would find a way to kill myself.*

But she was immediately stricken by a sense of guilt at the thought, and she quickly put it out of her mind.

Dear God, if only someone would come. If only someone cared, she prayed. *God, I can't take any more. I don't have the strength to bear anything else. Please, God, send an angel. Send us a deliverer.*

As Gail prayed, a sensation of calm descended upon her. Abutti's breathing settled a bit, just enough to give her a further glimmer of hope. And so, huddled beneath their blankets, while the storm raged outside and the room became ever more laden with the invading, insidious dust, the two captives fell asleep in each other's arms.

Gail came awake with a jolting start of fear. *What? What?* she thought. *Was it a bad dream? Another nightmare?*

Then she heard it again. Gunfire, somewhere outside. She lay under the blankets and listened, unsure of what, if anything, to do.

What's going on? What's happening out there? I'm so scared.

The sounds of the firing increased to a roar. A machine gun howled its demented anger into the night, and then there was the scream of a horn followed by the sound of a loud crash.

For a few seconds the shooting went quiet, before kicking back up again and rising to a new level of frenzy. Gail recalled the raging arguments between Yagmour and Boutari.

The soldiers have begun fighting among them-selves, she thought. *They've had a falling-out and have begun killing each other. They'll come for us next. We have to get out of here! Now!*

"Abutti! Come. Come, darling. We have to get up. We must go. Here, help me put on your shoes. Quickly. Help me, darling."

The child whimpered his fear as another burst of gunfire erupted, louder and closer this time.

Gail got the shoes on the boy's feet and had him sit on the edge of the bed as she reached beneath the mattress and found the thin strip of metal she had hidden there.

She took the boy's face in her hands and pressed her nose against his.

"Sit here and don't move, Abutti. Don't move until I come get you."

She gave him a kiss on the forehead and then turned to feel her way to the door. The light in the room seemed a little brighter now, better than when she had fallen asleep. Previously she could see nothing, but now she could just make out the door.

She took off her belt and took the buckle in hand. Turning the pin of the buckle at a ninety-degree angle, she tried to insert it in the keyhole, but she could not for the shaking of her hand.

Settle down. Take it easy; there's nothing to this, she told herself as the firefight swirled outside.

She took a deep breath and waited. *Yes. Yes, that's it. There's nothing to this. Come on, you can do it blindfolded.* She tried again, and this time she felt the pin slip easily into the hole.

That's it. That's it; easy, easy as you go, not too hard now.

She felt the pin touch the key. And then, as she applied pressure, the key began to slide backward and out the other side of the lock.

Smoothly. Carefully. I don't want the key to fall too far away. I've got to be able to reach it. . . .

At that instant, a powerful explosion rocked the building. Gail jumped, shoved the pin forward all the way to the buckle, felt the key shoot from the lock, and heard it hit the concrete floor outside. She dropped to the floor and tried to look underneath the door.

Too dark. I can't see a thing.

She took the strip of metal and slid it under the door as far as her hand would reach. Then, in a slow sweeping motion, she felt for the key.

Please let me reach it. Please, oh please, let it be close enough.

Nothing. She moved to the center of the door and felt again. Slowly she swept for the key.

There! I can feel it, she thought as she touched something with the very end of the strip.

She held the metal strip by the utmost tips of her fingers and nudged the key. It moved—and then she lost it. She reached again. Contact! Carefully, slowly, gently, she raked the key with the side of the probe. It moved again before slipping off.

Patience, patience, she told herself, as she got a better angle and tried again. She had it! She had a good angle and could feel solid, if tenuous, contact. She grasped the tip of the probe with the pads of her thumb and forefinger. The awkward grip made her entire hand hurt, but she kept at it. The key slid maybe a half inch closer this time, before she lost contact again.

There! Keep it up. Nice and easy now.

Gail got a better grip and reached out again. This

time she had a good angle on the key, and as she
raked with the strip, she swept in a wide arc and felt
the key slip under the door.

Her fingers scrabbled in the layered dirt of the
floor.

"I've got it!" she shouted aloud as she lifted the
key in triumph and elation.

She went back to the bed and helped the boy to his
feet. His breathing was becoming more labored again.
Gail tore a strip from a sheet and wrapped it loosely
over Abutti's nose and mouth. She knelt so they could
look each other in the face.

"Abutti, we must leave now, but I am frightened. If
you are brave—brave for both of us, then I won't be
so scared."

The little boy pulled the rag from his face and
looked her in the eyes. His voice trembled slightly,
but his eyes were steady.

"I'm not afraid, Gail. I'll take care of you," he said
in his little boy's voice.

Gail hugged the boy and kissed his cheek.

"I knew you would, Abdullah. You are so very
grown up. Now, come. Let's go quickly."

She put the cloth back over his face, took him by
the hand, and stepped resolutely to the door. She hesitated for just a second, then inserted the key and
slowly opened the door. She peeked out into the hallway but could see nothing outside. It was a black
abyss out there. But the firing came loudest from the
right.

Gail gripped Abutti's hand tightly, took a deep
breath, and slipped into the hallway.

"Wait here a second," she said to the boy.

She then turned, closed the door, and reinserted the
key into the lock.

"Okay. Now we can go," she said to the child.

Taking his hand again in hers, they set out down the hallway. She kept contact with the wall with her left hand and moved with careful and hesitant steps. She didn't know where they were going, but no matter where this path led, it was of her own choosing. And for the moment, at least, they were free.

CHAPTER 31

MY FOREHEAD SLAMMED INTO THE top rim of the steering wheel and bounced back like a rubber ball. Underneath my eyelids I literally saw stars, and for a moment was too stunned from the impact to make sense of the situation. But a burst of machine gun fire jackhammered the driver's side of the truck and snapped me back to my senses. I rolled to the right of the cab and shoved Terry toward the already opened passenger door.

"Go! Go! Get out, you red-ass baboon!" I yelled as I gave him a shove.

We tumbled out the door and crashed to the ground, almost on top of Roosty, who was firing at something in the dark.

I grabbed my machine pistol, held it at the ready, and shook my head, trying to clear my senses. I reached up and felt my face to make sure everything was still where God had placed it. It felt like I had been hit in the head with a baseball bat, but everything was still where it was supposed to be. Apparently the heavy wrapping of the *tagelmust* had saved me from any serious injury.

"The attack has stalled. Nobody's coming in! They're jammed up outside the gate," yelled Roosty.

I looked to our rear and saw flashes of gunfire outside. The attack had been tripped before we had gotten into position, and now our plan had gone all to hell.

"Well, we gotta make something happen," I called. "We can't let this turn into a standoff."

From above us and off to the right, a machine gun yammered away, firing into the street outside. I grabbed Roosty by the shoulder and pointed to the corner of the compound.

"We gotta knock out that machine gun. We put him outta action, Amayaz can rally his men."

"Yeah," he yelled, as a rattle of gunfire slapped the back of the truck. "You ready to go?"

At that second I realized that Terry was on the ground and not moving. I reached down and shook his shoulder.

"Terry! Terry, you hear me?"

He made no response.

"Hang on," I said to Roosty. "Terry's down."

I rolled him onto his back and felt his chest. *He's breathing, and his heart is beating.* I slid my hand up and felt his neck and throat. *Nothing there.*

I gently touched his face and felt a sticky liquid on my fingers. *Blood.* I ran both hands over the sides and back of his head, feeling for any wounds.

Nothing.

I felt his face again and found the problem: a broken nose. Terry must have hit his face on the dashboard of the truck and been knocked unconscious. I turned his head to the side so the blood wouldn't run down his throat.

Roosty fired another burst.

"Is he hit? he asked.

"No, he's knocked out. Must have hit the dashboard when we crashed," I called. "You lead, and I'll drag him. We can't stay here."

"All right. We're going for that corner over there!" Roosty pointed to a dim shape and yelled, "Ready?"

The machine gun let loose with another burst, and the walls of the fort blazed with gunfire.

"Go!" I yelled, as I grabbed Terry by the back of the collar.

Roosty bounded away from the truck, firing as he went. I held my subgun in one hand, the back of Terry's robes with the other, dug my toes into the dirt, and heaved with everything I had. I was head down and ass up, dragging Terry for all I was worth, as the bullets spat and slapped all around.

A bullet passing near your head makes a very distinct and unmistakable cracking noise. It is a miniature sonic boom that sounds just like those little round firecrackers boys throw against the pavement.

Crack—crack-crackcrackcrackcrackcrack!

That sound is one hell of a motivator. I was stretched out as low to the dirt as I could make myself, hauling with sincere gusto, and fairly skidded Terry across the ground. I slid in behind Roosty and shoved Terry's limp body under the protection of a tumbled-down stack of mud bricks.

I put my face next to Roosty's.

"You stay here with Terry and I'll take care of that gun," I said.

"Want me to fire while you run for it?" he asked.

"Dust is still so heavy, I don't think anybody knows where we are just yet," I replied.

I looked all around the interior yard of the fort. The lights on the walls looked like tiny beacons in the murk.

The only way you could be seen was to stand right next to someone. None of the combatants could see much of anything at all.

They're all just firing blindly in the dark, I thought, as several other rifles erupted from across the courtyard. But unaimed fire can kill you just as dead as a well-placed shot from a marksman.

"No, don't shoot. It'll just give away the position. Wait for me here," I said as I checked the magazine in my gun.

"All right. But don't take all day," Roosty said.

"I'll be right back," I replied as I got to my feet and headed for the corner of the fort.

I crouched low and moved toward the sound and flash of the machine gun. It was still firing wildly and indiscriminately in all directions—first a burst out into the streets, then a long sweeping trail of fire into the interior of the fort.

This guy is a menace to everybody around here, I thought as I reached in my pouch and palmed a grenade.

At close range, a hand grenade is the weapon of choice in the darkness. It doesn't give off a muzzle flash and give away your position, like a rifle or any other type of gun does.

Terry, Roosty, and I each had a pouch with several kinds of grenades. The one I had in my hand was a miniature fragmentation grenade. It is lethal in an en-closed area or at very short range but isn't as powerful as a standard grenade and hence not such a threat to the guy throwing it. A lot of soldiers have been killed and injured by their own grenades.

I edged near the tower and got ready to throw. I didn't count on the first one doing the job completely and had one in my other hand also.

The gun opened up again, giving me an angle on the tower. I pulled the pin, let the spoon fly, counted, "One, two," and threw. As soon as the grenade left my hand, I shifted the other grenade in my hand and repeated the act. Just as I threw the second grenade, the first one detonated.

Karumpf—Karumpf.

The sky overhead was brilliantly lit for a split second, closely followed by the flash of the second grenade's detonation. I heard something heavy hit the ground nearby. The firefight went silent for a few seconds as a patter of debris rained down around me.

I moved underneath the tower and felt something with my foot. Gun in hand, I bent down and felt a body. I ran my hand to the neck, pushed two fingers in under the jaw, and felt for the carotid artery: no pulse. Dead.

Above, from the remains of the tower, I heard a low moan. Someone was alive but hurt. I backed up several paces, readied another grenade, and threw.

Karumpf.

More debris showered down, but after that, I heard no further sounds from above. As I turned and retraced the steps back to my comrades, the firefight cranked back up again; only this time, it was minus one of the big players.

I knelt beside Roosty, and to my surprise found Terry sitting up, wiping his mouth and face.

"Bloody hell! I'm all wet," he said. "Has it rained?"

Then he seemed to notice the gunfire.

"What the hell—shooting's started! We better make for the fort!"

"We're in the fort, you nitwit," laughed Roosty.

"In the fort?" Terry said incredulously.

"You hit your head when we crashed the gate," I said. "Knocked you silly—and broke your nose, too."

"Knocked him silly? How could you tell the difference?" Roosty cackled.

Terry reached a hand to his face.

"My nose?"

He touched it with his fingers. "Damn, that hurts!"

Terry looked from me to Roosty, and then he got it.

"Oh yeah—the gate—the truck. Man, that was some bash-up, eh? But what the hell are we doing, just sitting around jabbering like a bunch of old women? We got things to do!"

"Yeah, but first we have to get Amayaz and his men through the gate. They're jammed up outside," I said.

"Then we have to show them the way in," Terry replied as he raised himself to a crouch.

Show them the way, I thought. *Yes, that's it.*

"Roosty," I called, "shoot the fuel tank on the truck. Several shots. I want a big spill. Terry, watch for return fire in case anybody sees it and fires on Roosty's muzzle flash."

Roosty took three steps forward, raised his subgun, and put four short bursts into the truck. The sounds of his shots were drowned out in the general gunfire.

I reached into my pouch and pulled out a concussion grenade. These are heavily made cardboard cylinders filled with flash powder. They give off a tremendous bang and a powerful blast of concussion, along with a brilliant and hot flash of light. If one lands next to you, you'll think you're dead, but they seldom cause much real harm. But they are notorious for starting unintentional fires. I was hoping now for the intentional sort.

I pulled the pin and pitched the grenade in an underhand toss.

"Grenade!" I called as it flew from my hand.

The three of us turned our heads, closed our eyes tightly shut, and buried our chins in our chests to protect our night vision. Anyone caught within proximity to the blast with open eyes would be temporarily blinded.

BLAMMM!

The grenade detonated with a flash and a roar. For an

instant, even with my head turned and eyes shut, the flash of light was as bright as the noonday sun.

Diesel fuel can be hard to light, but the grenade had done the trick. As I turned to see how effective my little spark had been, the flames from the burning fuel on the ground reached up and licked the belly of the truck.

Within a few seconds we had one heck of a fire going. It lit the interior of the compound in a weird glow that wasn't exactly illuminating but did show outlines and shadows in the heavy haze of the swirling dust. The sound of firing redoubled just outside the gates, and then I began to see the shapes of men as they came pouring in.

"Imouhar! Imouhar!" I yelled. "To the right! To the barracks! Amayaz! Amayaz!"

Running figures went fleeing across the yard of the fort, seeking refuge in the buildings. I called for Amayaz again, and suddenly he was at my side.

"You have them now, Amayaz. They are scared and routed. Hit the barracks hard, and I think they will quickly surrender," I said.

"If we give them that chance. Now I must go to my men," he said with urgency.

"We go to find the boy. God willing, we'll meet later," I replied.

As Amayaz set off at a trot, I turned to my companions.

"Ready?" I asked.

"As we'll ever be—lead on mate," Terry said.

"Let's go," said Roosty, as he slapped a fresh magazine in his gun.

I led us in a wide arc behind the advancing Imouhar, trying to stay as far as possible from the light cast by the burning truck.

From the sounds of firing, the Imouhar were just penetrating the barracks when Terry, Roosty, and I came to the corner of the headquarters building. We knelt at the corner, just outside the entrance to the building.

"I'll pitch a frag to the door," I said to my comrades. "You two follow it up with concussion grenades inside the doorway. Clear?"

"Yeah," they both replied.

I reached into my pouch and pulled out a standard American fragmentation grenade. This is the big kahuna, and it's one deadly device. It has a killing radius of fifteen feet, and a casualty-producing radius of fifty feet. But what I wanted it to do was take the doors off their hinges and clear the immediate entrance for us.

I pulled the pin, let the spoon fly, and rolled it to the door with a gentle toss. We retreated around the corner as I counted to myself, *One, two, three, f—*

Karummmmpf!

The grenade went off with a dull red flash, and the building shook from the stunning blast. The interior of the compound reverberated with the power of the detonation, and the firing in the barracks stuttered and slackened. I thought I'd heard a muffled scream in the building, but now it was quiet.

Immediately, Terry and Roosty bounded around the corner, tossed their grenades in through the open door, and turning their backs, dropped to their knees.

One, two, I counted.

Karumpf! Karumpf!

I lifted my head and plunged forward toward the smoldering doorway. My friends leaped to their feet, and without a further word, we hurled ourselves headlong through the smoke and debris into the enemy-held building.

CHAPTER 32

GAIL BURNS WAS COMPLETELY terrified. She couldn't tell what was happening outside. The shooting seemed to have reached a state of frenzy, and then there had been two explosions. After that, the firing had subsided for a while, but then it rose in intensity once again.

Soon there was another explosion. A faint wavering light played in the building, and she could smell something burning. She wanted to continue down the hallway, but for the moment her courage had deserted her, and she could go no farther.

Gail found an empty room, and they entered. Closing the door almost all the way, she left it cracked slightly open. Then, cradling the boy to her chest, they crouched quietly in a corner and made themselves as small as possible.

There were loud yells in the hallway, and a voice called sharply in Arabic.

"The boy! Get the boy and bring him here!"

Another excited voice yelled back.

"And the woman? What with her?"

"Kill her!" called the first voice. "The woman means nothing now."

Gail tucked her head deeper into her chest and clutched the boy even more tightly.

My God, oh my God. Please help me. Please, she prayed.

She heard footsteps running in the hallway, followed by more shouting, as the gunfire outside became louder again.

The voices were quiet for a bit, and then she heard a muffled, indistinct yell.

"What?" called the first voice, which she then recognized as that of Colonel Boutari.

The second voice was now more clearly heard.

"They're gone, my colonel!"

"You're crazy!" exclaimed Boutari. "They can't be gone. Look again!"

"I have looked! They are not in the room. Someone has let them out."

"It's Yagmour!" yelled Boutari. "He's trying to steal the boy. Find Yagmour and kill him. Then bring me the boy. But kill Yagmour first and I will reward you greatly. You already know what to do with the woman."

"Yes, Colonel!"

The sound of running feet swept down the hallway and past her door.

"You men!" shouted the voice of Boutari. "Search all the rooms. They may only be hiding. Leave nothing to chance."

"Yes, sir," called another voice.

There was the scuffle of footsteps in the hallway, the sounds of doors being thrown open, and the confused calls of many voices. The sound of slamming doors and pounding footsteps came closer and closer as the unseen men advanced down the hallway.

Gail lifted her head and tried to see if there was anything in the room that might hide them.

Nothing, she thought. *We are trapped. Oh, why did I stop? Why did I stay here? Better the unknown outside than to be cornered and helpless. Now I'm going to die in this horrible place.*

She heard footsteps just outside the door. Looking up, she saw the crack of the door begin to widen. Then Gail felt herself rocked by a terrible clap of thunder. The building shuddered as though it were about to fall.

My God! Was that an earthquake? Gail thought as the door was flung open by the force of the titanic jolt.

The sound of the thunder was still echoing when the building was hit again by two other equally loud detonations, one following immediately behind the other.

Explosions, her frantic thoughts told her. *They're trying to blow up the building. But who?*

From somewhere down the hallway Gail heard a pitiful and pain-filled voice calling, "Help me, someone help me. I am badly hurt."

"Shut up!" came the reply.

"But I think I'm dying. Help me please."

Then another, louder explosion shook the building, followed by a burst of gunfire and a strangled scream. Gail closed her eyes, held the boy tightly, and shook with fear.

What can I do? she thought. *Maybe in the confusion we can make a run for it. Yes, that's it. Right after the next explosion or burst of shooting, we'll just run. Maybe, just maybe, we can make it outside.*

Gail lifted the boy and put his arms around her neck.

"Hold on, Abutti. Hold tightly," she told him as she crept toward the door.

At that instant, a brilliant flash lit the hallway. The blaze of light was accompanied by another deafening explosion, and then a quick burst of gunfire. Gail took a deep breath and was preparing to run, when from the far end of the hallway, someone called her name.

"Gail—Gail Burns—we're friends. We've come for you and the boy. We've come to take you home."

It's a trick, she thought. *They are trying to lure me out.*

The voice called again.

"Hang on—we'll have you soon. The boy's grand-papa sent us. It's gonna be all right."

The voice, a Southern Appalachian voice; it was unmistakably American. No foreigner could feign that accent.

Gail's spirits revived, and she took courage once again.

"Down here!" she called from the edge of the door-way. "We're down here, at the end of the hall!"

Oh God, thank you. Thank you. We're saved.

Gail stepped closer to the door. As she did, her foot hit something that went skittering and rattling across the floor. Gail froze at the edge of the doorway and held her breath in suspense.

Maybe no one heard, she thought.

At that instant, the door smashed open, and a hand grabbed her by the neck, yanking her to her toes. A powerful arm went around her body. And before she could call for help or even make a sound, she was dragged from the room and into the hall.

She heard a peculiar popping sound and a split second later was blinded by a dazzling pulse of light. A gun erupted next to her ear, and her neck was scorched by the muzzle blast. Terrified, disoriented, and unable to resist, she felt herself being roughly hauled along, her toes now and then hitting the ground.

A vicious voice snarled in her still-ringing ear, "Do as I say, or I'll kill you."

Gail went limp with terror.

CHAPTER 33

WE CAME BURSTING INTO THE BUILD-
ing through the black smoke of the detonation. The shat-
tered doors opened into a short portico. There was a wall
to the left, and to the right the hall disappeared into the
darkness. Terry went to the right side of the hall, while
Roosty followed me on the left. Just ahead was an open
doorway to a room. From within came the faint glow of
a dim light.

As I slid closer to the door, I got a flash-bang ready in
my hand. I felt Roosty lean his upper body against me. I
whispered to him, "Flare down the hallway, just as I hit
the room."

I felt him squeeze my shoulder to signal, *Yes.*

I pulled the pin of the grenade and lifted it to shoulder height so Roosty could see it. When he squeezed my
shoulder again, I pitched the grenade in the room, held
myself near the door, and waited for the explosion with
closed eyes.

I heard the spoon fly from Roosty's flare as he tossed it down the hallway, and then the room erupted with the flash and bang of the grenade I had thrown.

I whipped through the doorway and turned hard to the right, hugging the wall as I went, checking from the corners to the center of the room. There was an explosion in the hall and a burst of gunfire, but it barely registered with me as I cleared the room.

I never stopped but kept moving at almost a run. From behind a desk, I saw movement. A man leaped up, pistol in hand. I shoved the little subgun to the limits of the neck strap and gave the trigger a slap. Two rounds hit the man at the base of the throat. He went down behind the desk like a trapdoor had opened beneath him. I continued around the room until I came to the man. Stooping for a second, I looked down at him. A glance was sufficient to tell me he was dead. I made a complete circuit of the room and came back to the doorway.

"Coming out," I called quietly.

"Clear, come," Roosty replied.

I slipped back into the hallway and fell in behind Roosty. Across the hall, Terry was at another doorway getting ready to enter, when bullets tore plaster from the ceiling over our heads. I stepped to the side, and we all opened fire on the muzzle flashes down the hall. Terry followed up with a mini-frag.

"Frag!" he yelled as he pitched it down the darkened hallway.

Roosty followed up Terry's throw with a quick burst of fire. We all three then dropped to our knees and turned our backs to the detonation.

The small grenade, in the confines of the hallway, went off with a crushing blast. I heard a scream, and then the whimpering of a wounded man.

"What happened to the flare? I asked Roosty.

"Dud," he replied.

"Get ready to throw another; on my command," I said.

I then called to Terry.

"Hold where you are; Roosty's going to throw another 'seeing eye.' Cover it; I'm gonna talk to the girl."

"Right," he replied.

"Gail—Gail Burns—we're friends. We've come for you and the boy. We've come to take you home," I called down the echoing hallway."

"Now," I whispered to Roosty.

I heard the spoon pop as Roosty's arm went forward.

I let the tin-roof-twang of my voice have full play.

"Hang on—we'll have you soon. The boy's grand-papa sent us. It's gonna be all right."

Then a small voice spoke in the darkness.

"Down here! We're down here, at the end of the hall!"

There was a shuffling sound, and then the metallic *snap* of the flare, followed by a blinding light that illuminated the far end of the hall. Caught in the circle of light was the writhing mass of a man, a woman, and a boy. The man lifted a submachine gun over the woman's shoulder and sprayed the hallway.

We dove to the floor as bullets tore the walls and ceiling overhead. I lifted my gun but had no shot on the man as he hastily dragged his human burden out a nearby door and out of view. I leaped to my feet and pounded down the hallway in pursuit.

"It's them!" I needlessly yelled.

A man, crouching inside a door, fired as I came near. His shots going high, I gave him a burst as I ran past. Then I was at the door that led outside. I hesitated long enough to change magazines, then launched myself outside. Behind me, I heard the crash of grenades going off.

I glanced all around as I ran into the open courtyard. The fight was still raging in the barracks buildings on the other side of the fort, the windows lit by the flashing strobes of gunfire within.

I swept the area with my eyes, looking deeply into the strange shadows cast by the flickering light of the burning truck. Off to my left, there was a single shot, and then I heard an engine roar to life. I ran in that direction.

Tires spinning wildly, slewing side to side, a jeep came bouncing from out of the darkness. I threw up my gun for a shot but saw the driver had the boy draped across his chest as a human shield. Instantly, I flung myself to the ground, just as he loosed a full magazine at me.

Then, as he roared past, I leaped to my feet and ran after him. The jeep was headed for the open front gate, and there was no one there as a blocking force; we were all inside.

As I ran, I extended the stock on the little gun and stuck it in my shoulder. The jeep was making an arc around the burning truck. He was almost to the gates. I slid to a stop, took quick aim, and tapped the trigger.

Pop-pop. Pop-pop. Pop-pop.

I held at the leading edge of the front tire, right where it touched the ground. The bullets found their mark, and the tire burst like a rotten balloon. The jeep careened suddenly to the left, then slid wildly to the right as the driver overcorrected, before crashing head-on into the gatepost.

I charged for all I was worth. I had to get down there before the man could recover from the crash. As I ran past the flaming truck, I saw movement in the jeep. I hurtled to the right to get an angle on the movement and be closer to the gate.

Then I saw the man stand up at the passenger side of the jeep. He had the boy held to his chest with one arm, and he pointed his gun at me with the other. The vehicle lay between us.

"No!" he screamed. "Stop. Do not come closer, or I kill the boy."

I kept my gun leveled on him.

"There's nowhere to go, Boutari. It is over," I called in a stern voice.

"No! No! I go. I go! Do not follow. If you follow, I kill," he ranted.

Boutari took a hesitant step to his right, closer to the gate. Blood ran down the side of his head and into his left eye. He took another step, a hesitant one, and then lifted his gun hand to clear the blood from his eye.

I dropped flat to the ground, hitting the trigger as I fell, and fired a short burst underneath the jeep. The bullets, skimming the dirt, cut the man's feet from beneath him. He crashed to the ground with a howl of agonized surprise, his gun falling from his hand.

I leaped to my feet and ran around the jeep. Boutari was rolled on his side, grasping his ankles. I picked up his gun and tossed it in the jeep. Boutari offered no resistance as I checked him for other weapons. The fight was out of him. He merely cursed and wept in pain.

I turned to the boy. He was still sitting on the ground where he had fallen when Boutari dropped him. As the child got to his feet, I knelt, so that our eyes were level. He was standing a few feet away and had the look of a scared rabbit getting ready to run.

I let the gun dangle from its strap and reaching up, unwound the *tagelmust* so that my face was in plain view. I held my hands out to the side, and spoke to the child in English.

"Abdullah, your grandfather sent me to find you. I am here to take you home," I said in a gentle voice.

The boy looked at me with wild eyes, and his head started to shudder and twitch.

"Abdullah, don't be afraid. You are safe now. We

will go home to your grandfather. He is waiting for you. He loves you and wants you with him."

"That is a lie!" screamed a voice from behind me.

I turned my head and saw Boutari lying on his side watching us.

"The emir is the one who had them all killed," he hissed in Arabic. "I only kept the boy to make the old man fulfill his promise. He wanted this child dead also. Now he's sent you to kill me."

"If that were so, wretched man, you would be dead already," I growled. "Not another word from your filthy mouth, or I will give you to the Tuaregs for sport. They will flay the skin from your living body and then let the women caress your raw flesh with burning embers. Be silent, dog."

"The Tuaregs?" He gulped.

He shook his head before lowering it into the dirt. "God punishes all sins," he whimpered in self-pity.

I turned to the boy.

"Abdullah, we must find Gail. Where is she?" I asked.

He looked at me closely, his eyes at first uncertain, then he lifted a small arm and pointed.

"Back there," he said in a tiny voice. "She is hurt."

"Will you show me?" I asked, as I extended my hand.

He looked from me to Boutari on the ground and then back into the depths of the fort, where the gunfire had now all but subsided.

His eyes came back to me, and he searched my face again. At last he reached out and took my hand.

"Yes," he said. "She needs our help."

I gave Boutari a glance as we walked by. *He's not going anyplace soon, at least not under his own power.*

I steered us away from the barracks as we crossed the grounds of the fort. I didn't want to risk a wild shot from there, not now. But it appeared Amayaz had things well in hand. His men were beginning to bring out the prisoners and set them on the ground in front of the building. As I returned, I heard the laughter of victorious men.

The wind had now almost ceased, and the atmosphere was already beginning to clear. I looked to the sky, and in the east, I thought I saw a faint streak of color on the horizon. It would soon be dawn.

I found Terry and Roosty where I had exited the building. They had Gail Burns under a light at the door and were tending to a wound on her scalp.

"A cut to the head always bleeds like crazy, love. There's nothing to worry about; it's just the body's way of protecting itself," Terry chattered amiably. It was his way of reassuring her that everything was okay. "Blood washes out any dirt, and the wound never gets infected. But we'll have you cleaned up in two shakes, we will," he said as he fussed over her wound.

Abdullah and I stepped into the light.

"And here's the bloke I was just on to telling you about," Terry continued.

"He ain't much to look at, that's for sure. But what he lacks for in presentability, he more than makes up for with bad character. Miss Gail Burns, may I present my old chum, Kennesaw Mountain Tanner—non-gentleman, non-scholar."

I sat down beside her and put the boy in her lap. They wrapped themselves in one another's arms, and Gail began to weep. This went on for a bit, and then she looked up and wiped her eyes. The boy kept his head buried in her shoulder. Gail shook her head slowly.

"There is so much I don't know. Who you are— where you came from—who those other men are."

She inclined her head toward the Imouhar in front of the barracks. "Much less what this is all about. But the one thing I can never do—I can never thank you men enough. You've given us back our lives, Abdullah and me. You saved us, right at the moment I thought all was lost."

"How do you feel?" I asked.

She reached up and touched her head.

"Very sore but very happy," she said with a radiant smile.

"She's going to be all right. Have a little scar there to show what she did on vacation with the lads," Terry said with a laugh.

"Where's Boutari?" asked Roosty. "Is he . . . ?"

"He's down by the gate; he's alive, but he's had better days. He's shot up some—but not too much. Would you go down and collect him before our friends find him? I want to talk to him some more. And if our friends get their hands on him first, things may get out of hand," I said.

Roosty nodded and took off.

"Miss Burns—Gail—let's get you inside," I said as I gave her a hand and got her to her feet. "We'll find some water and get you cleaned up. Then maybe we can rustle up some food; I don't know about you, but I'm hungry."

She took a couple of steps and staggered. As I put an arm around her waist to help steady her, she sagged and collapsed. I picked her up and carried her inside. She was as thin as a stray cat.

CHAPTER 34

THE SUN HAD BEEN UP FOR AN HOUR, and the dust was rapidly clearing out. Amayaz and I walked the yard and surveyed the results of the action. There were eleven killed among the militiamen and another four who were wounded. The Imouhar had shown no mercy to those who resisted but had been very lenient to anyone who gave up without a fight.

On our side, we had suffered two killed outright, and one man who I didn't expect to live much longer than another hour or two. Four others had wounds that would be the subject of many tales around the campfires.

We neared the gate and looked out into the street. As soon as the attack had swept the fort, the first thing Amayaz ordered was that the bodies on the fort walls be taken down and prepared for burial.

I stopped at the jeep and looked inside. There was a smear of blood on the windshield where Boutari had hit his head. It was a miracle the boy had not been hurt in the crash. I stood where Boutari had fallen to the ground and kicked dirt over a puddle of coagulated blood.

"I have summoned the mayor to a meeting," said Amayaz, as he watched me smooth the dirt with the toe of my boot.

"When the elders arrive, we will sit in conference with the town leaders and determine what to do with the captives," he continued.

"I think few of them are guilty of more than trying to make a living," I said.

"In many ways that is true," he replied.

"We will sort through their actions and decide on an equitable justice. The ones who gave orders and the ones who committed depredations will pay a stiff penalty. The ones who merely went along will be taught the error of their ways."

I looked down the street and toward the market area. The town was starting to come alive. The more intrepid citizens were beginning to venture forth, while the timid continued watching from behind closed doors, waiting to see what happened next. They would come out later, when they were assured that peace had broken out and was really here to stay. I had seen the same reaction under similar circumstances in other places, at other times.

I turned to Amayaz. "From what the prisoners all say, it appears this man Yagmour was the one who ordered the killings, the mutilations, and the other brutalities."

Amayaz nodded and said with a grim look, "I am told that Boutari was terrified of the man—though that does not excuse him. He was the commander of these criminals, and as such, he bears full responsibility for their crimes."

"True," I replied. "But he said something to me right after he was shot—pain sometimes loosens the tongue. I want to follow up on what he said; it may mean much to me."

"He is yours for as long as you need him. And I can have some men loosen his tongue even more, if it will help you," my friend said with a wicked smile.

I smiled in return. When Roosty brought the wounded Boutari from the gate, we carried him into the headquarters building, where we laid him on a bunk and treated his wounds. I then gave him some water and food and left him alone while we consolidated the capture of the fort.

I have a technique I use with captives that seldom fails to bring results. It works like this: Most people expect to be treated the way they would treat you if the circumstances were reversed. So I do just the opposite of what is expected. I tend to my prisoners' immediate physical needs and then show them a polite and decent indifference. They've prepared themselves to be brutalized, and when it doesn't happen, they have no idea of what's going on. It's completely confusing to them. And in that state of confusion, when I finally get around to talking with them, they tend to tell me the truth, if for no other reason than out of sheer relief.

But this time I modified my tactic. Twice I stopped by and checked on Boutari's wounds. I didn't speak with him other than to ask if he needed more water or food. Then, after the sun was up and the fort was filled with daylight once again, I found the biggest, roughest looking Tuareg in our group and had him come with me.

We crept down the hallway to the room where Boutari lay. When we arrived at the door, the Tuareg warrior stepped silently into the room, drew himself to full height, put a hand on the hilt of his sword, and stood staring down at the wounded colonel.

From my post in the hallway, I heard a gasp followed by muffled pleading and weeping. A few seconds later, the warrior emerged from the room, fanning his hand in front of his face. When we got outside, he told me, be-

tween fits of laughter, that Boutari had lost control of his
bowels and soiled himself.

I could not have asked for better results. I would let
the man stew in his own fears and filth for a while
longer. When next we spoke, he would be delighted to
talk to me.

We returned to the interior of the fort. Amayaz went
to supervise the gathering and accounting of loot. I went
to see about Gail and the boy. I found them sitting on a
bunk that had been pulled outside and placed under the
eaves of the building. A pot of tea sat on a small table,
and the remnants of a meal were on a nearby platter.

"Feeling better now?" I asked as I drew near.

The woman gave me a healthy smile, and the boy
looked up with wide, liquid eyes. Gail put her arm
around the boy and gave his small shoulders a squeeze.

"Much better than before," she said as she looked
from me to the boy.

"Think you can answer a few questions?" I asked as I
sat on the ground, picked up a cup from the table, and
blew the dust from inside it.

"I can certainly try," she said, as she picked up the
pot and poured tea into my cup.

Terry walked up at that moment. "Got Istvan on the
radio," he announced. "Said he's got a good horizon
now, the plane is prepped, and he'll be on the way
within the hour. Roosty has gone to mark the section of
road to use for a landing strip. He's taken a few men
with him to guard the plane while it's on the ground."

"Excellent," I replied. "How's the nose?"

Terry's eyebrows danced a fandango as he reached
up to touch his beak.

"Sore as bloody hell—begging your pardon, ma'am."
He nodded to Gail. "But it's okay. Ain't the first time
it's ever been broke, don't you know?"

I nodded in acknowledgment.

"Talmun and the elders on the way with Istvan?" I asked.

"Istvan said the old man was so eager to fly again, he and András were made to spend the night in the same tent as the old sheikh and the rest of the geriatric gang."

Terry shook his head and snorted with laughter at the thought.

"If we stay here much longer, Istvan will have to give them flight lessons," I said with a smile.

"Aye, that he would, mate, that he would," Terry replied. "But what gives next? What needs doing before Istvan and the air marshals arrive?"

"First, I need to speak with Gail, and then I'm going to have a conversation with Boutari," I said.

"Want me to go in and sweeten his attitude a bit?" Terry asked.

"That's okay. I think he's in a receptive mood. I'm letting him reflect upon his sins awhile. After that, he and I will kneel together at the altar of truth and have a come to Jesus," I answered. "But if you would check with that doctor, and if he's finished with the wounded, I'd like him to join me over here."

"You got it, mate. I'll just take a cuppa with me, if you don't mind," he said as he poured himself a cup of tea and took a grateful swallow.

I looked closely at my friend. His nose was black and swollen, and he was bruised underneath the eyes. He looked like hell, but as he lowered his cup, he gave me a huge grin.

I returned the grin and said, "Feels pretty good, doesn't it, partner? This being alive and all, once again."

"The spice of life it is," Terry said.

"But for a while there, especially when we dove into that building and started trading shots, I sort of wished I was home in bed with the wife. But now that it's all said and done—I wouldn't trade places with any man in the world."

"Yeah," I replied. "Now let's wrap this thing up and get the hell out of Dodge."

Terry set out to find the doctor, and I turned again to Gail.

"You said that Yagmour was the leader of the group that took you from the yacht. Is that correct?" I asked.

"Yes, he was the one—the one who ki—" She glanced at the boy. "He was the leader of the attack, yes."

"And you didn't see Boutari until you arrived here. Is that correct?" I continued.

She nodded. "Yes, that's right."

"In the last couple of weeks prior to the incident, did anything strange take place? Anything out of the ordinary?"

Gail lowered her face in thought.

"No." She shook her head. "Nothing really different that I saw. But you know, I was the tutor to the children and wasn't privy to everything that went on."

"But you were friendly with the wife, weren't you? She and you had a relationship through the children, yes?"

"We did, yes," she replied.

"Did she seem worried about anything? Anything at all?" I asked.

"No, she didn't. She was quite happy. It was a vacation with the family, away from the pressures of the palace and all its intrigues," she said.

"How about visitors—anyone unusual? Anyone who seemed out of place?"

She thought, and then I saw her eyes light with the recollection of something.

"There was one man," she said. "One man who upset the young emir so much that he had him sent away with orders never to return again."

"How did you know it was upsetting? Did you see a confrontation?"

"No," she replied. "But I heard it. They were on the patio deck, and their voices became quite loud and angry. I was walking on the deck near the bridge, and the man brushed by me as two of the crew members escorted him to the gangway and put him in a boat."

"Could you tell me what he looked like? Was he Arab or European?" I asked.

Gail gazed into my face for a few seconds before she spoke.

"He was American," she said, softly. "And I'll never forget him. When he glanced at me as we passed on the deck, he had a look of pure hatred in his face."

"Anything you can recall about his features?" I asked.

"His eyes," she replied. "They were so odd. I've read of such before, but I've never actually seen them."

Gail hesitated. "One was brown—and the other was green."

I felt a chill touch me.

Mayfield! What was that snake doing there?

"Did you hear him speak? What was his accent?" I asked, trying to keep the excitement from my voice.

Gail answered, "Flat—Midwestern—Chicago area, maybe."

That's Mayfield, without a doubt, I thought.

"Did you ever see him again?" I asked.

"No, no I didn't," she replied.

I need to talk with Terry and see what he thinks this is all about. He has a good nose for dirty dealing, and it's a sure thing, something is certainly foul with this.

I took a sip of tea and reflected on everything that had happened so far—the little oddities about this whole setup—and the fact that something, in the back of my mind, in a voice that I hadn't been quite able to hear, had been whispering a warning to me all along. But that voice was speaking louder now and becoming more and more clear.

"I want you to wait here until Terry returns. I think it's time I spoke with Boutari. If you need anything, just yell. I'll be within earshot," I said as I rose to go inside.

Boutari seemed to be expecting me. I pulled a chair close to the side of his cot and let him talk. He looked at me with the eyes of a supplicant—like a man pleading for his life, and in many ways, he was. Whatever remained of his shriveled soul, he dumped it all now.

What he had to say filled in a number of perplexing voids. And as he told his tale, I could feel the stirrings of an old hatred begin to grow again within my breast. This entire matter was worse than I had ever imagined. The levels of duplicity and deadly intrigue at work would baffle Machiavelli himself, and I felt my head spin with the sheer evil of it all. It left me unsure how to proceed and what steps I must next take.

But what the hell—nobody ever said this would be easy. I've gotten through rotten situations before, and I'll get through this one, too. It's just a matter of taking problems one at a time.

CHAPTER 35

THE PLANE LANDED ON THE DIRT
road as gently as though it were carrying a fragile
cargo of fresh eggs. Roosty stood in the road with his
hands and arms raised above his head and guided Istvan to a spot where he taxied off the road, spun the
plane around, and made ready again for the next takeoff.

The door slid open as soon as the engine died and the
propeller came to a halt. András quickly hopped from
the plane and then turned to give a hand to Sheikh Talmun and the other elders of the tribe. Amayaz and I
went forward to greet the new arrivals.

"My lord, I give you news of success," said Amayaz
as he embraced the tribal leader and gave him a kiss on
each cheek.

"We had expected no less," said the old man in a
voice for all to hear. "Your victory means we live again
as a people. You have restored our honor and our place.

We give you the thanks of your tribe, Lord Amayaz. You are the champion of your people."

Amayaz said nothing in reply but made a slight bow in humble response to those words of praise. However, when he glanced at me and our eyes met, I saw in them a gleam of great pride. We then greeted each of the elders in turn before climbing aboard a truck and returning to the town.

Amayaz led the elders on a tour of the fort and gave them an account of the battle. He started at the front gate and took them, step by step, across the yard and into the buildings, recounting the deeds of each and every man of the attack force. The men who had made the assault followed closely behind. And when Amayaz spoke of a particular act of bravery, the man who had committed the act was singled out and brought forward for recognition by the elders of the tribe.

We next stopped by a storeroom, where the assembled loot of the fort had been placed under guard. Sheikh Talmun and the others fingered the guns and other equipment, and I could almost hear the calculations in their heads as they tallied this newfound wealth. At last, we sat in the portico of the main building to confer on what to do next.

When everyone was settled and tea had been served, I led Gail and young Abdullah into the presence of the sheikh and his companions.

"Emiri Abdullah bin Sultan bin Mohammad al Jemani, Miss Gail Burns, I wish to present you to the men who are responsible for your liberation—Sheikh Talmun and his tribal council," I said in Arabic.

Gail stepped forward, leading Abdullah by the hand. She glanced at the boy and, reaching down, gently removed his thumb from his mouth before turning and speaking to the Imouhar elders.

"Gracious and courageous lords. I can never give you

sufficient thanks for our release—for our lives—for our liberty. You will have my heartfelt gratitude for the rest of my life," she said, then bent down and whispered something in the boy's ear.

Abdullah looked at the men with shy eyes and quivering lips. I thought he was going to melt to tears, but instead he whispered, "Thank you, my lord," before sticking his thumb back in his mouth.

The sheikh motioned for us all to sit. We were served tea, and Gail was asked to recount the tale of how she and the boy were captured and their experiences here in the fort.

I'd say she did a pretty credible job. In concern for the boy, she left out some of the gorier details but indicated to the elders that she could fill those points in more fully at a later time. The old men listened with rapt attention and asked only a very few, but pointed, questions.

At length Gail finished the harrowing tale. The men remained quiet, each one thinking, no doubt, of the ordeal suffered by this slight woman and the brutal orphaning of the young boy.

Finally, Sheikh Talmun spoke: "What would you have now, young lady? How may we give you justice?" he asked.

Gail looked directly at the sheikh. "I want to take the boy to his grandfather, and then I wish to return to my home."

"Is there nothing else?" asked Sheikh Talmun. "Do you not desire vengeance? Do you not wish to see punishment inflicted upon the men who have treated you and the boy with such cruelty? You need but say the word, and it will be carried out."

Gail shook her head. "No. No, I do not. It would give me no pleasure and would make of me their equal. I wish but to depart. I leave matters of justice in your hands."

The sheikh nodded his head and then conferred in a low voice with his confederates. He turned once again to Gail. "It is as you wish. As soon as you all are ready, you may take the boy and go," said the sheikh.

I cleared my throat and got the attention of the sheikh.

"Sheikh Talmun, I have a request of you and your council," I said.

"If it is ours to give, yours it shall be," he replied. "Our being here in this place, sitting in judgment of our enemies, is principally by your doing.

I nodded my head in acknowledgment of his courtesy.

"I wish to take the man Boutari with me. I have further need of him in order to bring this matter to a finish. Lord Amayaz and I have spoken, and we have determined that it was the man Omar Yagmour who bears the main responsibility for the deaths of your men, and he now lies among the dead. As for Boutari, he will receive justice at the hands of the boy's grandfather, Emir al Jemani," I explained.

Amayaz spoke up. "It is as he says, my lord. We have questioned the captives and found this to be so. Yagmour—who now answers his crimes before Allah—was the one who tortured and killed our kinsmen. And we have identified the ones who carried out his orders. These, we will try in our council and administer unto them their richly deserved justice."

The sheikh conferred again with his peers before looking up at me once again. "Take the man with you. He is a gift. Use him as you will."

"Thank you, my lord. Thank you all," I said as I bowed my head and placed my hand over my heart.

I stood and turned from Amayaz to the elders, letting my eyes rest on each man in turn.

"With the permission of you all, I would take my re-

gretful leave. I must return the child to his anxious
grandfather, and we have many leagues of journey before us yet," I said with a feeling of gratitude.

Everyone stood, and I embraced each man, one by
one. Sheikh Talman held me by both arms and looked
into my eyes.

"Return to us when you can," he said. "You bring us
luck."

"I make that to you a solemn promise," I said as we
embraced and kissed.

Terry was standing nearby. He had taken Gail and
Abdullah in hand and had them ready for departure.
Roosty had backed an open-bed truck to the headquarters building and was supervising the loading of what
little we would take with us.

The final task was at hand, and that was the loading
of Boutari onto the truck. I had saved that for last, as I
didn't want the Imouhar to become unduly inflamed at
the sight of him. They might yet do something rash, and
I didn't want to lose him at this late stage.

As I walked to the building, I signaled Terry to get
the woman and child into the truck. He helped them into
the cab and then turned to come with me. We stepped
into the building and turned down the hall. The floor
was littered with debris from the assault, and the air still
held the smell of gunpowder, blood, and fear. We entered the room where Boutari lay on a cot, being tended
by the town doctor.

As soon as the fighting was over, Terry had dug
the doctor out of hiding and marched him to the fort.
Once the poor man realized that he wouldn't be harmed,
he had performed yeoman's duty patching up and tending the wounded.

"Doctor, I must take him now," I said as I stepped
close and looked down on his patient.

The doctor was checking the dressing on Boutari's

leg wounds. He stood up and gave me a stern look.

"This man should be in a hospital. He has several broken bones, and though I have cleaned the wounds, there is the danger of infection," he said, peering at me over the tops of his glasses.

"That's where we are taking him, Doctor. We are flying him out of here immediately."

I reached under my robes and pulled out a sheaf of currency.

"I hope this will be sufficient to cover the treatment of these men and the care of the injured who yet remain here under your tender ministrations," I said as I handed him the money.

I saw his tongue flicker as he licked his lips and extended his hand for the cash. He riffled the stack with his fingers before quickly stuffing the wad into his shirt.

"Most sufficient—generous, even," he said. "I have given this man a pain reliever. He is conscious and somewhat lucid but will not be in undue pain, at least for several hours."

The doctor handed me a pill bottle.

"There are six more capsules here. Give him one every four hours. That should get you to your destination."

I put the pills in my pocket and thanked the doctor, who then scurried from the room without a backward glance. When I think of the death and brutal action that had emanated from this place in the last few weeks and months, I can't say that I blamed him.

Now it was time for us to clear out also. I turned to the door and gave a loud whistle. Within a few seconds, András and Roosty came down the hall to the room.

"Let's each grab a corner of the cot and use it as a litter," I said, as I looked down at Boutari.

Terry pulled the waist sash from his robe and bent over the cot.

"Need to tie him down so he doesn't tumble out while we're moving the old boy. Last thing we want is to go to all this trouble and effort, and then have him fall out of bed and break his bleeding neck," Terry said as he fastened the knot securely at Boutari's waist.

"Right—on three," I said as I took a corner of the old army cot.

We picked up the cot and our human burden and carefully maneuvered through the door and down the hallway. As we neared the exit to the building, I heard a woman's voice raised loudly in excitement and consternation. My heart quickened.

I hope nothing is wrong with Gail; she's suffered enough, I thought as I quickened my pace and almost pushed us to the door.

We stepped into the yard, and I saw that the voice I'd heard belonged to the woman Rahab. She was remonstrating loudly with Amayaz, but as soon as she saw us, she threw her hands in the air and let out an anguished wail.

"My love," she shrieked, as she came running over, the tail of her robes flying behind her. "What have they done to you? Why are these men taking you from me?"

Who the hell is she talking to? Certainly not me, I thought as we stopped and set the cot on the ground.

Boutari, restrained by the tie-down, sat halfway up on the cot and reached his arms out to the woman.

"My darling, I knew that you—you of all people would not desert me. Help me. Tell these men to let me go. I have done them no harm, yet they take me away to be murdered," he pleaded.

"They will take you nowhere, my heart. You shall remain here with me and never leave," she said as she spread her arms and leaned over to give Boutari a kiss. But it was a kiss of a very different sort.

Snarling like a lioness taking down her prey, the

woman pounced with blinding swiftness. Her hand flashed high, and I caught just the tiniest glint of reflection as she slashed downward and plunged the knife deeply and with deadly effect straight into Boutari's throat.

Boutari, as he collapsed backward onto the cot, issued a loud gasp and then a strangled gurgle, while the crimson blood gushed proudly from the severed artery of his throat.

Still, Rahab was not yet finished. Quick as a mongoose, she struck again—two, three, four more blows into the chest of the dying man. She swung back her arm to make a slashing cut across Boutari's face, when Amayaz snapped out a hand and grabbed her wrist.

Rahab struggled like a demon to free her hand and strike again. But then she stopped and, turning, looked at Amayaz as though seeing him for the first time. She nodded, and then I saw her relax.

Slowly, she opened her hand and let the knife drop onto Boutari's chest. When Amayaz released his grip on her arm, Rahab took a step back, and looking down on the bloodied man, studied the effects of her work.

The attack had been so sudden and so completely unexpected that no one else had even moved. I had been mesmerized by her vicious and fatal attack and found myself just now releasing my astonished breath.

I looked down on the dying man and watched as the last few beats of his heart pumped the blood from his gashed throat. Then it was over. The look on his dead face was one of utter confusion and puzzlement.

Rahab leaned over and looked long and closely into those dead and staring eyes. Then, straightening herself to her full height, she turned to look first at Amayaz and then at me. There was a smile of satisfaction on her face.

"Justice," was all she said.

Wordlessly, but with the bearing of a queen, she then

turned and simply walked away. No one made the least effort to impede her passage. And as she walked, with each step she took, the blood dripped slowly from her hand, leaving a trail of dark and glistening drops to mark her regal passage.

As fascinating as a cobra, and just as deadly, I thought.

I watched until she exited the gates and was lost to my view. Then I turned back to our unfinished work.

Amayaz had some men take charge of the body and carry it away. It would be buried with all the others, victors and vanquished alike; for the hall of the dead makes no distinction among the ranks of its new arrivals.

Amayaz and I bade each other a quiet farewell. We both, I felt, were in a hurry to finally leave this place of sorrow and bad memories. Terry, András, and I climbed into the back of the truck. I banged on the top of the cab, and Roosty cranked the engine.

I lifted a hand in a departing salute as we wheeled slowly across the yard, first past the burned-out hulk of the truck we'd used as a battering ram and then past the crashed jeep at the gate.

Turning into the deserted street, we headed for the outskirts of town. When we arrived at our improvised airstrip, Istvan was standing under the wing of the plane waiting for us. Within minutes, we were all aboard. András closed and locked the door and then went to join Istvan in the cockpit. The engine coughed to life, and in a few seconds, I felt us begin to move. A minute later, we were airborne.

I glanced over to where Gail and Abdullah were curled up together, asleep. I closed my eyes and tried to sleep, too, but somehow, the oblivion of unconsciousness eluded me. My mind refused to rest and continued to replay recent scenes over and over again. I kept seeing those bodies hanging from that wall and the glittering knife in Rahab's bloody hand. And the words of Boutari, when he spoke to me from the cot, kept playing in my mind, over and over, like a broken recording that refused to stop.

Jemani had them killed—his own son, the wife, and the children. I only kept the boy to insure that he'd make the final payment.

I looked out the window again, and in spite of the warm air in the plane, felt a shiver run down my spine.

CHAPTER 36

WE LANDED IN TAMANRASSET WITHOUT incident. This was the place, an outpost of civilization, where we would start to reimmerse ourselves into the supposedly legitimate world of papers and governmental permissions.

Istvan had earlier backstopped the other aircrews with a cover story that, with a liberal application of baksheesh, had easily held up under scrutiny. With my permission he now sent those crews on their way out of the country. They would be back in Europe by the next day, each man sitting in his favorite bar, regaling his friends with bogus stories of his adventures on the Algerian oil exploration project.

It was late in the afternoon when we landed, and we were all exhausted. So we took the hotel rooms of Istvan's departing aircrews and settled in for a night of civilized living. I gave the hotel porter some money and sent him out to buy a couple of changes of clothing for Gail and Abdullah.

The porter returned with his old wife in tow. They had bought not only clothes but also toilet articles for Gail and a few toys for Abdullah. When Gail saw the hairbrush, makeup, and other things the kindly couple spread out on the bed, she burst into tears. I thanked the porter and his wife and sent them on their way with a nice tip. Once I saw Gail and the boy comfortably settled in, I decided it was time to look after myself.

"Gail, I'll be in the next room if you need me for anything—anything at all," I said as I stood in the open doorway that separated our rooms. "Terry and Roosty have the room on the other side of you. Open your door to one of us only, and under no circumstances to anyone at the door to the hallway. Understood?"

"You're not worried about anything happening here, are you?" she asked, a startled expression crossing her face.

"No, just being cautious is all," I replied with what I hoped was a reassuring smile. "We'll rest here tonight, and then tomorrow we'll go on to Tunis. We can get you a new passport and repatriation assistance at the American Embassy. And I can make arrangements there for Abdullah. While waiting for those wheels to turn, we can stay with a friend of mine. He has a large place, and it's safe."

I looked down at the boy as he played on the floor with a toy truck.

The resilience of children is remarkable, I thought, as I watched him play. *I just hope I can find the right way to get the boy back where he belongs. Wherever that may be.*

I looked up and caught Gail watching me intently. We were silent for a few seconds before she said, "Don't worry too much about what may happen next. You've gotten us this far. I know you'll get us the rest of the way."

I smiled. "Thanks for that vote of confidence," I said. "It helps."

I turned to my door. "Remember," I said with authority, "all doors locked. Never open the front door for any reason at all—never. And open the side door only to me, Terry, or Roosty—*mafoun*?"

"Yes," she replied, "I understand. *Mafoun*."

"Okay," I said. "Now, why don't you get a nap, and I'll call for you at dinnertime. It might be a nice change to sit down for a decent meal served on china and a linen-covered table."

"A nice change," she said with a smile.

I nodded my head and closed the door behind me.

Back in my room, I let the hissing cascade of water play over me, and took a long time scrubbing the ground-in dirt and grime from my weary body. After toweling off, I put my filthy robes and *tagelmust* in a kit bag and changed into a set of old, well-worn khakis.

I hung the little Skorpion machine pistol back around my neck and buttoned the shirt over it. You couldn't tell it was there unless you were looking for it. I then stuck my pistol in the waistband of my pants and clipped my knife to my belt. Lastly, I pulled on an old, loose-fitting safari jacket. Checking myself in the mirror, I now looked the part of the European/American visitor to the North African Sahara.

The evening was uneventful. We had dinner in the hotel dining room, and I fancy we looked the part of outback adventurers after a desert vacation trek. There were several other groups of foreign travelers in the hotel. So, all in all, we blended into the background pretty well, with no one paying us much attention at all.

After dinner, Terry and I walked Gail and Abdullah to their room and saw them safely in for the night. At the door, Gail hesitated a second and, reaching up, placed a gentle hand alongside my cheek.

"Thank you," she said in a quiet voice as she held her hand against my face.

I took her hand in mine and brought it to my lips.

"You are welcome," I replied before releasing her hand.

I then stepped back, and before closing her door, I said, "Remember—me, Terry, or Roosty—no one else."

"Got it," she said. "Good night."

"Good night," I replied as I closed and locked the door.

Terry crossed the room and sat in the chair. I took a seat on the side of the bed. We looked at each other and held our silence, both of us thinking of the next steps.

"Well, what's the final song, maestro? How do you close out this symphony?" Terry asked.

I thought a few seconds before answering.

"The murders and kidnapping took place in Italian territory. If I get Gail and the boy to Italy and tell the story of what I learned from Boutari, the system there will take charge. Gail will give a deposition and be released. The boy will go into the hands of the Children's Protective Service, and the courts will figure out what to do with him after that."

Terry leaned forward in his chair. "But they'll only turn him over to the emir. You know that, don't you?"

I thought for a second before replying. "Eventually— yes. But the Europeans are more resistant to political pressure than, say, my own country. Maybe it will buy some time and allow other information to come out. Something that will prove the old man had his family murdered. And no matter what, it will tell the emir that someone is watching. It may sway him from trying to harm the boy in the future."

"Always the optimist, aren't you, mate?" he responded.

"I have a few friends in the Carabinieri, some of them

highly placed, and the Italians are no strangers to intrigue. If I can make my case, the boy has a good chance," I said. "But I'm making this up as I go along, old friend. So if you have a better plan, let's hear it. I need all the help I can get."

"I'm just a worker bee, me lad. This sort of thing is beyond me ken. If you need some shooting, I'm your man. But when it comes to outthinking Middle Eastern potentates—well, you're on your own. But you know whatever I can do, I will," he said with a grin and a fluttering of eyebrows.

"I know that, Terry. And thanks," I said as I rose. "So, if you will wait here until I return, I'm going to give Pope Donnelly a call and let him know our ETA tomorrow. Then I look forward to getting a good night's sleep."

I went downstairs and placed the call to Tunisia. I had expected to have to wait while the call was routed, but instead I was connected immediately. Donnelly and I spoke in an innocuous business code. He reported all was well and that he was looking forward to the return of our group. He concluded by saying that he would meet us at the airport upon arrival.

I returned to my room and bade Terry a good night. And just for the pure enjoyment of it, I took another long shower before turning in and settling down for the night. But after sleeping on the ground these past days, the bed seemed unnaturally soft and uncomfortable. So, after an hour of tossing and turning, I pulled the blankets onto the floor, rolled up, and finally drifted off. But I woke at the slightest sound—real or imagined, and would lie awake in the darkness, a hand on my pistol, listening for surreptitious footsteps in the hallway.

CHAPTER 37

BACK AT THE AIRPORT THE FOLLOWING morning, we climbed aboard for the next leg of our journey. Istvan had filed a flight plan to the central Algerian town of Mecheria; this way, we wouldn't have to declare out of customs and immigration as we would on an international flight. Once under way, Istvan would amend the flight plan, and we would continue on to Tunisia and its capital city, Tunis.

It was a long flight from southern Algeria to the shores of the Mediterranean. I spent the intervening hours contemplating my next moves and how I would handle the situation with the boy. If what Boutari had said to me had any truth to it at all, it was apparent I couldn't turn the child over to his grandfather. That would only amount to a delayed death sentence.

I tried to come up with some explanation as to why any man would commit such a horrendous crime: the murder of his own offspring. But nothing I thought of made even the least amount of sense.

Perhaps Jemani is mad, I thought. That seemed to be the only explanation that made sense at all. But when I had met and spoken with him in Beirut, he seemed as sane to me as anyone else. No, it was something else, but what that could possibly be, I just didn't know.

It was clear to me that I had to turn the boy over to the Italians. It wasn't a perfect solution, but it was the best one I could think of at present. And after that, I would figure out where Mayfield's hand lay in this and what I would do about him.

A hundred miles an hour is the cruising speed of the AN-2. On land that is a criminally fast pace, but in the air, it seems you are almost standing still. However, as the day wore on, the miles slipped steadily beneath us. And it was a pleasure to look out on the vastness of the desert and upon the rugged mountains and know I was crossing in thirty easy minutes what would take a full day of grueling effort by camel.

Inexorably, the sun began its descent in the west. As the shadows lengthened on the ground below, I began to see signs of civilization, and I knew we couldn't be far from Tunis. A bit later, Istvan stuck his head out of the cockpit and announced we would be landing in thirty minutes.

One step closer, I thought as I looked at Gail and Abdullah, asleep on a pallet of blankets.

Before long I felt our descent, and as the sun dropped below the western horizon, we began our approach. I reached over and gently shook Gail's shoulder. She sat up and looked at me with tired eyes.

The madness of her ordeal will take some time to wear off, I thought. *But she's a strong woman, and she'll make it.*

"Landing soon," I said. "Wake Abdullah, and let's get ready."

She gave me a smile before waking the boy and getting ready to land.

The lights of the city sparkled in full view as we swung out over the inner gulf and the harbor below. Then Istvan banked us on final approach, and within a minute I felt us touch Mother Earth once again.

We taxied to the northwest corner of the airport and parked at a commercial aviation facility that caters to the business of oil field service aircraft. Istvan shut down the engine, and as soon as András popped the door open, I saw Pope Donnelly standing nearby.

He came over to greet us as we climbed down from the plane.

"Glad to have you lot back in town," he said as we shook hands.

I introduced him to Gail and the boy.

"And it's right glad I am, Miss, to see you here, safe and sound at last," he said, as he shook hands with Gail and tousled Abdullah's hair.

"And I am so very glad to be here," Gail said in reply.

"Well, great, mate, so what's the arrangements? I hope you got us in some first-class digs. Some of us has been living rough for a spell, while others has had a soft time of it," Terry said to his friend with a mocking laugh.

Donnelly ignored him and turned to me.

"Kennesaw, I've got the lads here booked in a hotel nearby—I take it they'll be flying on in the morning. As per instructions, you, the lad, and the young lady will be staying at Jean Marc's place," he said as he handed me a set of car keys.

"Keys are to that white Land Rover parked just over there." Donnelly gestured. "Clicker to the gate is on the sun visor. Jean Marc and his *chef de sécurité* are expecting you. I'll take this lot to the hotel and then check in with you later."

"Thanks, Pope," I said as I took the keys.

It was the time of parting. I looked and saw that everyone was gathered around, watching and waiting quietly.

"Boys, I may not see you tomorrow, so scatter out of here first thing in the morning. Take a commercial flight or hop across the Med with Istvan, whichever suits your fancy. But know this," I said as I looked from one man to the other. "Terry, Roosty, Istvan, András, there are few men who can do what you do—and fewer still who have the guts to do it. I thank you for putting yourselves forward again. I'll see you the next time around, when things are bad, and brave men are called for."

We shook hands all around. Gail gave the guys a hug, and then we went to our vehicles. Pope stood at the back of his Rover and collected the guns from the other men. Later, they would be left with Jean Marc Lavalier. Since that was where I was going, I hung on to my own iron.

The streets were full of traffic as we maneuvered through the city. Tunis is a remarkably modern place with a great admixture of the old and the new. From the airport into town we drove down a wide boulevard that led to the center of the brightly lit city. Jean Marc's compound lay near the port, just off Avenue de Mohamed V.

I soon left the main street and wound us through a series of small neighborhood side streets and alleyways. I had to search carefully in the dark, because there was no streetlight at the corner of the narrow paved track that led to the back entrance of the compound. Slowing down, I looked, and there it was. As we turned into the alleyway, I switched off the lights and hit the clicker that activated the heavy metal gate that allowed entrance to the compound.

The gate slid smoothly open, and as we passed

through, it closed automatically behind us. I parked the car beneath an open-sided garage, switched off the engine, and let out a breath of relief.

A safe place at last, I thought. *We can relax a bit before the next stage.*

"You'll like Jean Marc and his wife Sophia," I said as I looked over at Gail.

"They're both descended from French colonists and local Tunisians. Their home mixes the best of both cultures, and each of them is a magnificent cook. They set a table that will make you groan. You'll enjoy it for the few days we are here."

Gail smiled in reply, but I could tell she was heavily fatigued.

The letdown is beginning to hit her. Best thing she could do is sleep for a couple of days. Well, this is a good place for that, I thought as I got out and went to help her with Abdullah. The boy had gone to sleep on the way from the airport.

I took the sleeping child in my arms and picked up my bag.

"Come on," I said as I bumped the door closed with a hip. "They're probably in the kitchen, whipping up a world-class dinner for us."

Gail followed closely as I walked to the covered entrance to the back of the house. I motioned her to open the door and lead the way in. We stepped into a large anteroom—something like a combination pantry and mudroom—that gave way to the kitchen and the rest of the house.

The room was barely lit by a light from the hallway ahead. I turned to close the door, and as I did, I heard an ominous *click*. Then an unseen voice spoke to me from the darkness.

"Stand right there, Tanner. Don't move," said the voice.

A gun safety going off is an unmistakable sound, one that will put a chill in you when heard at close range. And that voice, too, was unmistakable; I had known it for years.

The light in the room was suddenly switched on, and there he was, with a pistol leveled on my face: *Mayfield!*

Another man, an Egyptian from the looks of him, stood near his side. He, too, had a pistol pointed at me, but I kept my gaze on Mayfield. His eyes were lit with a sardonic gleam, and the tight-lipped smile frozen on his face had the look of unmitigated malignancy.

"Over here, Miss Burns. You and the boy step to that corner," he said, as he gestured with his free hand.

I felt Gail's eyes on me.

"Kennesaw, what, what, what should I . . . ?" she stammered.

"Do as he says, Gail. Take Abdullah and do as he says," I said, keeping my eyes on Mayfield.

"That's a good girl. Do as the man says, Gail," he sneered in a mocking voice as Gail hesitantly took a step.

When she was away from my side, the Arab man grabbed her by the arm, shoved her roughly into the corner, and made her sit.

Mayfield never let his eyes or his gun stray from my face.

"So, big man, how does it feel to be on this end of a gun for a change? Do you like it? Does it make you feel wanted?" he said with a face twisted in hatred. "Did you really think you could get away with treating me the way you did back in Savannah? Huh, did you? By God, I've lived for this moment."

"Where are Jean Marc and his people?" I asked in a level voice. "What have you done with them?"

"They're okay, for now," he said, with a laugh. "But when your body is eventually found along with theirs, it will look just like a bad falling-out among thieves."

"I know what you did, Mayfield. Before he died, your man Boutari told me all about you. And what I know, others know also."

I was fishing here. Boutari had said nothing about Mayfield, but I knew for certain now that he was a principal actor in the affair.

Mayfield guffawed, "Boutari! Why, that inept buffoon couldn't so much as scratch his ass without help. I had to coach him and that idiot Yagmour every step of the way. But in the end, the fool tried to double-cross me and kept the kid. But now you've done the heavy lifting for me and brought him back, just as I knew you would. I've always had confidence in you, Tanner. You always bring 'em back alive, don't you?"

"Why did the emir have his family killed, Mayfield? And what do you have to do with all this?" I asked.

Mayfield laughed again. "Because I told him to, that's why. The son was plotting a coup against the old man. And if he had come to power, he would have bounced us out of the country and cut a deal with the Iranians. But I was able to bring that to a screeching halt. It's what we used to call *geopolitics*, you moron."

"But what do you get out of it, Mayfield? A maggot like you never does anything without calculating his gain. So what's in it for you? If you think this is gonna get you a general's star, you're wrong. The army knows you for the punk you actually are," I spat.

Mayfield's eyes narrowed to mere slits in his face. I had touched him with my insult, and now he really was angry. I saw him start to form a reply, and then I saw him make a supreme effort of will to choke it off.

He looked at me for a second and then said in a voice that was menacing for its flat, emotionless tone, "Put your hands behind your head, Tanner, and do as you're told. Screw with me, and I'll shoot the woman."

Slowly, I lifted my arms and put my hands on the back of my head.

From the side of his mouth, he spoke to the Arab.

"He always carries a gun. Search him, and then come back here and watch the woman."

This is it, I thought. *As soon as I'm disarmed, Mayfield will shoot.*

As the man stepped near, I willed my body to relax. I took a deep breath as the man reached underneath my jacket and found my knife. He pitched it to the side.

"Keep looking," Mayfield said. "I know he has a gun. It's on his other side."

The man started to move, and for a fraction of a second, he was between Mayfield and me. I struck.

I hit his gun hand, knocking it aside with my forearm. At the same time, with my other hand, I clasped the man on the back of his head, buckled my knees and, dropping, jerked him forward and down. As he toppled over, off balance, I sprang back up, smashing my forehead into his mouth and nose. I felt his lips split and nose and teeth crunch, as the front of my skull plowed into his face.

Two gunshots exploded in the room, followed immediately by two more. I felt the man shudder with the impact of the bullets and then go limp.

Mayfield yelled something unintelligible. Gail screamed in shock and terror. As Mayfield fired again, I heaved the dying man with all my might and threw him on top of his boss.

As the two men crashed backward in a tangle, I tore open the front of my shirt and whipped out the little subgun that lay hidden beneath. Plunging forward, firing on full auto as I went, the rounds of the little gun tore into both bodies, hammering them to the floor.

From beneath the man, Mayfield struggled to get his arm clear. He was just able to get off one wild round before I emptied the magazine into his face.

I stood panting, staring down at the bloodied men on the floor. With my foot I shoved the Arab off of Mayfield and had a good long look at what I had done. Both men were dead.

Putting a fresh magazine in the Skorpion, I went hurriedly to where Gail and the boy were crouched in the corner. Reaching down, I helped them to their feet.

"It's all right," I said, as her arms went around my neck and the boy buried his face in my side.

I put my arms around them both. "Come. Don't look down. Just come with me. I have to find my friends."

I led us into the kitchen, closing the door on the reeking carnage behind.

CHAPTER 38

ANDRÁS WATCHED AS I GOT INTO the harness. When I fastened the last buckle and gave him a nod, he turned and opened the door. The wind rushed into the airplane, filling the cabin with the clean, pure smell of the ocean below.

I checked the anchor point of the safety line and then joined András near the door. At our feet lay two long shapes. Bending over, we grabbed the canvas-wrapped bundle nearest the aft side of the door and gave it a heave. It slid halfway out the door, and then, turning in the wind, jammed against the doorframe. I put a foot on what felt like a shoulder and shoved. The body tumbled out the door and disappeared into the darkness.

We shifted the next figure just to the lip of the door. I sat down on the floor, and with both feet, gave it a shove. The weighted body of Colonel Forrest Mayfield joined his comrade in death as they fell through the night sky to the Mediterranean below, to sink in a watery grave, where they would be seen again, nevermore.

I turned and stepped forward in the cabin. Terry handed me a pillowcase that had our guns inside.

"That everything?" I yelled, over the wind and roar of the engine.

"Yeah!" Terry called in reply.

I stepped back to the door and pitched the bag of guns and knives out into the slipstream. Then I reached up, and pulling the sling of the Skorpion from over my neck, held it in my hand a second before tossing it, too, out the open door. We were clean.

"That's all," I called to András, who then closed and locked the door.

I returned to my spot and sat down. The plane droned on as before, though its burden was now slightly lessened.

After searching the house, we had found Jean Marc and his wife locked in the wine cellar. Thank God, they were unharmed. After dispatching Gail and me, Mayfield apparently *had* intended to come back and kill them, too, making it look as though we had died in a shoot-out. I hadn't believed him when he said it and had fully expected to find my friends dead.

I sent the Lavaliers, along with Gail and Abdullah, to the hotel with instructions for Istvan and the rest to get ready for an immediate departure, and for Donnelly to return and give me a hand.

Pope and I cleaned the blood from the floor and walls and removed all evidence of the break-in and the fight. We put the bundled bodies in the back of the Land Rover and went directly to the plane, where the rest of our people were waiting in readiness. We got everyone aboard and then loaded our final cargo. I turned to Donnelly.

"Get out on the first thing flying to Europe in the morning. After that, make your way to someplace warm, say perhaps, the Bahamas, and lay low for a while," I said, as we shook hands.

"Don't worry about me, lad. I'll be all right," he replied.

"I'm not worried," I said. "Just glad you're still alive. If Mayfield had caught you back there, we might just have three bundles on the floor of the plane instead of two. Now, go on, get out of here."

Pope gave me a grin and ducked his head.

"See you next time around," he said and then walked to his Rover and pulled away.

I climbed aboard just as Istvan cranked the engine. András closed the door as I found a place to sit. We taxied to the darkened runway and once again took off into the night.

We landed at Malta and were on the ground just long enough to drop off Terry and Roosty. I didn't want them involved in what was coming next. From here they would catch a commercial flight to parts unknown and rest awhile, their ears open for any murmurs or rumors of recent kidnappings and murders.

I watched my friends as they walked to the terminal building and back into the legitimate world of ticket-buying passengers and peaceful travelers. Istvan contacted the tower for instructions, and within minutes we were airborne again.

From Malta to the southern coast of Sicily is a short hop, less than sixty miles. I stood in the cockpit just behind Istvan and watched as the water changed to land, and then as the mountains of Sicily grew larger and larger. It was mid-morning, and the day was bright and beautiful.

Below us, covering the southern slopes of the mountains, were hundreds of greenhouses that glittered and shone like crystal ornaments. Before long we were over the center of the island, looking down on ancient villages tucked here and there in the folds and slopes of this timeless and rugged land.

Then, far away in the distance, I saw the sea once again. Istvan spoke into his microphone, then looked at me over his shoulder and pointed out the windshield ahead.

"Palermo," he said. "Landing in ten minutes."

I nodded that I understood, then went back into the cabin to ready Gail and Abdullah for what next lay ahead.

When we walked into the terminal building, I held us back in the customs and immigration line until I was sure Istvan was under way again.

"Okay, Gail," I said, as I took her in one hand and Abdullah in the other. "Just as we've rehearsed it— simple and to the point. They will separate us as soon as they realize they have a problem on their hands and try to get us to contradict one another. Just keep saying that you need medical treatment for yourself and the child and you want to see the American consul.

"My friend will get the call about us and be here very soon to take charge of the matter. Remember, the most important thing of all is the safety of Abdullah. We have to ensure that nothing further happens to him. We have to get him to someone who will ensure his protection."

As she nodded her understanding, I looked down into her eyes and saw they were steadfast and unwavering.

"Ready?" I asked.

She gave my hand a squeeze. "Ready," she answered.

We stepped into the short queue, and within a few steps we were at the immigration kiosk. I slid my passport over the counter. A middle-aged man took my passport, stamped it, and looked at me with bored eyes. Gesturing to Gail and Abdullah, he asked in a sour tone of voice, *"Famiglia?"*

"We are together but not family," I answered. "Neither the woman nor the child have passports. They are kidnap victims who have just escaped from captivity. We desire the sanctuary and protection of the state of Italy. And I wish to be placed in immediate communication with Brigadiere Alberto Rossi of the Carabinieri. The matter involves a crime that was committed upon Italian territory."

For a few seconds the man looked at me like I had a male member growing out of my forehead. Then he picked up a phone and spoke in it while he stared first at Gail and then Abdullah. As he listened to the reply, I saw a light of recognition come into his eyes. He put down the phone and stood.

"Will you please come with me?" he said in a kind voice.

And coming from behind the kiosk, he led us a short distance to a small room. Closing the door behind us, he gestured to several chairs.

"Sit. Please," he said. "Fear no more. Help will arrive momentarily."

If there's one thing the Italian security services know about, it's murder and kidnapping. Within minutes, the ball was rolling, and we soon had all the help we needed.

CHAPTER 39

THREE DAYS LATER, WE WERE LED into the inner office of the special court judge. A tall, courtly man with a head of abundant white hair rose from behind his desk and greeted us with cordial sympathy.

"Please sit," he said as he indicated the chairs arrayed in front of the desk.

"You have been through a most trying ordeal," he said as he lowered himself into an ornately carved chair. "But now you are safe. And it is the mission of this office to see that as long as you are on Italian soil, you remain safe."

I looked from Gail to the boy and back to the judge. I nodded to the American consul who sat in the chair on the other side of Gail.

"Judge Guadagno, sir, for the woman and myself, that is a simple matter. But as for the boy—you've heard what Miss Burns and I have both related—Abdullah cannot be returned to the custody of his grandfather. It is just impossible," I said in what I hoped was a business-like tone of voice.

The judge was seated deeply in his chair. As he listened, he kept his eyes lowered and his fingers templed just beneath his nose. When I finished speaking, he lifted his head slightly and looked directly at me.

"The safety of the child is a duty of this court, Signor Tanner. It is no longer your responsibility. And what you have presented to this court so far is testimony only, not fact," he said in a sonorous voice.

I felt the blood begin to rise in my neck, and my hands clenched the arms of my chair.

Watch what you say, buddy. Don't blow it now. There is too much at stake.

I took a breath and released it. The judge was watching me with a severe look on his face.

"Su Honore," I said, trying to keep the heat from my voice. "I was tasked with returning the child safely to his family. As I do not at this time know if that is entirely possible, I have not yet discharged my duty. And until I do so and am fully satisfied that Abdullah is safe and will continue to be so, I cannot, and will not, just wash my hands and walk away. I will not be a latter-day Pontius Pilate!"

I expected and was prepared for a rebuke. Judges the world over generally have little to no tolerance for anyone disputing their pronouncements. And they particularly dislike hearing it when it comes from the mouth of a foreigner. But I would be *damned* before I would walk away and see Abdullah returned to the hands of that murderous fiend because of political cowardice or any other reason.

The judge had lowered his face again and was tapping his upper lip with his fingers. I saw a slight smile touch his lips.

Here goes, I thought.

"I see you reference another Italian, one who some may say once abrogated an important duty of his own. I hope, for your own sake, Signor Tanner, you do not include *this* judge in that estimate," he said as he tapped his lip.

"I was speaking of myself, *Su Honore*. I have nothing but thanks and gratitude for what you and your government have done for us. I speak in this manner only because, at present, the child depends entirely upon Miss Burns and myself. Until someone else can present themselves with a conflicting claim and satisfy a court as to suitability, she and I serve in the position of what I think is termed in loco parentis. I believe, *Su Honore*, that it was your forebears who coined, not only the words, but the very concept in law."

The judge looked at me over his fingertips.

"And if someone should present a conflicting claim, are you prepared to contest that in court?" he asked.

"*Su Honore,* I am," I replied.

He looked to Gail.

"And you, signorina—you, who have been so quiet. Do you, too, make this claim?" he asked.

Gail nodded her head and looked over at Abdullah by her side.

"Sir, I have been his tutor since he was three years old. He loves and trusts me, and I love him. I am all that remains of what he knows as family. You have heard, and had evidence, of the atrocity committed by his closest relative. So, yes—I will do whatever is necessary to protect this child."

The judge looked from Abdullah to Gail to me and back to Abdullah.

"Excellent," he said.

Then, turning to an aide standing nearby, he said, "Renzo, will you ask His Eminence to come in, please?"

The young man opened the door and gestured someone in.

A dignified man, dressed in the white robes and *ghutrah* of the Persian Gulf emirates, entered the room and stood quietly. After a bit, Abdullah turned in his chair and looked at the man. The boy's eyes grew wide and then a smile lit his face. He leaped from his chair and ran to the man, throwing his arms around the man's legs and burying his face in his robes.

"Uncle!" cried Abdullah. "Uncle! Uncle!"

The man picked the boy up and cradled him to his chest. He showered the child's face with kisses and gently stroked his hair.

We all stood as the man said, "Shhh, shhh, Abutti, Abutti, shhh, shhh," over and over again, as he rocked the boy in his arms.

At last he sat Abdullah in a chair and stood next to him, a reassuring hand on the child's shoulder.

The judge had come around his desk and looked from the man to me.

"Signor Tanner, may I present to you His Eminence, Khalid bin Ali al Jemani, great-uncle to the child and brother to the child's grandfather," the judge said with a courteous smile.

I extended my hand and took his.

"Sir," I said with some uncertainty.

Al Jemani held my hand for several seconds and looked at me intently before releasing his grip.

"You have done a noble thing, Mr. Tanner. My family thanks you, and I thank you," he said, placing the tips of his fingers over his heart.

I hesitated before speaking. Was this some trick? A subterfuge on the part of the emir to get the boy back in his clutches?

"I don't know what—" I began, before the judge cut me off.

"Signor Tanner," said the judge. "If you will listen to what His Eminence has to say, I think it will allay your fears. I can vouch for the veracity of his every word. I have seen the proofs he presents, and our embassy in his country has verified the facts."

The judge indicated the chairs, and we all sat.

Al Jemani began, "My brother, the former emir, has been deposed. Shortly after you and he met in Beirut, we became fully aware of what he had done. A council of the heads of our family was convened, and he was removed from his position as chief of state. . . ."

"Yes, but—" I interrupted.

He raised a hand to signal silence.

"Hear me out, please. My brother has been placed in a hospital for the insane. He will never be released. And in the fullness of time he will die where he now sits, locked in his madness, awaiting the judgment of Allah."

"But why?" I asked. "Does anyone know why he would do such a horrible thing? There is no worse crime on earth than the one he committed."

"Madness," he replied. "There is no other answer. His fears were played upon by the whispered lies of others. He became convinced he was about to be deposed and murdered by his only son. In my brother's twisted mind, what he did was an act of self-protection."

I sat there for a second to let this sink in.

Madness indeed.

"You spoke of the whispered lies of *others*. Do you happen to know who those *others* may be?" I asked.

"We do," he replied. "We have all but one of them in custody now. The other is a countryman of yours, a military man. We have requested the cooperation of the American government, but they inform us that this man cannot be found and that he has been missing for more than a week."

I took a breath and slowly let it out. *Mayfield.*

I looked al Jemani in the eyes and waited until I knew a connection was established. I would say this only once.

Placing my hand on my heart, I said, "Sir, I do not think the man you speak of will be seen on this earth ever again."

Al Jemani looked down at the boy at his side. He ran his fingers through Abdullah's hair and smiled.

"Shuhkran," he said in a low voice—*Thank you.*

"Afwan," I replied—*You're welcome.*

We all rose. The judge looked from one of us to the other.

"Are we satisfied that justice has been served this day?" he asked.

Everyone responded that this was so.

"Then it has been a rare day indeed, one seldom seen in my years of judicial experience. Now, I wish you all Godspeed on your journey home," he said and then rose and shook hands with everyone.

We filed from the room, and from there, out of the building. I blinked in the bright sun and fished my sunglasses from my jacket pocket. Gail stood with al Jemani and Abdullah, as a large chauffeured Mercedes with blacked-out windows pulled to the curb.

"Will you come with us, Miss Burns, and continue in your old job? The child will need your comforting presence while he settles into my household," said al Jemani.

"I will come," said Gail as she wiped tears from her cheeks. "But first I wish to see my own parents and family. It has been a while since I saw them last, and I have a great desire to be with them now."

"When you are ready, there is a place for you in our home. Please know that you are always welcome," he replied.

"Thank you," she said. And then she kissed Abdullah and gave him one last hug.

An assistant opened the door for al Jemani, who leaned over and handed Abdullah to a nurse inside. He then slid in beside the child. The assistant started to close the door, but al Jemani stayed his hand.

"Wait," he said, and then, looking up at me, he took a folded piece of paper from within his robes and extended it to me.

"You will find the remaining funds deposited as per the agreement you had with my brother. Here is the confirmation," he said.

I held the paper in my hand.

"Sir, I don't want—" I began to reply.

But al Jemani waved his hand and smiled. The assistant closed the door and got in the front seat. Pulling smoothly away, the car was soon lost from view in the snarling whirl of the Italian traffic.

I turned to the small young woman at my side.

"Let's go home, Gail Burns."

"Let's do," she replied.

I whistled and waved down a cab.

"To the airport," I said to the driver as I closed the door.

CHAPTER 40

WE CAUGHT THE NEXT FLIGHT TO Rome and were lucky enough to grab two seats on a plane to New York leaving in a few hours. Gail had gotten a new passport from the American consul in Palermo, and I thought that was the end of our government connection. But while waiting for our flight, we were joined by the regional security officer from the American Embassy.

Now, most good American citizens labor under the misimpression that, should they get in real difficulty overseas, they will be taken in hand and given every assistance humanly possible by the good folks at their nation's embassy. I wish it were so, but it seldom works out that way. Not unless you happen to be a senator, film celebrity, or an NBA star.

More often than not, the poor traveler is viewed as a nuisance if not a downright embarrassment: a problem to be ignored, if possible, and one to be quickly gotten rid of, under all circumstances.

So when Gail showed up out of the clear blue as not only a kidnap victim but also a witness to the murder of foreign dignitaries—well, let's just say that nobody thought their career would be greatly enhanced by dealing with that sticky problem.

That actually worked out in our favor. Gail had a new passport within hours. The consul was more than happy to sit quietly and let the Italians handle the situation. And let's face it, nobody is more experienced in dealing with organized murder and kidnapping than the Italian government. And fortunately for me, no one really wanted to look into what Signor Tanner had to do with all of this.

The regional security officer, or RSO, as he is called in the trade, sat with us until boarding call. It was his job to make sure we actually got on the plane and did nothing silly, such as holding a press conference or extending our stay on Italian soil.

The boarding line moved steadily, and just as I entered the concourse, I turned and gave our watchdog a cheery wave. He responded by touching his fingers to his forehead in a salute and then turning and walking away. His babysitting job accomplished, he, too, was now free to go.

We settled into our seats and got ourselves situated with blankets and pillows. It is a long flight from Rome to New York, one I wasn't particularly looking forward to, in spite of all that had happened during this expedition. But the cabin steward soon came through the aisle taking drink orders, and it wasn't long before I was able to savor the spiritually uplifting taste of a good Irish whiskey.

Gail and I both slept through most of the flight, and when I awoke, I felt like I had been ground between two millstones. It was the post-mission letdown that was hitting me. All the built-up tension had to go somewhere, and it expressed itself by a physical manifestation of severe fatigue. It wasn't unexpected, and I knew it would dissipate in due time.

I took the complimentary toilet pack with me and went to the lavatory to freshen up and try to make myself presentable. While I washed my face, shaved, and brushed my teeth, I stared at the guy looking back at me in the mirror and asked myself if I recognized that man.

Who are you really, Tanner? I silently asked the guy in the mirror.

Do you actually know what you're doing, or do you just crash around on this planet, leaving destruction and mayhem in your wake, like some sort of brainless automaton?

But wait a minute, I answered. *I've just saved two lives. That's a good thing, isn't it? Certainly that has to count for something.*

Sure, but how many lives did you take in the process? And how many other lives did you put at risk? And what gives you the license to do these things, anyway? Did any of those people you killed come to your home and threaten your life or the lives of people you love?

But if those kinds of people aren't stopped, what becomes of us? You yourself told me that the first duty of the strong is the protection of the weak. So tell me, if you won't do it, just who the hell will?

You've got me there, buddy. So now, why don't you just clear out of here and let someone else use the facilities.

Okay, I said to the man and, returning to my seat, dozed quietly the remainder of the flight.

Upon landing, Gail and I zipped right through customs and immigration. It goes pretty fast when you have no luggage and can jump to the head of the line, though Gail's new passport got her a questioning look from the plump lady in the glass booth. But it was stamped without an interrogation, and a few minutes later we were officially back in the United States.

We shouldered our way through the bustling crowd that thronged the JFK terminal and out to the ground transportation area.

"Where to, Gail?" I asked, as the buses and taxis roared by.

"Home," she replied. "I'll get a ride to LaGuardia and catch a flight to Seattle."

A chill gust of wind caught her hair. Shivering, she pulled her jacket closed and reached up to smooth her hair back into place.

"Colder here than I expected," she said. "I guess I've been away a long time."

"Yeah," I replied as I looked about at nothing in particular.

Some partings are awkward, and this was one of them. Gail felt it, and so did I. We had shared an intense experience. And even though we had not spent much time in any sort of deep and meaningful conversation, there was a connection we were both reluctant to break. But it was time.

"Well, if you're ever down South, give me a yell," I said, as I leaned over and we exchanged a hug.

"Sure," she replied, blinking away a tear.

Just then a taxi pulled up, and the man running the place said, "This is yours, lady."

I opened the door, and Gail got in.

"Take care," I said.

"You, too," she replied as her lower lip trembled.

"And think about staying in the States. There are a lot of kids here that would love to have you for a teacher," I said as I closed the door.

Gail gave me a parting smile. Turning in her seat, she waved through the back window until the cab disappeared into the mass of other hurrying vehicles. I watched until she was out of sight and then turned to the taxi meister who was standing nearby.

"Think a veteran can get a taxi in this place?" I asked the man.

"Sure thing, General. Take this one right here," he replied with a flourish.

He opened the door of a cab that had just stopped.

"Thanks. But don't call me general, partner; I work for a living," I said as I handed him a five and got in the cab.

Slamming the door, the man laughed and banged on the roof of the cab, shouting, "Get outta here."

"Where to, sir?" asked the Pakistani driver as we pulled away.

"Times Square," I answered.

I settled back in the seat to enjoy the ride. I love New York and thought I would enjoy the city for a bit. A few more days would make no difference to me, and for some reason I was slightly reluctant to go home just yet.

CHAPTER 41

I DID THE TOURIST THING FOR THE next few days. New York is one of the great walking cities of the world, and I made the most of my stay. A few years ago I had a Saudi prince as a client who owned a penthouse apartment on Park Avenue. I had spent several summers here as his bodyguard and came to know the city quite well. I have several friends and any number of acquaintances living in the five boroughs, but really didn't want to see anybody. I preferred staying to myself and enjoying the anonymity of the crowd.

The national myth is that New Yorkers are a cold and surly race, but I find them to be some of the most gregarious people on Earth. You can start a conversation with someone on any street corner, and if you're not careful, you'll get your ear chewed off. I've stopped before to ask directions and soon had three or four people shouting and giving assistance, and wound up going for a drink with new acquaintances.

No, I like New York. I'd like to come here and live for a year. I'll bet I could find a nice little marina somewhere on the East River that *Miss Rosalie* and I would really like. But after a few days of big-city hustle and bustle, I felt it was time to make my way south. I didn't fancy the idea of flying again, so I booked a sleeping berth on the train and headed down the coast in style.

The train is a civilized mode of travel, one I wished I used more often. I sat and watched with delight as the towns and countryside rolled by in an ever-changing and fascinating pattern. I took my meals in the dining car on real linen tablecloths, with genuine silverware. The club car was a favorite place to sit quietly with a drink or engage in conversation with a fellow traveler. I find that people who like train travel tend to also like other people. All in all, it is a pleasant and relaxing way to travel, and I could feel myself unwinding as the rumbling wheels of the cars counted the passing miles.

All things, good or bad, eventually come to an end, and the next day we were in Savannah. I stepped out of the car and onto the platform and immediately I felt the warm, moist, pine-scented air wrap me in a blanket of welcome. A quick cab ride to the airport where I picked up my old Bronco, and within an hour I was parking under a wide live oak tree and looking down on my dock, where *Miss Rosalie* rocked contentedly at rest.

Place looks pretty good, I thought as I got out and scanned the broad, rippling surface of the river and the waving grass of the great salt marsh beyond.

As I ambled down to the dock, I took a deep breath and savored the taste of the clean ocean air. *Miss Rosalie*'s dock lines were nice and tight, and as I stepped aboard, the scrubbed and tidy condition of the deck told me that Danny Ray had given the old girl his lavish attention. I sometimes believed that my shy friend had come to love the boat almost as much as I did.

I descended to the cabin and dropped my small travel kit on the bunk. The place was a little musty, so I opened the ports in the salon and then checked my secret hiding spots to make sure nothing had been tampered with. Satisfied that everything looked the way it should inside, I went back out and walked the deck from stem to stern.

Boats always need constant attention, and when you find a small problem, you have to get right on it, or it will become a large problem in a hurry. I found a couple of spots that needed some scraping and painting, but overall, she looked good.

Next I unlocked and went in the pilothouse to check over the mechanicals. First I looked under the instrument board, checking the wiring and all electrical contacts. On a boat, corrosion is the death of electrical instruments.

I then dropped down into the engine room, where I checked the oil and fluids. Diesel fuel has an affinity for water, so I drained a cupful of fuel from the filters and checked it for contamination.

I then checked the condition of the batteries with a critical eye and followed the cables from the battery bank all the way to the starter. The electrical system was in good shape also—nothing missing, nothing added.

Satisfied that all was in order, I hit the starter button and fired up the engine. She surged with power for a second and then settled down to a rhythmic, pulsing throb. I climbed back to the pilothouse to scan the instruments and make sure they were all in working order, while I let the engine run.

Everything looked normal, but I had an unsettled feeling. I could feel the residual presence of an unwanted visitor. Someone had been aboard in my absence, and it wasn't Danny Ray. Whoever it was had been very good—they knew what they were doing and had missed all my telltales except one.

On the handrail going down to the engine compartment, I had placed a tiny drop of oil and had laid a hair on it. Undisturbed by a human hand, the hair would have stayed where it was until doomsday. But it had been swept away by the violating touch of an intruder. Whoever he was, he had gone throughout the boat, looking, feeling, sniffing—and leaving behind who knows what.

I knew who had sent him. The question was, had Mayfield left someone behind in his place? Did he have a lieutenant to pick up where he left off? It was critical that I find the answer to that question. Tonight, after everything was settled down, I would go over the boat with a fine-tooth comb, and I would do it again for the next several days.

After fifteen minutes, I shut the engine down. Now it was time to go ashore and make my reappearance to the world. I washed my hands, shot a little cologne in the direction of my face, and put on my old beach bum hat.

It was just about the start of happy hour as I stepped through the open doors of Captain Flynt's.

"Hey, Kennesaw! Good to see you, boy! Just get back in town?" called my friend, Bob Martin.

His wife, Fran, spun around on her stool and gave me a sunny smile over the top of her drink.

"Hey, handsome—come here and give us a kiss. It'll be the only one I'm likely to get tonight," she said as she presented me with a pair of bright red lips and elbowed Bob in the ribs.

I gave Fran a smooch and a hug and shook Bob's hand. The Martins are two of my favorite friends. Bob is an old retired army warrant officer and probably the most sensible man I've ever met. But his health isn't too good. He's already lost one lung to Agent Orange exposure, and the remaining lung isn't doing that well either. But Bob hangs in there without complaint. A rare man,

Bob would rather know how you are doing than to talk about his own difficulties.

Fran is a buxom, bubbly blond. I once asked her if, when she was younger, she had patterned herself on Marilyn Monroe.

Fran laughed and told me, "Why, hell no! I never wanted to look anything like that flat-chested little trollop!"

She then thrust out her bosom and struck a pose.

"Back home in Anniston, Alabama, everyone used to tell me I looked just like Jayne Mansfield. I even met her once, when she came to Birmingham to the opening of a Cadillac dealership. And you know what she said to me? She said, 'Why, honey, me and you look just like twins. What a pair we would make.'"

Bob looked over and drawled, "That wouldn't have been a pair, Fran. It would have been four of a kind."

In reply, Fran pouted her lips, shook her endowments like an exotic dancer, and let out a shriek of delight. The entire bar broke up with laughter.

"How was the trip?" Bob asked quietly as I settled in on the next stool.

Bob knows a little about what I do, and he is the very soul of discretion.

"It was okay, Bob. Nothing out of the ordinary to report," I replied as I caught the attention of the bartender.

"Come back with everything you left with?" he asked.

"More or less, Bob. More or less," I responded, as Tyrone came over and plunked a cold Dos Equis in front of me.

"Huhhh!" he said as he poured the beer in a tall glass. That's Tyrone's way of saying, "Hello, Kennesaw, good to see you again."

"Thanks, Big Tee," I said and took an appreciative pull on the beer.

Fran wandered away to speak to some people at the other end of the bar. Bob took a sip of his drink and looked at me in the bar mirror.

"Day or two after you left, there was a guy seemed to take a real interest in your boat. Since no one was there, he must have thought it was for sale. Yeah, real interested, he was," Bob said in a low voice.

I took a sip of beer and wiped the foam from my lip.

"Do tell," I responded.

"Yeah. But I don't think he'll be back to talk to you about it," he said.

"No? Why not?" I asked.

"A couple of the local shrimpers—you know 'em, the Bohannon brothers—were headed to their boat before daylight one morning and found him sprawled in the parking lot. Said it looked like the old boy had run into some sort of trouble."

"They did, eh? What kind of trouble?" I inquired as I watched Bob in the mirror.

Bob took a sip and then said, "The kind of trouble you find at the wrong end of a couple of axe handles. They figured he must have pissed somebody off real bad."

I nodded my comprehension. "The old boy survive the encounter?" I asked.

"Oh yeah, he was young and tough. He'll heal up eventually, but I tell you, from what I heard, his dentist is going to make a fortune off of him. Probably send one of his kids to Harvard for a year off that one case alone."

"Uh-huh," I said as I took another sip. "Danny Ray didn't run into anything troublesome, did he?"

"No, Danny Ray is okay. Since you've been gone, I've had him out at my place, working on my dock," Bob replied with a smile.

"If you see the Bohannons before I do, tell them I said they're a couple of Good Samaritans, helping out that stranger the way they did. If there were more people like them, this world would be a better place," I said to the mirror.

Turning on my stool, I looked directly at my friend. "And thank you, Bob, for looking after Danny Ray. I'd hate to think of anything happening to him."

Bob lifted his drink in salute.

"To the good life," he said.

I returned the salute.

I stayed for a while and caught up with the rest of my fellow barstool barristers. I was hoping to catch Dolores, but Tyrone told me she was up in Atlanta getting one of her kids out of jail. After a quiet dinner of freshly caught speckled trout and deep-fried hush puppies, I decided it was time to call it a day. I said my good-byes and then headed down to the docks and back to *Miss Rosalie*.

I was almost to the ramp leading down to my dock, when I saw a dome light come on in a car nearby. Instantly alerted, I reached to the waistband of my jeans and put a hand on my knife as a man stepped out of the car.

"H-h-h-h-hello, K-K-K-K-Kennesaw."

It was Danny Ray.

"Hey, friend," I called out as I strode over and shook my buddy's hand.

Danny gave me a strong grip and looked at me shyly from beneath the brim of his cap.

"Uh-uh-uh—I gu-gu-got somebody wants to t-t-t-talk to you," he said.

I felt another presence and, turning, saw a woman get out of the car. I looked at her closely as she came over. She was dressed in an old sweatshirt, a pair of jeans, and sneakers. As she came closer, I saw that she was in late middle age. Her hair was pulled back in a thin ponytail, and as she took a nervous drag on her cigarette, I saw the hollows of her cheeks collapse over some missing teeth.

She walked with her elbows tucked in to her sides and one arm across her body, as though she were protecting her ribs from an anticipated blow. Her sallow skin and hangdog demeanor spoke of the soul-crushing effects of generational poverty. Growing up back in the hills, I had known dozens of women just like her.

This must be Danny Ray's mother, I thought.

The woman stopped an arm's length away and looked me searchingly in the face. She took a deep pull on her cigarette and then flipped the butt toward the parking lot.

Blowing a stream of smoke from the corner of her mouth, she stepped even closer and in a whiskey-and-smoke voice said, "Danny Ray tells me you the one who helped when y'all found my little girl out in the swamp."

"Are you Mrs. Causey?" I asked.

"Yeah, I am," she replied as she studied my face with shifting, flitting eyes.

"I'm very sorry for your loss, Mrs. Causey," I said as I returned her gaze.

"Yeah, well—thankee. I 'preciate it," she replied. "But I come here to ask you for something. Danny Ray tells me you might could help me out," she said as tears came to her eyes.

"What's that, Mrs. Causey? What can I do for you?" I asked as I looked at this sad and forlorn woman.

She sniffed twice and rubbed her nose before saying, "My little girl, Tonya, she ain't committed no suicide Mr. Tanner. She was kilt. She was throwed off'a that bridge. I know it. I know it deep down inside. I went to the po-leece in Savannah, and I told 'em so. But the law won't help me, Mr. Tanner. The law, they don't never help pore people, no sir; they just piss on us. The law only works for the rich folks.

"Mr. Tanner," she pleaded, "I ain't got nowhere else

to go. Danny Ray told me you might could help. I need you to help me get them sorry som'bitches that kilt my baby. I need 'em to answer for what they done."

She buried her face in her hands, and her thin body was racked by the choked sobs of grief and frustration.

I put an arm around the woman's frail shoulders, pulled her to my chest, and let her cry. When after a few minutes her sobbing had diminished, I kept an arm around her shoulder and steered her toward the dock ramp.

"Come on, Mrs. Causey. Let's go sit on my boat, and you can tell me what you think happened."

As we walked, I could feel her body trembling. Glancing over my shoulder, I saw Danny Ray hovering uncertainly behind.

"You, too, Danny Ray. Come on—you're part of this, too."

Danny ran ahead of us and held the boat securely against the dock as we went aboard. As she stepped on deck, Mrs. Causey hesitated and then turned to me, our faces level with one another.

"Mr. Tanner, I want you to know, I ain't got no money to pay you with."

"Ma'am," I replied, "that's one worry you don't need to concern yourself with. Someone else has already taken care of that problem."